We've Hit
TURBULENCE

We've Hit TURBULENCE

JESSICA L. COZZI

Delacorte Romance
An imprint of Random House Children's Books
A division of Penguin Random House LLC
1745 Broadway, New York, NY 10019
penguinrandomhouse.com
getunderlined.com

Editor: Alison Romig
Cover Designer: Ray Shappell
Interior Designer: Michelle Canoni
Production Editor: Jamie Johnson
Managing Editor: Tamar Schwartz
Production Manager: Shameiza Ally

Library of Congress Cataloging-in-Publication Data is available upon request.
ISBN 978-0-593-90485-5 (trade pbk.) — ISBN 978-0-593-90486-2 (ebook)

The text of this book is set in 11-point Sabon MT Pro.

Manufactured in the United States of America
1st Printing

The authorized representative in the EU for product safety and compliance is Penguin Random House Ireland, Morrison Chambers, 32 Nassau Street, Dublin D02 YH68, Ireland, https://eu-contact.penguin.ie.

For James P. Egbert
I felt your encouragement in every word of this story and wish more than anything that you were here to see this. Somewhere, in some way, I'd like to believe that you are.

And for Matthew, who showed me exactly why a happily ever after is always worth hoping for. More than you'll ever know.

Part One

DEPARTURE 

Chapter One

Jack Cameron *probably* isn't cheating on me, but one can never be too sure.

At least, that's the thought running on a loop in the back of my mind as I shuffle, bleary-eyed, through the airport. How the hell are there humans in this universe who consider themselves morning people?

The airport at 4:00 a.m. is a lawless place—evidenced by the fact that the sun hasn't even peeked over the horizon yet and I can already see a businessman in a tailored suit barking into his phone at whatever poor soul is on the other end. Nearby, a sleepy-looking woman is perched on a barstool sucking down a Bloody Mary like her life depends on it. And a few feet from where she sits, a rumpled-looking girl in a faded Loyola University sweatshirt is spread out on the floor, snoring peacefully, using her carry-on duffel as a pillow. The only unifying factor among the three is that they've made it past the dreaded airport security line, which I'm still inching my way through, staring at them enviously from the other side of the metal detectors.

With nothing better to do, I check my phone one more time, hoping a text has materialized. While it's obscenely early on the

East Coast, it's not even midnight in Honolulu, so there's no reason Jack should be ignoring my message.

Or the fifty messages I sent throughout the week.

Going for broke, I pull up his contact and hit the call button one more time, crossing my fingers. It rings for an entire minute before the voicemail clicks on.

"Hi, you've reached Jack Cameron. Leave a message and I'll get back to you. Thanks!"

I hang up, dejected. While my boyfriend and I have never been the attached-at-the-hip type, we still manage to communicate every day—whether through a brief phone call, sporadic texts, or sharing funny memes and TikToks. But for the past seven days, I've barely heard from him at all. No likes on my silly stories or responses to my Snapchats, just a half-hearted text here and there. What started as a slow trickle of worry in my chest has already morphed into an all-encompassing panic.

I stare at our last messages from a week ago on my tiny screen until my eyes water—from the lack of blinking or the hurt, I'm not entirely sure.

Jack: Got a lot of studying ahead of me tonight—night, Olive.

Olive: Night, Jack. See you soon for spring break. :)

Well, maybe it's a *touch* impulsive, but that's the reason I'm hopping on a flight a whole week earlier than I originally planned. Because Jack isn't answering me, and something feels weird, and it's the spring of my senior year at Becker High, so it's not like I'm really missing anything. Which is exactly why it was easy to convince Mom, the die-hard hopeless romantic, to let me move up the trip and head to the University of Hawaiʻi a week early, using the excuse that Jack will have a bunch of exams next week and we won't be able to spend much time together.

Maybe I forgot to mention to her that Jack has no idea I'm coming this early . . . but that's not something I can worry about right now.

My bigger focus is that I can't untangle the knot of worry in my stomach—because my boyfriend, a year older than me and already in the second semester of his freshman year of college, is ghosting me. I swore to my mother and my friends—and most importantly, myself—that we wouldn't be the cliché. That what Jack and I had was more than a high school fling that would fizzle out in college. It *had* to be. But now here I am, with unreturned texts and unplayed voicemails and a level of anxiety steadily increasing with each passing moment.

"It was supposed to be a surprise, but I kinda told him about it already," I semi-lied to Mom when she asked what Jack thought of my early arrival. It *is* going to be a surprise, but maybe not in the *I'm here early; let's spend more time together!* way.

That's the way I *want* it to be.

But I may not have mentioned to Jack that I was coming early.

There's a very real possibility it'll be more of a caught-him-in-the-act surprise. And part of me feels like I'd rather see what's going on with my own eyes and be able to accept it at face value than over a stilted FaceTime conversation or text. I don't have time to dwell on that, because the grumpy-looking TSA agent is already waving me forward and instructing me to drop everything in the scratched plastic bin making its way down the conveyor belt.

The trek through security is as agonizingly slow as expected. I fight down a spike of anxiety as I watch them loosely search through my backpack, probably bending the pages of my planner in the process—my meticulously organized, detailed-within-an-inch-of-its-life book that I never leave home without. *Relax, Olive. It's just an ordinary planner.*

Maybe so, but this isn't any ordinary trip.

I eventually make my way to the gate (breathing a sigh of relief that my planner is unharmed once it's returned to me), throwing on the hood of my sweatshirt and slinking down in the uncomfortable seat at the gate's waiting area, checking my phone the whole time for messages that I know aren't going to be there.

At least I'll have an answer for Jack's weirdness in thirteen hours, no matter what it is.

I just hope it's a good one.

I've never flown on my own—a fact that didn't stress me out before, but now as I stand in line worrying the glossy paper of the boarding pass between my fingers, I can feel the panic starting to creep in. What if the plane crashes? Or someone gets sick? Or worst of all—what if I'm stuck next to an annoying seatmate for the next thirteen hours, crushed in the middle?

The last thought makes me shudder, but at least I'm armed with several downloaded true-crime podcast episodes and have my neck pillow for what will hopefully be a very sleepy flight.

When I sprang my last-minute decision to leave early on Mom, she didn't put up a fight. Honestly, it's exactly what I'd expect from a woman who falls hopelessly in love with a new man every three months, morphs her life to be with him, and then realizes, as she always does, that it isn't going to work out.

For Mom, flights—and going on spontaneous journeys in the name of love—are some of her favorite things. Instead of deterring me, as an attentive parent would, she squealed with delight and dragged her laptop to the kitchen table to help me book my ticket. When I expressed my worry about taking a direct flight—as someone who isn't too keen on flying, it's a *long* time to be trapped in a giant sky tube—she scoffed.

"Don't be silly, Olive," she chided me, her cherry-bright nails flying excitedly over the keyboard as she searched through airline offerings. "You'll get there quicker if you fly direct, and the sooner you see Jack, the sooner your love story continues."

It's honestly a surprise she never turned into a romance writer—her missed calling. At least she has her soap operas.

The flight attendant's chipper voice declaring, "Now boarding group B," breaks through my thoughts, and I spring up from my seat, my heart jackhammering in my chest. It's not the first time I've flown—I've been on a few of those making-the-trek-for-love trips with Mom—but like the hundreds of other things you start doing for yourself as an almost-high-school-graduate, it seems scarier when you're doing it solo.

I eye the plane through the tall glass windows as I get closer to the front of the queue, unease swirling in my stomach. This isn't the same as the first time you deposit a paycheck by yourself or go to a doctor's appointment without your parent there. This is getting on a metal death trap in the *sky* and hoping it doesn't plummet to the ground.

The gate attendant scans my boarding pass without much fanfare and ushers me forward, and I try to convince myself that my mother is standing right behind me, riffling through her purse for ChapStick or complaining loudly about forgetting her headphones at home. But it doesn't work, because the only sound behind me is the irritated sigh of a woman in her fitted suit, tapping her toe impatiently at how slowly the line is moving. I almost want to spin around and ask her why she's wearing a full suit and heels for a thirteen-hour flight to Honolulu, but I bite my tongue at the last second before I can make trouble.

Eventually I reach my seat—23B, the dreaded middle but the only last-minute seat available on the flight—and settle in, catching a glare from the elderly woman sitting against the window.

"Good morning!" I chirp, a bundle of nerves, trying to make nice with the person I'm destined to sit next to for thirteen hours. But she doesn't take well to my kindness, instead sniffing haughtily and sticking her nose back into her glossy gossip magazine, making it clear I'm going to be ignored for the duration of this trip.

Fine with me. I shove my backpack under the seat in front of me and pop in my earbuds, slinking low in my chair and queueing up the first of the true-crime podcasts I have on deck. Not that I think I'll be listening to them for long—I'm already yawning uncontrollably, and the sky is turning a dusky pink through Cranky Lady's window, which reminds me I've basically been up all night.

I glance next to me at the aisle seat—still empty. The TV screen in front of me tells me the plane's due to take off in ten minutes. I mentally cross my fingers that the poor soul misses their flight, because this seat being empty means after takeoff I can scoot over there and put a buffer between me and my hostile seatmate. The odds look promising, but we still have some time to wait, so I fire off a text to Mom to let her know we're leaving soon, switch my phone into airplane mode, and press play on my podcast while closing my eyes.

A couple of minutes go by, and I'm being lulled to sleep by the gruesome reenactment of a woman being brutally stabbed and disposed of by her lover, when some rustling in the aisle gets my attention. I pop my eyes open and blearily blink at the bright lights, watching a woman skirt by with three young (whining, cranky) children in tow, making their way down the row. Luckily, none of them slide into seat 23C, which elicits a sigh of relief.

The pilot's voice crackles overhead, and I pause my podcast to listen. "Good morning, ladies and gentlemen. The time is five-forty-five a.m. local time here at JFK, and we'll be closing the doors and departing for Honolulu shortly. Please fasten your seat belts and prepare for takeoff. Thank you."

Still no seatmate. *Perfect.* I straighten up and make sure my bag is correctly stowed underneath the seat in front of me, accidentally jostling Cranky Lady in the process. She clears her throat loudly, and I count down the seconds until the door is sealed and I can slide one seat over, away from her snark, at least marginally.

There's more rustling at the front of the plane, the flight attendants moving aside to let someone pass, but I can't see over the sea of heads in front of me. Even Cranky Lady perks up, curious, before furrowing her brow and diving back into her magazine.

I do one more quick scan of my surroundings—there are a few empty seats remaining. Someone's moving down the aisle, still too far away for me to see, but I resume listening to my podcast and lean my head back while closing my eyes, toying with the hood of my sweatshirt and preparing to taxi. The exhaustion of this whole morning finally starts to get to me, and I feel myself tipping toward the beginnings of a deep sleep when my arm is bumped and I'm jostled awake by someone sliding into the seat next to me. *Damn it.*

"Oof—sorry." A deep, distinctly male voice is muffled through the sound of the podcast host reciting the grisly murder, but it's clear enough for me to make out what he's saying. "Didn't mean to bump you. Been in a bit of a rush this morning."

I pop out an earbud in response, cracking one eye open and getting a glance at him while he's busy shoving his bag under his seat. But as soon as I catch a glimpse of his profile, the blood turns to ice in my veins.

Oh shit.

I tug my hoodie farther down my head, jerking away before he can spot me. *Relax, Olive. Don't freak out.*

Don't freak out.

Okay, I think I'm freaking out.

"Hey," I lean over and whisper to Cranky Lady in a moment of panic-induced weakness. "Is there, um, any way that we can switch seats for this flight?"

She looks up from her magazine disdainfully. "Sweetheart, why on earth would I willingly take the *middle seat* when I paid for the window?" She says it with a wrinkled nose, as if moving literally one seat over is worse than a death sentence. And as if she isn't sitting in coach right alongside me.

Because I can't sit next to him for the entire flight, I want to plead, but instead I keep pushing. "*Please*? Is there any way at all?

I can, um . . ." My eyes quickly dart around the cramped space, trying to find something to use as a bribe before the guy stops fiddling with his luggage and has to look up. Based on the way the flight attendants are beginning to shut the overhead bins at the front of the plane, I don't have much time. "I can give you my dessert when they come around with meals later?" I'm even mentally counting all the cash in my wallet right now to give to her, but if her Prada tracksuit is any indication, my measly tips won't be enough to sway her. "Please," I whisper again, more frantic this time as the flight attendant helps the guy with the final shove of his luggage.

Cranky Lady looks less than impressed, picking up her magazine with a huff and going back to ignoring me, this time with even more disdain radiating off her than when I first sat down. It's going to be a long flight for all of us.

"There we go," the guy says, and I'm not sure if he's talking to me or himself as he leans back into his seat. His seat belt makes a distinctly metallic *click* as it snaps shut, breaking through my super-eloquent thoughts that are just long strings of expletives. "Thank God I made the flight. The security line got a little crazy back there," he continues, talking to the air.

I'm still tugging my hood over my eyes, pulling at the strings so the fabric cinches into a smaller and smaller O. Maybe if I just ignore him, he'll leave me alone. Maybe he won't even recognize me.

"You know," he tries again after a beat, his voice softer and less cheerful this time as the flight attendants encourage people to take their seats, "this doesn't have to be awkward if you don't want it to be, Olive."

Fuuuuuuuuuuck. I want to crawl in a hole and die. Or jump

out of the emergency exit of the plane. But I can't really do either of those things, so right now, I'm forced to take a deep breath and turn toward him instead.

Staring back at me is Tyler Ferris—the boy whose heart I'm responsible for breaking.

And if I'm being honest, it's one of the bigger regrets of my life.

Chapter Two

There are a lot of places I fantasized about running into Tyler again outside the halls of Becker High School, but the cramped economy seat of a thirteen-hour flight was not one of them. It's almost 6:00 a.m., I've been up all night, and I'm *not* prepared for this conversation, so I do what any self-respecting eighteen-year-old would do: I pull the strings of my hood tighter around my face, pop my earbud back in, and pretend it's not happening. *What the hell is he even doing here? It's a week before break—is he skipping school?* Somehow, that seems totally on brand for him. And sure, I may be skipping, too, but that's for . . . reasons. Reasons that are definitely far more important than whatever stunt Tyler's trying to pull.

Still, I'm curious and can't help taking a peek. Next to me, Tyler goes back to getting settled. He looks the same as he did a week or two ago when I saw him in the cafeteria and breezed right past him as he tried to say hello—long, slender frame, slouchy black hoodie, his signature dark brown flip of hair that matches the muddy brown of his eyes. Eyes he always said were boring but I used to find endlessly fascinating when the light hit them just right and lit up all the flecks of gold nestled there. Eyes that still track my movements whenever I catch a glimpse of him across our school hallway, instead of us walking side by side like we used to. He's usually laughing with Delia about some inside joke, the kind that I used to be a part of.

I can't force myself to look in Tyler's direction any longer, instead staring down at my hands in my lap, the petal-pink polish now chipped and gnawed away from the stress of the last few days. The soul-sucking panic after leaving Jack voicemail after voicemail after voicemail, text after text after text, and not hearing anything back. The kind of stress that makes you do something irrational, like convince your mom to let you start your spring break a week early and fly nearly halfway across the world.

Yeah, that kind of stress could wreak havoc on even the best manicure.

I was already exhausted, and now I'm really not in the mood to have an awkward, stilted conversation on what is now becoming the Flight from Hell. Next to me, Tyler says nothing, giving me the floor to get my feelings out, like he always does.

Or, rather, like he always *used* to.

I stare hard at my hands until I weaken and take out my phone, not blinking for so long that the letters of the podcast episode title start to blur together in front of me. In my peripheral vision, I see Tyler taking out his own phone. My mind immediately starts swimming with possibilities. *Is he texting his friends about this? Has he given up on trying to talk to me?*

Two seconds ago, I was considering emptying my wallet to the woman next to me to avoid having to speak to Tyler, so I'm surprised by the painful twist in my gut at the thought that maybe *he'd* already given up trying.

Before I can open my mouth and finally force myself to say something, the screens on the in-seat televisions all synchronize and start their safety demonstration. *"Aloha and welcome aboard."* The screen flashes through examples of how to tighten your seat belt, use your oxygen mask, find the emergency exits—all wonderful things to put into your mind right when you're about to take off into the skies in a giant metal death tube.

Another scene: an awkward (and scarily in sync) group of rowers slicing through the churning ocean, all of the men turning to the camera at once and saying in cultish unison, *"It is a federal offense to remove any vests from the aircraft."*

It's so creepy and campy that Tyler and I both snort in surprise at the same time. He turns to me, eyes skimming over mine before quickly jerking away at the intense contact, pocketing his phone. "That's mildly disturbing for nearly six in the morning, huh?" His tone is light and easy, clearly letting me off the hook for not answering his previous statement. It's a gift that I'm not sure I deserve, but I feel my shoulders relax in relief anyway.

"Yep," I mumble, angling myself away from him.

After another second, from the corner of my eye, I see Tyler turn back toward his own screen, getting the hint that the conversation is over. "Well, it's good to see you, Olive."

Shit, shit, shit.

I jam my eyes shut in a weak attempt to fake sleep, praying the hot flush of my cheeks isn't visible. Of course he'd actually try to make small talk with me—I must be out of my mind to think he'd pretend to be semi-strangers for this entire journey. But that never stopped me from being irrational when it comes to Tyler Ferris and my stupid, fickle heart.

And now, Olive Austin, you're well and truly fucked.

Chapter Three

When I first met Tyler Ferris, I was being peer-pressured by my mom.

I wasn't particularly thrilled about having to work at a greasy, sweaty pizza joint. Sure, the food was good, and I wasn't the poor soul stuck doing deliveries, but coming home smelling like yeasty dough and simmered sauces isn't high on your list of priorities when you're sixteen. But Mom was insistent that, now that I was growing into semi-adulthood, I needed a semi-adult job to prove it. She'd already successfully coerced me into joining the field hockey team freshman year—arguing that spending *all* my time with her probably wasn't the most healthy—and now she was on a kick to get me employed, too.

"Besides," she'd added jovially as she drove me to the interview. "It'll feel nice to make your own money. You'll certainly be making more here than you do for your weekly allowance taking out the garbage." (She was right on that point, but not by much.)

I'd walked into Suburban Slices feeling wary, eyeing the chipped cement sidewalk outside and the hopelessly outdated glass brick window design, a pit forming in my stomach. As much as I wanted to go to the mall with my friends on the weekend with my own bit of cash to spend, I suddenly wasn't sure if it was worth working *here*. I made a mental note to see if any of the stuck-up shops at the mall were hiring. All the while, I was gripping the handle of my bag, feeling the reassuring weight of my planner inside. *Hey, even if this interview is a bust, at least I got to put a cute pizza sticker next to the interview note in today's date box.*

I pushed open the door and stepped inside, enveloped by the comforting smells of warm tomato sauce and crispy dough. The place was nice, if not a little small, with a few mismatched tables and chairs and a glass-topped pizza counter where two people were busily working. One was an older-looking man, all dark, wiry arm hair and bushy eyebrows, radiating the aura of being in charge, twisting dough between his fingers and spreading it out into a circular shape. His accomplice was younger, around my age, and was intensely stirring a vat of sauce before ladling some onto the stretched-out dough. At first glance, his face looked vaguely familiar, in a way that I couldn't quite place. Had I seen him around before?

"Hi." My voice came out embarrassingly squeaky and nervous, so I cleared my throat and started over. "Is Nunzio here? I'm supposed to have an interview for a position."

The boy just looked up from where he was helping the chef sauce a doughy circle of uncooked pizza, one eyebrow quirking up curiously, dark eyes studying me. "Interview?" he repeated, as if it was a foreign word, turning to the chef for confirmation. "I didn't even know he did those."

The chef responded with a grunt, sprinkling soft-looking cheese onto the pizza. When it became obvious that he wasn't going to say anything else, the boy turned to me apologetically.

"Sorry about that." He laughed awkwardly. "Let me go try to find him." He returned the ladle to its vat of sauce and disappeared into the swinging back doors of the kitchen.

I tried my best not to be awkward—and certainly failed—by wandering over to the fridge of bottled sodas, checking out their collection. The chef at the front continued his pizza-making task, completely ignoring me, and I couldn't help but think that maybe this *was* a bad idea after all. Sure, the stores at the mall were filled with snobby employees who seemed to resent you for wanting to shop, but it was probably better than working here.

I heard the doors swing back open and turned around just in time to see a short, gray-haired Italian man strolling out from the kitchen, the dark-haired boy in tow. Nunzio, the owner, judging by the way he clapped his hands and studied me, came to a stop practically nose to nose with me.

"Olive, yes?" He squinted as he looked at me, whether from old age or old-school Italian scrutiny, I couldn't be sure.

"Yes, sir." I worried that it sounded too formal, and the quirk of the boy's smile as he stepped back behind the counter and resumed his pizza-making tasks confirmed it.

"You're here for the job, yes?"

"Yes, sir."

Nunzio chuckled. "This is not the military, Olive. No need to be so formal."

Face burning in embarrassment, all I could do was nod.

The boy piped up from the counter, saving me the mental anguish. "Said she's here for an interview."

"Ah, yes, that." Nunzio waved his hand flippantly, dismissing any concern. He turned his full focus back on me. "Are you able to follow directions?"

I forced myself to sound grown up and mature, straightening my spine, hoping I was pulling it off. "I am."

Nunzio hummed a noise of approval. "And can you count?"

"I . . . I can." Previous math classes may have put that statement into question, but it was nothing he needed to know.

He clapped his hands together excitedly, decision made. "Perfect. You'll start tomorrow. Tyler can show you everything you'll need to know. Come in at three." Oblivious to my shock, Nunzio spun on his heel and disappeared back into the kitchen, stopping to declare something in rapid-fire Italian to the chef (who again grunted) before vanishing.

The boy at the counter—Tyler, apparently—looked at me again, impressed. "I mean, that's pretty standard for Nunzio's version of an interview, but I've never seen it happen that fast. He must really like you."

I shifted from foot to foot, face reddening. "Thanks." It must've been the pizza ovens making everything feel so stuffy and hot.

Tyler studied me for another second, lower lip jutting out slightly in concentration as he took in my dark, messy curls and green eyes, my summer freckles no doubt already making an appearance in a spray across my nose and cheeks. "Do I know you from somewhere? Do you go to Becker?"

Oh, great. "I do." Becker High wasn't the biggest high school in the world, but it was definitely big enough not to know every single person there, and it looked like this Tyler guy was one of them. "I'm guessing you do, too?"

He flicked a handful of cheese in my direction with a wicked grin, laughing as I blinked in surprise. "Guilty."

"Interesting." The giggle that slipped past my lips surprised even me, and all I could do was blink again as I picked a stray piece of cheese out of my hair. "I don't think I've ever seen you around."

Tyler gasped dramatically, clutching at his chest. "You wound me, Olive Austin. I've certainly seen *you* around."

My brain hooked on to the fact that he clearly *did* know me—he mentioned my last name without me ever bringing it up. Which brought on another hot flush of embarrassment, because not only did I have no idea who this guy was, but he also caught me.

I opened my mouth to start to apologize, because really, what else *was* there to do, but he just waved it off with a good-natured smile. "It's all good. My friends and I have always been more of the stick-to-the-sidelines type. But I'm sure you'll get to know me a lot better now that you're a fellow Suburban Slices pizza slinger." He puffed up his chest proudly, which jerked a laugh out of me.

"Here," he said, reaching out his hand. "Let me give you my number. In case you have any questions."

"Questions?" I raised my eyebrow at him unconvincingly. "About what? Directions to get to my place of employment, which I'm clearly already at and need no help getting to?" Still, I placated him and slipped my phone out of my back pocket, placing it in his palm. He tapped the screen for a few seconds before passing it back, proudly displaying my new contact—the name *Tyler* with the slice of pizza emoji next to it.

"Nice," I deadpanned. "Real clever. I never would've guessed."

He shrugged in response. "Sometimes you gotta go for the

obvious, right?" His teeth were nearly blinding in the fluorescent lights when he flashed them at me playfully.

The sound of Mom tapping the car horn outside shattered the moment, and I turned back to Tyler apologetically. "That's my ride. I have to go." I hurriedly combed the last stray flecks of cheese out of my hair and headed toward the door. "See you tomorrow, I guess?"

Tyler nodded at me, an undeniable warmth radiating from him. "See you tomorrow, Olive."

And while that was the first night I fell asleep thinking about his deep dimples and meltingly perfect brown eyes, it certainly wasn't the last.

Chapter Four

Well, at least I had the foresight to bring a decent pillow. I mean, *thirteen hours*. Good thing it's comfier than I remember, because my fake-sleeping shifts deep into a real dream about a kidnapping gone wrong—too many crime podcasts—when I'm jerked awake by the sound of the flight attendant's overly chipper voice.

"Drinks, anyone?"

I crack one eye open, adjusting to the dim lighting of the plane and the hum of the engines. And it's in that moment I notice the pillow I'm smushed up against isn't a pillow at all, my own pillow forgotten in my lap. Rather, my head is resting on the broad shoulder of a boy who I've nestled against many times before—but definitely don't have permission to do that with now.

"I . . . *shit* . . . sorry." I rocket away from Tyler as if his skin is on fire, while it's actually *my* cheeks that are burning. In doing so, I accidentally bump into Cranky Lady, who gives me the side-eye and sticks her nose further into her magazine. I'm not entirely sure, but I think she's still on the same page that she was when I tried to barter for her window seat. Either she's the slowest reader of all time or she's just unsociable as hell.

To his credit, Tyler doesn't look annoyed but is rather mildly amused as I flounder. "Was I snoring?" I ask through a yawn, feeling the dried drool in the corners of my mouth and immediately wishing I could evaporate into the air the plane is coasting through.

"Not at all." He's trying so hard to keep a straight face that he has to be lying. It wouldn't be the first time I've snored horrendously on his shoulder.

My gaze narrows. "Like a cow, huh?"

His quiet laugh seeps into my skin, warm and comfortable, like it's belonged there the whole time. "Nah."

"A bear?"

"Definitely not a bear."

"How about a—"

Tyler reaches over and gives my wrist a gentle, calming squeeze before letting go, searing me with his touch in a way that feels both shockingly new and achingly familiar. "Ol, it was fine. Nothing I haven't heard before. If you really want to know, it was like a white noise machine at most."

The flight attendant standing in the aisle next to us clears her throat, pointedly looking at the drink cart and dragging us back to the matter at hand.

"Two Cokes, please," Tyler says primly, adhering to the Law of Air Travel, which is that soda or alcohol is acceptable any time of day because time doesn't exist in airports or on planes. My throat is too fuzzy and dry to thank him, and I instead focus on the dark spot on his shoulder while the attendant fixes us our drinks.

Tyler glances my way, probably wondering why the hell my eyes are burning a hole into his hoodie, before his gaze flickers down and a quiet snort escapes his lips. There's no denying where the giant wet mark on his shoulder came from.

"Olive Austin." His voice is playful. "Did you just . . . drool on me?"

It takes superhuman strength not to pull the hoodie strings tight over my head again—that type of disappearing act is only effective three times maximum, and I've already used it twice. May as well save it for when things inevitably go even further south. I force myself to scoff, weakly playing it off as unperturbed. "Did not."

"Oh yeah?" He gestures to his sleeve as he passes over one of the cups. "What's this, then? Phantom drool?"

"I think the air-conditioning is leaking."

Another deep laugh, this time stirring Cranky Lady from her stupor as she glances at us curiously. "Definitely not."

I still can't tear my eyes away from the drool stain, shame heating my face. "I'm so sorry. I'll pay to have your hoodie cleaned when we get back."

He chuckles gently and jerks his chin toward my bag peeking out from underneath the seat, the corner of my planner poking out with its million tiny sticky note flags, a riot of colors. "You're gonna jot that down in your to-do list? I remember how much you were obsessed with that planner of yours."

I want to curl up and die—is there anything more embarrassing than being perceived by an ex who really, truly knows you even though you really, truly wish they didn't? "Really, Tyler. I'll get the hoodie cleaned, I promise."

Tyler looks at me, not saying anything. He's probably thinking the same thing I am, causing my cheeks to heat uncomfortably: We've swapped spit before. What's a little drool on a hoodie? Eventually, he clears his throat and takes a sip of his soda. "That's not necessary, but thanks." An odd formality has creeped into his voice, back to being strangers who don't banter about the decibels of my snoring.

It's like cold water over my head, a reminder of why I'm on this plane in the first place. *Jack.*

I'm on my way to see Jack.

My boyfriend.

Tyler doesn't hold that title anymore.

I glance down at my tiny plastic cup for a distraction, bubbles fizzing toward the surface. "You remembered my drink?"

Now it's Tyler's turn to scoff. "Of course I remembered, Ol. You practically waxed poetic about how a cold Coke was the best cure for nerves. And it's not like it's a particularly obscure soda to remember. It was the only thing you'd ever drink when we had shifts together at the pizzeria." Just the mere mention of the greasy, sweltering kitchen of Suburban Slices has me cringing.

I still remember the nervous tingle I felt all the way down to my toes when I walked into that bustling restaurant and saw him for the first time. The embarrassment I felt when I realized he knew me and I couldn't even place him. Imagine it, not recognizing the boy who would ultimately become the failed love of your life just a short year and a half down the road.

My first day at Suburban Slices wasn't what I expected—Nunzio, who for all intents and purposes was my *boss*, was nowhere to be found. He was busy puttering around town picking up ingredients and ensuring deliveries, so it was just me and Tyler, and the surly chef who I found out was named Bono.

"Don't even," he'd grumbled when Tyler opened his mouth to point out the U2 resemblance. "You guys need to start coming up with something more original."

"I was going to pivot to a more Sonny-and-Cher-style joke, but something tells me you won't find that funny, either," I deadpanned, and he cracked the smallest of grins.

"Ignore him," Tyler chirped good-naturedly as he waved me to another side of the counter, piled high with stacks of flat cardboard. "He skipped his espresso today and has been cranky ever since." He leaned forward to whisper conspiratorially to me, and I caught a whiff of his spicy cologne. "But between you and me, I can't tell the difference between when he's had it and he hasn't." The quip caught me off guard and I tried to stifle a snicker, but to no avail. Bono waved his hand in our direction and muttered something in Italian at Tyler, who took it in stride with a grin and told me that he had absolutely no idea what he said.

"All right, boss." Tyler's joking and good nature were warming me up toward him, and I was ready to get down to business. The place smelled less like pizza grease and desperation and more like warm, comfortable tomato sauce and bubbling cheese, and things felt like they were looking up. "What's on the agenda for today?"

Tyler schooled his expression into mock seriousness. "Before you can learn the sacred art of putting toppings on a pizza, you have to learn the crucial base skill of working at Suburban Slices." He lowered his voice to a hushed, awed whisper. "Folding pizza boxes."

I blinked at him as my eyes traveled to the flat pile of cardboard on the counter. "You mean they don't just come pre-folded? I never would've guessed."

When Tyler threw back his head and laughed, a hot rush of pride surged through my chest, pleased that I was the one to elicit such a reaction out of him. He was still wiping the tears from his eyes when the front door to the restaurant opened, the little bell chiming to signal a new arrival.

"What's got you in stitches, Ty? Anything good?" a purple-haired girl asked as she strode up to the counter, ears glinting with an array of piercings. Her lips were painted a dark berry red, so deep it was almost the color of her hair. Her gaze hesitated over me for a few seconds before turning back to Tyler. "New hire?"

Tyler nodded between the two of us. "Yep, this is Olive. Nunzio hired her yesterday, so we're going over the ancient art of pizza box folding as her first training exercise."

"Nice." She nodded appreciatively, but her stoic expression didn't change. She didn't seem mean per se, but she definitely seemed prickly.

Tyler gestured in her direction. "Olive, this is Delia Franklin, my best friend and resident pain in my ass at all times."

"It's nice to meet you," I said primly, arranging my face into a warm smile. "I'm Olive Austin."

Delia simply looked at me coolly, expression unreadable. "I know who you are, Olive. We go to school together."

I felt my smile slip a little bit, concerned. *How come I don't remember any of these people?* "Right."

Delia heaved a sigh like the world was on her shoulders and leaned against the counter, rapping her knuckles on it lightly, silver rings and indigo nail polish glinting in the fluorescent lights. "Well, I'll let you guys get back to your riveting task. I'm just here to pick up my check." She gave us a wave and disappeared into Nunzio's back office, and all I could do was stare at the spot she'd been standing, taken aback by the entire exchange.

"She works here?" I'd asked, perplexed.

Tyler nodded as he pulled sleeves of cardboard from the counter and settled them in front of us, ready to begin my training. "Not behind the counter. She's the delivery driver most nights. It's how we became such good friends. She can be a bit much when you first meet her, but she'll grow on you eventually."

I hummed in acknowledgment as I followed Tyler's steps and started folding the boxes. It seemed like there was a comfortable rapport between the two of them, and even though I'd only known Tyler for twenty-four-ish hours at that point, I was startled by the low simmer of jealousy in my stomach.

I just had to hope that she'd grow on me, like Tyler said. It didn't seem like there was anything romantic there—but at the time, there hadn't been anything romantic between me and Tyler yet, either. Delia was another person in his world, someone I had to hopefully charm into liking me.

And grow on me she did. It didn't take long for us to become a trio, constantly spending all of our weekends together walking around the mall, going to the movies, or making Taco Bell runs late at night and eating our hauls in Delia's ancient, idling Camry in the fluorescent-washed parking lot. As someone whose household only consisted of myself and my mother, I often felt shy and awkward around my peers—it was the default that I hadn't even realized I was leaning back on. But Delia and Tyler had a way of making me feel like I was meant to be there with them, and it was like my shyness evaporated into thin air.

At one point that summer, my mother commented that she always knew where all three of us were at all times because wherever one of us was, it was inevitable that the other two would follow. She was thrilled that I'd finally found some friends that I was hanging with regularly, even though I knew she secretly *did* love the nights—even if they were getting rarer—when the two of us would curl up on our couch with fresh popcorn and put on a movie for some mother-daughter time.

And for the first time in my high school life, I found myself sinking into a group of friends who weren't just polite acquaintances on the field hockey team, making idle chitchat at mandatory team bondings and pasta dinners. I was more of a floater at school, bouncing between groups with surface-level friendships, never able to really get past the stilted and awkward phase of getting to know someone—at least, not until Tyler and his extrovert tendencies helped break me out of my shell. With him and Delia, I finally felt like I was part of a *unit*. That I was a puzzle piece that fit effortlessly, clicking into a place in their lives with no force at all.

That is, until I blew everything up, and suddenly Delia didn't want anything to do with me anymore. And it's not like I can point any fingers with my role in the entire situation.

The summer Tyler and I worked at Suburban Slices was when we really got to know each other. All the chitchatting in between flipping pizzas, building boxes, and doling out saucy, gooey slices gave you a lot of time to get to know someone. We talked about everything from our favorite types of movies (early 2000s rom-coms for me, superhero films for him), movie theater candies (I'm a Sno-Caps girl, but Tyler is a popcorn loyalist and thinks it shouldn't be tainted with any kind of chocolate), and other hobbies (tabletop games for Tyler and field hockey for me). The conversations even continued after work when he'd occasionally offer to give me a ride home, since he had his learner's permit and his parents let him take their rusty Jeep to and from work—and I was the contraband passenger, where our chatter would continue right until he pulled up to my house and put the vehicle in park.

Right away, I knew that I was drawn to Tyler, that I liked him, but I didn't realize how much. He always had an easy smile, the kind that made your blood fizzy when it was directed at you. He had that tantalizing dark hair and dark eyes combo. And even though it wasn't legal at sixteen to have tattoos, he had a few stick-and-pokes from his guys' nights of various little things—an old Atari gaming system, a slice of pizza (which he swore wasn't related to his job at Suburban Slices), and even a random piece of toast.

Now, on this plane, I watch his hoodie sleeve on the armrest next to me, thinking of the ink that rests beneath it. It makes my heart pang in an uncomfortable way.

Back when I first met Tyler, he was quirky and funny and friendly in all the right ways. He was filled with adventure and promise—exactly the things you want at sixteen. Before you understand that life requires a lot more stability than stick-and-pokes and flimsy life plans.

Adventure and throwing caution to the wind are cute when you're young. But if I've learned anything from Mom's string of heartbreaks, it's that those things don't hold up in the real world for too long.

But I didn't know that back then. In the moment, Tyler Ferris charmed me, and I wanted to stay in his orbit. That much I *did* know. Especially when, a few weeks after meeting Tyler, he asked me to be his girlfriend via a sweet, clumsily scrawled message on the inside of a Suburban Slices pizza box. I don't think I'll ever be able to forget the nervous grin on his face as he presented the cardboard to me, speckled with grease and cheese from the heart-shaped pie he attempted, which resembled more of a blob but tasted as perfect on my tongue as when I told him yes.

Chapter Five

Now I watch the flight attendant make her way back up the aisle to collect garbage, everyone passing empty cups and napkins and cans. Tyler gives his over, wordlessly reaching out his hand to collect mine, too. It's not something that should be that big of a deal, but chivalry on a plane thirty-five thousand feet in the air is hard to come by.

"You know," he says quietly once the flight attendant has moved on to the next row. "It's been really weird running into you at school and just . . . not getting to talk to you like we always used to. I kind of hate it."

I do, too. But I don't voice that out loud—instead I nervously twist my fingers around the edge of my hoodie sleeve, wishing that the next few hours could burn by so we don't have to do this awkward slow dance with each other. It's much easier to handle in school, where I can always make an excuse about being late for a class or needing to run to my locker or disappearing in the fold of my field hockey teammates before a practice. But here, with no handy distractions or excuses, there's no escaping the awkward conversation that Tyler seems insistent we have.

"It's just different now," I eventually mumble into my lap,

my heart breaking further with every single word. It's hard to believe there are still pieces of it left to break after everything that happened, and judging by the pained look on Tyler's face, that seems to be how he feels, too.

"Okay, Olive," he responds softly, hurt still echoing across his face—rolling over his cheekbones and eyelashes and the gentle slope of his nose that I always used to love tracing with my fingertips while lying together. "I get it. We don't have to keep talking about it." He shifts back in his seat toward his own TV, popping his headphones in and giving me the silence I thought I'd been craving. But now that I've got it, I'm not so sure.

But that's always been Tyler for you—aware of other people's feelings to a fault. Sometimes before you even realized that it's how you felt.

Tyler and I dated from the start of sophomore year until the fall of junior year. Moving from friendship to dating him felt as natural as breathing, swimming, the seasons changing. Our date nights were filled with all sorts of adventures—late nights taking the leftover pizza slices from work and having picnics in the open trunk of his Jeep, movie marathons spent curled up on the couch arguing over the merit of putting Sno-Caps in the popcorn, grabbing Coke slushies and sitting on the sun-warmed concrete while watching Tyler practice new tricks on his skateboard at the park. Every second I wasn't with him, I was thinking about the next time I would be, and every time we were together, it felt like magic.

That was the start of what I thought would be forever.

But *boy,* was I wrong.

Tyler was like the easygoing, adventurous antithesis to my more structured nature. Spontaneous date nights and day trips were one thing, but when it came to our futures—something that, at sixteen, felt both light-years away and eerily pressing at the same time—Tyler had absolutely no idea what he wanted to do with his life. Whenever I brought it up, he'd get cagey and change the subject or laugh and make a joke about how he wanted to be a professional skateboarder, pizza slinger, or something equally ridiculous.

"I'm thinking about being a professional tattoo decider," he'd joked the fall of our junior year as we were heading to class, pausing in the hallway to gesture at the career-fair poster tacked up on the big community board. "Like, my job would be to hang out at the tattoo parlor and help people decide between the two designs they aren't sure about."

I hummed noncommittally, fingers tightening around my backpack straps. I'd grown tired of Tyler's cheeky jokes about his future, which were funny at first but then shifted to annoying, then downright stressful. Delia and I had several conversations about it, which already felt like crossing a line, because discussing one of us behind the other's back was *not* something we were prone to doing.

I think this is why you need to talk to him, she'd pointed out over text just the night before, which I found rather unhelpful. *Clearly you guys aren't on the same page about things, and it's time to shape up or ship out.*

While some may find that harsh, I was unfazed, because that was Delia Franklin for you—blunt to a fault, even when you didn't want to hear it. If she knew it's what you *needed* to hear, that's what you were going to get, whether you liked it or not.

Granted, I don't think she expected everything to fall out the way that it did. Even after, when I'd occasionally scroll through our now-silent text thread in heartbroken dismay, I'd think about how the *ship out* part of her statement was meant to be rhetorical.

Junior year was when everything was supposed to start falling into place—SAT scores, career fairs, college visits, life planning. I'd been meticulously studying the list of company attendees at the career fair for a week, internally memorizing the layout and planning who I was going to talk to at which point, what I was going to say, who I still needed to research, and what I was going to wear. Tyler, on the other hand, just seemed thrilled about the fact that the last two periods of that day were going to be cut short.

"Ol?" Tyler nudged my shoulder to get my attention, jerking his chin toward the poster. Even though his joking attitude about our futures was grating on me, I couldn't fight the flip in my stomach at his beaming smile.

I was addicted, for better or for worse. "Sorry, what?"

"I said, what do you think about that? Being a professional tattoo decider?"

Bite your tongue, Olive. I knew that snapping at Tyler or pushing him away wasn't going to get me anywhere—it never does with free spirits like that. They don't respond well to directness. It's better to approach things as recommendations. "I think that there won't be a professional tattoo decider booth at the fair, so you should probably expand your options a little bit."

Something in Tyler's face subtly tightened. "Yeah. I told you, I'll look at the list before the fair."

"The fair's on Tuesday. It's Friday." Even then, I hated the nagging in my voice, but I couldn't stop it. The thought of spending my life with a professional tattoo decider, whatever that was, filled me with the same sinking feeling I got whenever Mom walked out the door for a date with whatever man she'd been seeing, swearing this one was *the* one when I knew later that night she'd walk back in with a crushed look on her face that told me she'd been wrong, again.

Tyler adjusted the strap of his backpack and didn't look at me. "Yeah, um, about that." He took a deep breath, visibly steeling himself in a way that sent warning bells off in my stuffed-to-the-brim brain. "I'm . . . I'm not even sure if I'm going to go, Olive. I don't know if there's anything there for me."

We rounded the corner toward a quiet hallway, and I couldn't stop from turning on my heel and looking at him, dumbfounded. "What do you mean? You don't even know what you want to do! How do you know you won't find something that you like there?"

He answered with a shrug. "I don't know, Ol. I just . . . I don't have a ten-step life plan the same way you do, okay? I don't have a planner in my backpack that weighs more than a small child, organizing my life to a T. We're only juniors. There's a lot that can change between now and when we graduate and choose entire *careers*." He tugged at the collar of his Modest Mouse shirt, face flushed. "The thought of locking myself into a life path right now makes me feel . . . itchy."

Looking back, I should've told Tyler that things could change over time, that what he chose then didn't necessarily have to be his forever path, as long as he put himself on *some* sort of path. That anything was better than wandering around aimlessly, not having a care in the world about the future because you're all about *living in the moment*, that while it's fun to be young, it's also important to put stock in your future, to put yourself on a track that gives you the ability to put down roots. Anything that saves you from a string of heartache after heartache when you realize that being young, wild, and free isn't forever.

If anyone knows firsthand what that looks like down the line, it's me.

I could've said any of those things, but I didn't. What came out of my mouth were the seven words that I wish more than anything I could've delivered differently.

I don't think we're going to work.

"Olive?" Tyler's voice nudges me now, breaking me out of my trance. "Are you feeling nervous being on this plane right now? You're doing that thing with your hands again."

I immediately force myself to stop worrying the hem of my sweatshirt between my fingers. "No."

"Okay," he says slowly, eyes scanning my face like he doesn't believe me. "Are you feeling nervous sitting next to *me*? Because if so, I can see if the flight attendant is willing to—"

"I'm not nervous," I blurt, an instant lie that betrays me immediately, judging by the way Tyler shakes his head. "Besides, the flight is full. I bought the last seat."

"Unless you've changed completely, Olive, you forget how well I know you." He says it flippantly, but there's a slight edge to his voice. A quiet sting that reminds me of exactly what I gave up by stepping away from us. The conversation is tipping toward awkward and stilted territory, fast.

After a beat, I sigh into the fresh cup of Coke that the flight attendant passes over on her route back toward the cockpit, then take a tentative sip, relishing the feeling of the bubbly, sugary liquid coating my tongue. "You're right. I did forget."

Tyler blows out a disappointed breath and takes a big swig of his own drink, nearly draining the tiny cup. "Forgot that fast, huh? It's been less than two years." His voice is equal parts casual and biting—as if the war on how he should feel right now is wearing on him, too. Cranky Lady must sense the tension, because she yawns dramatically and puts on her headphones and eye mask, snuggling up against the window and leaning as far away from the two of us as she can possibly get, which is not very far when you're sitting in coach.

When I make no move to answer Tyler, instead staring into my cup of bubbles like it holds the secrets of the universe, Tyler tries again.

"So, Ol—"

"Olive," I interrupt, firm. "Nobody calls me Ol anymore." *That name only ever belonged to you.* But now, *Tyler* doesn't belong to me.

He swallows, clearly thrown off but attempting to recover. "Right. So, how's Mr. Two First Names?" Jack's last name being Cameron made this a joke Tyler came up with right before we started dating—one I used to laugh about but now no longer find funny.

"Don't call him that," I snap, the bite in my voice surprising me.

Tyler, however, is unfazed. His mouth quirks up in the corner in his telltale smirk. "Right, sorry, let me rephrase. I meant to ask, how's that Jack*ass*?"

"*Jack* is great." I give him a pointed look when emphasizing his name, but Tyler's expression is unreadable. "I'm on my way to visit him right now, actually."

Understanding dawns on Tyler's face, and he leans back in his seat. "Ah, right. I forgot he went to UH. Heard it's a pretty great school."

The mere mention of Jack being away at school causes the fizziness in my chest from the soda to be replaced with something much heavier—panic. Because Tyler just unknowingly reminded me why I'm on this plane in the first place.

The unanswered texts. The unanswered calls. The fear that when this plane lands in Hawai'i and I step off of it and go see Jack, I may not like what I find.

But as quickly as those thoughts flash in my mind, they're replaced by another. As I watch Tyler fiddle with his headphones, eyebrows knitted in concentration, it becomes crystal clear. I pop in my own headphones in a wordless response.

He can't know anything about what's going on. I couldn't take the gloating if he did, the *I told you so* that I rightly deserve to hear but want to avoid anyway.

I can't question if the decision I made back then was the right one.

I have to believe that it was.

Chapter Six

"So." Tyler's voice interrupts the podcast I'd gone back to listening to, and I pause it in mild annoyance. "How's Mr. Two First Names doing at the University of Hawai'i?"

I straighten up, narrowing my eyes a little. "I told you, *Jack* is doing fine," I reply in a voice that better translates to *You have no right to ask*. "Mom said I could start my spring break trip a little early."

"Ah, Sherri. I miss her." His tone is wistful, bringing me back to all the jokes they shared over our kitchen table, and the appreciation he had for Mom's truly out-of-control mug collection. "How's she doing?"

"She's fine." *As fine as she can be, for someone who was just broken up with again*. Tyler must read it in my tone, because he frowns and sits up straighter.

"Another one?"

My grim nod confirms it. "Another one."

"Damn." He sits back and shakes his head, disappointed. "Was it Neil? I was really hoping he was the one for her. They got along so well."

It's surprising to me that he still remembers who my mother

was dating a year ago, but then again, that's Tyler Ferris for you—thoughtful to a fault. I think Mom took our breakup even harder than I did, especially because even though I told her when it happened, I still haven't told her why. "Yeah. She really was sure he was going to be The One, you know? She spent a whole month fixing her chipped nails every single day, because she swore a proposal was on the horizon. Really thought it was about to happen when he showed up and took her on a surprise dinner date—but it was more of a breakup date." As soon as the words leave my lips, Cranky Lady gasps in the seat next to us, and both Tyler and I glance her way.

She lowers the magazine she'd gone back to reading in the middle of my spiel, having given up on trying to sleep. "What? That's too good of a story to pretend I didn't hear it."

"I know, right?" The easy way Tyler immediately jumps into the conversation with our less-than-pleasant seatmate is a reminder of how he possesses the scarily easy ability to connect with anyone he comes across. "I mean, a *breakup dinner*? That's worse than breaking up over a text message, in my opinion. Thank god I've never been broken up with that way." His eyes skirt over me and my face heats up in shame, because while I may have had the heart not to break up with Tyler over text, I'm still not entirely proud of how I *did* handle it. And judging by the quick look he gives me, it seems like he isn't quite over it, either.

Cranky Lady nods sagely, placing the magazine in her lap. "Oh, definitely. Entirely inexcusable."

Tyler points at her as if to say *exactly,* before turning back to me. "When are you finally going to break through as her voice of reason and convince her to ditch these deadbeats?"

Yeah, right. This gets a mirthless laugh out of me. "Please.

We both know that the only voice of reason Sherri Austin listens to is her own. And that's probably why she keeps ending up in these situations." It's not even like this is close to her worst heartbreak, either. Tyler nods in agreement.

The worst heartbreak of my mother's that Tyler had ever seen was when some guy named Asher from LA proposed to her during a whirlwind weekend together after dating for a few months. Mom swore it was the real deal, as she often did—and it was right around the time that Tyler started coming over to the house, so he got a firsthand look at all the wedding planning she'd started doing, before she and Asher (read: mainly Asher) decided to scrap the whole thing and elope in Vegas. Tyler had been helping me pack and talking me through my jumble of nerves, being that I'd only been to Vegas with my mother one other time, and there was particularly bad turbulence that left me wary of planes ever since.

I remember, as soon as I'd heard about her harebrained idea, how quickly I'd pulled out my phone and texted Delia and Tyler in our group chat.

Olive: OMG, you guys, Asher and my mom decided they're going to ELOPE.

Tyler: ??? What happened to the big white wedding she was going on about?

Delia: Wait, she's actually going through with marrying that weirdo?

Olive: Guess so. Gets worse—they're doing it in Vegas

Delia: OMG. This, I have to hear about. Are we all invited?

Olive: Ha, probably not. I'm shocked *I* even snagged an invite.

Delia: Well, I'm sure it's bound to be the party of the season. Send lots of pics!

Delia: Oh, and if you manage to sneak yourself into a casino, give me a call first.

Delia: My uncle taught me some blackjack tips that could come in handy.

Olive: Yeah D, I'll be sure to keep that in mind 🙄

Tyler: Ol, this is crazy.

Tyler: Hang tight. I'm coming over.

Delia: Wish I could join, but Nunzio has me doing double duty on deliveries tonight.

Delia: Pray that the customers tip well so I have some Vegas betting funds to contribute xo

"Is your mom sure about this?" Tyler whispered to me when he showed up fifteen minutes later, concern lining his features.

We listened to the sounds of Mom struggling to zip up her suitcase in the den downstairs, humming "Chapel of Love" under her breath while she worked. "She seemed so excited about the big wedding every time I came over. She was literally showing me her Pinterest mood board the other day."

"Pinterest?" I looked up from where I was folding the last few T-shirts that would fit into my bag. "I didn't realize she even knew how to *work* Pinterest. Or that she knew what a mood board was."

Tyler shrugged. "I didn't even know what Pinterest *was* until she showed me. It's kinda cool."

I grunted as I tried to close my own suitcase, which was nearly bursting open and one step away from vomiting its contents all over my bed. Tyler was perched on my desk chair, watching the whole thing in bemusement, since I refused to let him help. I watched him glance over at my planner, open on my desk, the Vegas wedding date inked in bright pink pen with a tiny diamond ring sticker next to it. Even if I wasn't totally on board with the plan, it was in the planner, and so it shall be.

"It's what she wants," I explained with a sigh, even if I knew that deep down, I agreed with him and the whole thing felt like a mistake. "Who am I to stand in the way of that?"

Tyler's eyes tracked my hands as, frustrated, I jerked the zipper of the suitcase closed. "Well, for starters, you're pretty much her only voice of reason."

I couldn't help but snort at that. "Please. I couldn't get through to her even if I tried. She's a lost cause when it comes to these men, and she's going to wind up pushing forward with whatever she wants to do, anyway."

And lo and behold, she did—twelve hours later, Mom and I

were standing in our still-dark kitchen waiting for the cab to the airport, which is exactly when Asher texted her to call off the wedding. *Texted her.* He couldn't even bother to call her or, I don't know, actually show up to tell her to her face. My mother'd had some close calls with love before, but until that moment, she'd never been *en route to the wedding itself* when everything fell apart.

I wasn't even thinking when I did it—my brain was on autopilot. It was five in the morning, my mother had just crumpled to the ground wailing in heartbroken agony, and I didn't know what to do, so my muscles took over. I hadn't even known I'd taken the phone out of my pocket until I heard Tyler's sleepy voice on the other line.

"Ol?" he mumbled, punctuated by a yawn. "Is everything okay?"

"Yes . . . and no. We're okay," I hurriedly explained, because while it *was* a heartbreak emergency, thankfully nobody was actually dying. I was so ashamed that in that moment, the biggest thing on my mind was that I would have to scratch out the pink-inked note about Mom's wedding day in my planner. That the tiny diamond ring sticker would probably rip the paper when I pulled it up. That my perfectly organized planner would look ugly and ruined—not unlike the state of my mother's relationship.

"Did you guys get to the airport okay?" Tyler's voice interrupted my mental self-shaming.

I sighed into the receiver as I watched my mother curl up on the couch, her body shaking with unreleased sobs, not unlike an infant whose face turns all purple before letting out a piercing wail. "That's the thing, Ty . . . I don't think we're going to the airport." *And that stupid diamond ring sticker is going to ruin this week's layout,* I wanted to blurt, but I didn't, even though Tyler would've immediately understood why that bothered me so much, because he's Tyler.

The clock on the microwave hadn't even hit five-fifteen before there was a knock at the door. When I swung it open, I was still surprised to see him there, even though somewhere deep in the chambers of my heart, I knew he would be.

"I got here as fast as I could." Tyler yawned again, standing there in the purpling dawn with his rumpled pajama pants, hoodie, and a pillow-creased face. "How can I help?"

And while there is no medically documented cure for heartbreak—nothing but time, and wine, and ice cream, unfortunately—Tyler was the biggest help that day, whether it involved sitting on the couch with Mom while she vented her frustrations, or fixing her a mug of tea, or quietly lowering the volume on the TV after she dozed off watching *Jeopardy!* He helped me cancel the flight and get back the hotel deposit with no problems.

Tyler Ferris spent the whole day, from sunrise to sunset, helping me nurse my mother's heart back to health, and he had no idea how grateful I was for it. I told him that much after dinner, when Mom finally slunk up to her room with a piercing headache, and he and I were sprawled across my bed, my head in his lap while his fingers toyed gently with the roots of my hair, giving me a much-needed scalp massage after a day of nonstop caretaking and stress.

I was certain that, after witnessing an entire day of my mother's mental unraveling and the drama that was our two-person family, Tyler would want out. Or at least wouldn't want to hang around my house anymore. But when I told him that it was getting late and it would be okay if he left, he looked down at me incredulously.

"You want me to leave?" He looked a little bit wounded. "But what if your mom needs either of us? I'm happy to stay, Ol—I already talked to my parents about it."

"You talked to your parents about my *mom*?" I bolted up, and a hot lick of shame slithered across my face, and the shock on Tyler's face let me know it was visible. I'd met Tyler's parents before, and they were so sweet and somewhat sickeningly picture-perfect, the epitome of finding your soulmate and building a life with them. The complete antithesis of me and my mom. It was, to put it lightly, mortifying to think about them knowing the details of our life.

"No, no, no—I would never." He reached out and grabbed both my hands, squeezing reassuringly. "I told them you needed me here today because you're going through something. They said it's fine, Olive. They know I'd never leave you if you needed my help."

First the embarrassment of Tyler potentially telling his parents about my crazy, reckless mother, and then the mortification of being someone who needed help—it was too much. I'd pulled my hands out of his grip and started pacing my room.

"I appreciate it, I really do," I said, and the words were true, even if it hurt to say the rest of it. "But I don't need your help. This isn't the first time she's been like this. We'll be just fine."

I expected Tyler to be agreeable and leave, or, on the other hand, at least put up some sort of fight. But he did neither of those things. He simply leaned back against the pillows on my bed, nodding seriously. "Of course you'd be okay," he said after a few quiet seconds, seeming to choose his words carefully. "It was never a question about whether you'd be okay. I just didn't want you to have to go through that alone if you didn't have to."

Oh, I remember thinking, *when did someone light a sparkler in my heart?*

I already knew I loved Tyler, but up until that moment, I'd never known what people meant when they said they fell more and more in love with a person every day. Once you've given someone your whole heart, how could you fall any deeper? But that was the moment I knew love wasn't just contained in the four chambers of a human heart—it was a well with no bottom.

Or rather, with a very *far down* bottom—but eventually, pennies and wishes tossed over the edge would crash against the cold, dark stone below.

Life taught me that lesson, and fast.

I just didn't know it yet. I still had the naïve belief that all wells were bottomless, catching your wishes and storing them safely. Not sending them down into a darkness they can't climb back from.

Chapter Seven

Tyler sucks in a breath through his teeth, letting it out with a quiet *pop,* jarring me out of the uncomfortable memory and pulling me back to our plane conversation. "I mean, Neil broke up with Sherri over a *dinner*? That's just brutal. Did she take it okay?" I can see the question in his eyes that he isn't quite asking. *Is she taking it as poorly as she did last time?*

"She's okay. Hurt, but okay." I can still see her face behind my eyelids if I think about it, so crushed and hopeless. At least there was no sobbing on the kitchen floor this time. And Cranky Lady is nodding right alongside me, as if she could see it, too.

Tyler laughs quietly. "That still sucks. Worse than being broken up with in a school hallway, am I right, Ol? At least you had the decency to not get my hopes up over dinner first."

Cranky Lady's eyes widen and pinball between the two of us, piecing it together. *Oh,* her expression seems to say, quickly morphing from surprised to apologetic. Maybe she's regretting not switching seats with me earlier.

Tyler grimaces, realizing what he laid out in the open, while I consider the chances of the emergency exit opening and sucking me into the stratosphere—and if that would really be the worse option right now. Cranky Lady, to her credit, picks her magazine back up with one last *Good luck* glance at the two of us, resuming her reading. Or not-reading. Either way, the shame is bubbling fierce and hard in my stomach.

"All right," he mumbles awkwardly after a few painfully silent seconds, scratching the back of his neck. "Let's just . . . let's just agree not to talk about that."

"Yeah," I respond tightly, twisting my knuckles together in my lap. "I think that's for the best."

He huffs out a short laugh. "Wouldn't want this flight to get any more awkward than it already is."

Another thought dawns on me suspiciously then, and I turn to Tyler. "Why are *you* on this plane a week before spring break? You don't have a secret girlfriend hiding out in Waikiki, do you?"

The accusation just makes Tyler laugh as he shifts in his seat, absentmindedly clicking through the seat's television channels to avoid looking at me. It's hard to tell in the dim plane light, but I think his cheeks are a little red. "Nope, no girlfriend." An odd rush of relief sweeps through me at his words, and I have to mentally poke myself and remember that *I am currently on a plane to Hawai'i to visit my actual boyfriend.*

"Got it." I nod. "Any plans for after graduation?"

Tyler suddenly looks even more uncomfortable than he did a mere few seconds ago, not meeting my eyes now as he tugs on the hem of his hoodie. "I, uh, don't think so. I talked to my parents, and taking a gap year makes the most sense for me right now. I can always assess things later to see how I feel."

Even though that's the complete opposite of what I'd choose for myself, it's so very Tyler. It makes my chest ache to push out the next words, but I force the conversation to continue, because we've come this far into talking to each other again and I'm not quite ready to back out yet. "Do you have any idea what you're going to do in the interim? Work? Travel?"

He shrugs. "I'll figure it out as I go, I guess. That's not why I'm going to Hawai'i, though. I'm heading out there to visit Lucas and Ella—they just had their first daughter. Lucas is going to be away for some military training next week, so we figured I'd go out to see them now. I went back when they first moved, and it was pretty cool."

The mention of Tyler's older brother brings back hazy memories of photos of him in his marine uniform scattered throughout the house. Although my family is incredibly small—no siblings or living grandparents, and a father I never knew—Tyler's is absolutely massive. Tyler's older brother, Lucas, had married a lovely woman named Ella. Both of his parents are also one of six children, so there were plenty of aunts and uncles and cousins to go around at the family events I attended. While it was warm and inviting to be enveloped into his family, it also drew attention to the emptiness of my childhood, of dinners alone with my mother, of the barbeques and holiday dinners that I never had or could invite Tyler to.

But of course, I can't escape the coo that comes out when he mentions a baby. "That's adorable. Congratulations! Wow, Uncle Ty at only eighteen years old. Impressive."

"I know, right?" He beams and thanks the flight attendant as she passes by with a basket full of chips, handing me a bag before opening one of his own. "It's kind of weird to think that once upon a time, my brother was trying to shove my head into the toilet pretty much daily, but now he's the father of an adorable little human being."

I can picture that bullying clear as day, and even witnessed it once or twice. "What's her name?"

He grins excitedly, clearly animated when it comes to his newborn niece. "Mele. Her name means 'music' in Hawaiian. I don't know if you remember, but Ella's a really good flute player. She—"

"Oh, don't worry," I interrupt with a laugh. "I remember." I can recall the beautiful, crisp notes floating along the wind at many of Tyler's family's barbeques during the summer we were together. "She's incredible."

Tyler nods and glances into his bag of chips, lost in thought and suddenly looking a little sad. "Yeah. They moved out to the base in Kāneʻohe Bay that fall." He doesn't say the words we're both thinking, but my brain ad-libs them in anyway. *The fall we broke up.* "They're living a great life out there, don't get me wrong, but it's weird being the only child at home."

"Tell me about it." He's preaching to the choir with that one, and he knows it.

Tyler blinks in surprise and breaks his intense stare down into his chips, realization about what he said dawning on his face. "Sorry, Ol—Olive. I didn't mean—"

"It's okay." And I mean it. Tyler already knows how I feel about being an only child—the product of a two-week stand with a sailor eighteen years ago, back when Mom was even more serious about trying to find The One. Only that time, the man she'd been with (my dad, I guess, although he never was one to me) didn't break up with her because they'd fallen out of love. He broke up with her because he was already *married*.

Clearly, I've never had any desire to connect with my sleazeball of a father, and Mom never settled with someone long enough to give me that long-desired sibling. So I've lived vicariously through Tyler with Lucas, as well as with Jack and his sister Isabelle. They're both lucky to have those coveted older siblings, mingling at family gatherings, calling each other on the phone. Another thing I wanted and never got.

Tyler coughs in an awkward attempt to redirect the conversation. "Enough about me. Why are you visiting Mr. Two First Names before spring break? Just because?"

Because I'm pretty sure he isn't cheating on me, but I want to check to make sure. Because he's been weird lately. Because something about us doesn't feel right, which is throwing me off because I never felt that way when I was with you. I don't say any of this, instead settling on a simple lie. "Because I love and miss him, obviously."

Shock registers across Tyler's face, as if I've slapped him. "You love him?"

It's only been a year, but he can't seriously be that clueless. "Why wouldn't I?" While me visiting Jack may not necessarily be just because I miss him, it doesn't mean that I still don't love him. Those things don't have to be mutually exclusive, right?

Tyler coughs and hurries to course-correct. "No, you . . . you should. Obviously. He's your boyfriend. You *should* love him." His neck flushes pink, clearly out of his element. He's a long way from being the carefree, charming boy I first fell in love with at Suburban Slices. For only the second time in all the years I've known him, the first being a day we'd both rather forget, Tyler Ferris is at a loss for words.

Finally, he manages to find them. "And how are things with his friends? You get along with them all okay?"

"We get along fine." And that really is the truth—there isn't much more to say about it other than yes, I do get along with them *fine*. If falling in love with Tyler felt as easy as breathing, falling into a relationship and life with Jack felt like a well-executed plan.

Technically, if anyone was to blame for putting Jack in my path, it's my junior-year chemistry teacher. It was an AP class, which usually had a bigger mix of all the grades, and so, for our first lab assignment that fall semester, I found myself paired up with a senior.

Not just any senior, though—the elusive, illustrious Jack Cameron. Golden boy of the senior class, the one that everyone wanted to know and be known by. But the thing that made Jack so charming to me wasn't his money, or his parents' connections, or the fact that he was older and thus, by the laws that governed high school logic, wiser. From the very first day where we slid onto the stools of the workbench in the back of Mr. Thatcher's classroom, he was . . . completely normal. Just a tall, toned teenage boy with wheat-gold hair that shone in the sunlight beaming through the windows and piercing blue eyes to match.

"Jack," he offered by way of explanation as I started lining up glass beakers for the in-class experiment, trying to keep my cool because one of the most popular senior guys in school was speaking to me, which the field hockey girls would go gaga over at practice. "Your name is Olive, right?"

I remember being taken aback. "Uh, y-yeah. How did you know?" The class had started a few days ago and Mr. Thatcher was mercifully not one of those teachers who made us do those embarrassing icebreakers, so it's not like Jack had any reason to know me. But he'd only smiled at my question as he picked up one of the pipettes and the sheet of instructions, looking curiously at my planner stacked neatly next to me on the bench.

"I've seen you around," he said simply. "And I've seen you on the honor roll list, too. Couldn't have been paired up with anyone better, which is a relief, because I suck at chemistry, and you seem organized enough to help us both out."

I felt myself light up at his praise, pleased to be recognized. I didn't have a lot going on once I scaled back on field hockey—moving to the intramural team—to focus on SAT prep junior year, so it made my heart feel fizzy to get some recognition for throwing myself into my studies (and my planner-stickering). "Thank you. I've heard you're not too bad yourself." This got him to chuckle, but we didn't say much else as we got to work.

"Are you doing anything tonight?" Jack asked, cheeks a dusky shade of pink as he kept his eyes trained on the bubbling liquid in front of us. I was in the middle of jotting down the final notes about the conclusion of the experiment, and my pen halted.

"Me? Why?" This was not following the laws of high school politics. Juniors did *not* hang out with seniors. Not unless they were required to, like in gym class or in labs. They were acquaintances at most. And they definitely did *not* pass party invitations among each other unless you qualified for one of the only two exceptions:

A. You were a junior or a senior with a sibling who was in the other grade, so you got automatic VIP status. Or:
B. You were inter-grade dating (which I was not, Tyler being only a few months older than me).

Jack, clearly flustered, scratched the back of his neck, the shade of his cheeks darkening even further. "Nothing major. My buddies and I are throwing a party at my house . . . It's open invite, and, ah, I was wondering . . . if you and your friends wanted to come. No limit."

It at least felt like a compliment that Jack thought I had a wealth of other acquaintances close enough to invite to parties, other than Delia and Tyler. Little did he know that one of the reasons I was so good at school was because that was really all I focused on, other than hanging out with those two. The field hockey girls and I were fickle friends at best, and my shy tendencies made it kind of hard to get close to anyone who wasn't my boyfriend; his best friend, who thus became by best friend; or my mother.

Though I doubt Jack Cameron would've wanted to invite me to the party if he heard *that* sob story.

"I'm sorry," I said apologetically. "I can't tonight. I have plans." I promised Tyler we'd have a movie night and watch the latest Marvel release, a genre I wasn't a huge fan of until he got me into them, but seeing his face light up throughout the action sequences made it totally worth it.

Jack nodded, blowing out a tiny breath, probably relieved that the awkwardness was over. He'd flashed me a warm smile, letting me know that it was all good. "No worries, Olive. Another time. Fun plans tonight?"

"Yeah." I couldn't look at him as I picked my pen back up and continued writing out the lab notes. "Watching a movie with my boyfriend." I didn't see Jack's expression when I dropped the B-bomb on him, but I heard him shift in his seat, and he cleared his throat.

"No worries," he said again, slightly less enthusiastic this time. "Hope it's fun."

The bell rang and class filtered out into the hallway. I beelined straight for Delia at her locker, which was open and vomiting nearly all of its contents out into the hallway. While Delia was a great friend, she was a terrible organizer, and the small space was crammed to the gills with crumpled-up sweatshirts, discarded pens, and dusty textbooks from classes that she hadn't taken in years.

"D," I breathed, afraid to speak too loudly in case the Becker High rumor mill caught wind of my exclusive invitation and the party wound up being busted before it even got a chance to start (which would ensure I never got an invite from a cool senior like Jack Cameron again). "I have to talk to you."

"Hmm?" Delia muttered from the depths of her locker, poking her head back out with the shiny wrapper of a granola bar between her teeth. "What's up?"

"Um, first of all, are you sure that thing isn't expired?" I pointed accusingly at the snack still wedged between her teeth, the glimmering foil bumping up against her septum piercing. "Things kind of have a habit of living in your locker for all of eternity."

Delia shrugged and pulled the granola bar out of her mouth, examining the label for what seemed like too few seconds before unwrapping it and giving it a bite. "A little stale, but I'll survive." She swallowed and eyed me. "Anyway, what's up?"

I stepped closer, lowering my voice even further. "I just had to partner with Jack Cameron for an assignment in chemistry, and it ended with him inviting me to a *senior party* tonight."

It took Delia a few extra seconds to process this, the cogs in her brain practically turning in front of my eyes. "Jack Cameron?

Is that . . . a good thing?" She frowned. "Or is it supposed to be a bad thing?"

Right. I'd forgotten that she was accustomed to spending her weekends either at the skate park, with me and Tyler, or running pizzas around the neighborhood for Suburban Slices. (Not that I was one to judge—the fact that I was treating a measly house party invitation like a personal invite to the Met Gala was giving me away, too.) "He was actually pretty nice, and it's a good thing, I think. That he thought I was cool enough to get invited and everything. But I told him no."

Delia now looked *very* confused. "Er, I'm not following you, Ol. It's a good thing, but then you said no?"

"Tyler and I have plans tonight. That new Marvel movie that he's been dying to see." Delia nodded in recognition. "Also, I don't really know if Ty would want to go in the first place, and asking him feels, I don't know, *weird*, I guess." *Does it?* Even though it just happened, it was already becoming muddied in my mind from the shock of getting the invitation in the first place.

"Got it." Delia's tone made it clear that she very much did not get it but was willing to humor me anyway. She took another bite of the stale granola bar and chewed thoughtfully for a few seconds. "Well, how did he react when you said no? Was he a dick about it?"

"Not at all." It was actually surprisingly refreshing, how kind he'd been. "When I told him I had plans with Ty, he said to have fun and then just let it go."

"Then I wouldn't worry about it." Delia slammed her disorganized locker shut with a bump of her hip. "It's not like you would've really known anyone else there, anyway. And you and

Tyler are going to have fun watching whatever superhero crap it is that you two are obsessed with."

And I did. But still, that night, even as Tyler and I were curled up on the couch under one of my softest fuzzy blankets, warm bowls of popcorn in our laps, I couldn't help but wonder what was going on at Jack's party. If he and his friends actually wanted me there. If I was really cool enough to be invited to a senior party. If I had actually brought Tyler and Delia along with me, and we'd had a good time, it may have been exciting. It may have been different. We would've been *in* with the cool kids, which is the kind of thing that everyone scoffs at until it happens to them, and then everything's different. *Then* suddenly it becomes an exciting invitation.

And I couldn't shake the confusing, twisting feeling in my gut that I wasn't sure if I wanted to be there or not.

Chapter Eight

Tyler shifts in his seat awkwardly, looking like he'd rather be anywhere else than on this flight with me. *That makes two of us, buddy.* "That's, uh, good to know that you get along with his friends." He doesn't wait for me to ask about Delia. Even now, he knows an update on her would be less helpful and more a papercut to the heart.

"All right, this is getting weird," I blurt. No time like the present to acknowledge the elephant in the too-small, very cramped room in the sky. "We've got a long way to go on this flight still, so why don't we just . . . go back to doing whatever it is we planned on doing back when we expected our seatmate to be a complete stranger." It feels brutal to be this blunt with him, but for both of our sanities, it's the option that makes the most sense.

Another flush from Tyler. "You're right. A good plan."

The plane's engines hum in a weak attempt to fill our awkward, uncomfortable silence. Tyler and I both do our best to ignore each other for the next hour (not that it's working very well with the less than two inches of personal space between us in these economy seats), but there's only so much movie watching, snacking (Tyler's already on his third bag of plane-issued chips), and fake sleeping one can do before you finally have to succumb to making conversation. Even Cranky Lady has nodded off against the window, so we can't ignore each other by talking to her. Instead, she's snoring in a nature that isn't very dignified, and I'm sure she'd have something to say about it if it was one of us.

As for Tyler and me, we both do a pitiful job at pretending to be preoccupied, eventually caving and facing each other once again.

"So, Mr. Two First Names." He straightens up and shoves his crumpled-up chip bag into the back pocket of the seat in front of him, once again passive-aggressively ignoring my plea to call Jack by his name. "You're *really* visiting him for no reason? Or something's going on?"

My heart's hammering too fast to wonder if I'm really that transparent, or if Tyler's still able to see through me like he always has. "I'm just going to visit him because I miss him. I already told you."

He doesn't seem to buy it, brow furrowing. His lower lip juts out the way it always does when he's confused—the way that makes me feel like my heart is hiccupping. "A week before spring break?"

"A week before spring break." I grind my teeth and grip my phone tighter in my hand, wishing it wasn't defunct on this plane so I could at least spend the rest of my flight falling into the social media vortex and avoiding this conversation. We both know all there is to do is listen to my pre-saved podcasts or scroll through my camera roll—which is thankfully empty of any photos of us together, purged back when I was trying to heal my heart, even though I was responsible for breaking it. "Is there a problem with that?"

Tyler holds his hands up in surrender. "Nope, no problem. Just trying to make conversation, because it doesn't sound like you to just impulsively hop on a plane and skip school."

The exhaustion of the morning and the stress of the flight is getting to me, as well as the sharp stab in my heart from being read so well by a boy who shouldn't know me at all anymore. I can practically feel the frayed strands of my patience giving way. "Well, stop making conversation about my relationship. You and I are broken up, Tyler. We've been broken up for a long time."

He looks chastened, staring down at his lap with an unreadable expression on his face. "Trust me, Ol—Olive, I know exactly how long it's been." The way he says it, like he's been counting the minutes or the hours or the days, makes me inhale quickly.

"It's been over a year, Tyler." I try to stand firm, but my voice sounds small.

His cough interrupts me, sharp and quick. "Fifteen months. I'm well aware."

My neck starts to feel warm and itchy, and if possible, the already cramped plane makes it harder to breathe. I don't even justify Tyler's rebuttal with an answer, crossing my arms and staring pointedly at my TV screen, which silently shows the map of our plane over the United States. Right now, we're coasting somewhere above the Midwest, still a while to go before we hit the open ocean.

I wasn't foolish enough back then to think that Tyler and I would return to best friendship after the breakup—that's never, in the history of *ever,* worked out for anyone. Still. I thought there would be a few weeks of total isolation and heartbreak and weirdness, and then we'd at least find our way back to each other as acquaintances, or we'd get to a shaky point where we could at least give each other small smiles in the hallway. Where we could look back at our relationship as something that may not have worked out but was fun and nice while it lasted. Where we could wish each other the best and move on.

I had every intention of getting to that point, but Tyler didn't seem to be on board. Because that last moment together in the hallway was the final time I heard from him. In the days that followed, still reeling from the shock and hurt of everything that happened, I felt numb to it all. And the silent, dark, cold brick that was my unused phone was another painful reminder. Our nonstop chatter in the hallways became awkward glances darting away from each other as we carried our trays to opposite sides of the cafeteria. Hangouts before homeroom became me skirting into the building at the last possible second so I didn't have to awkwardly riffle around my locker pretending to be busy so I didn't look lonely. And even if it broke me from the inside out, I know the pain I felt then was entirely deserved.

Tyler's voice is quiet now, breaking through my thoughts. "It's just . . . I don't know, Ol. Skipping a week of classes before spring break to see your boyfriend who you were already going to see a week from now, anyway? That's not like you." He runs a hand through his hair, visibly distressed. "None of this is like you."

"I told you to call me Olive. I don't use that nickname anymore." It's out of my mouth like a reflex, but I immediately wish I could take it back when I see the hurt on his face. But I'll do anything to distract myself from the tight, squeezing feeling in my chest, knowing no amount of hoodie wearing or arm crossing is going to hide how I'm feeling from Tyler. He's always been good at reading me.

"Just talk to me," he pleads in a hushed voice. "I know you, Olive. I may not have dated you in over a year, but it doesn't mean I don't know you. It doesn't mean I can't tell when something's going on."

The gentle caring in his voice is what pushes me over the edge, makes me cave in like it always has. The words rush out before I have a chance to stop them. "I don't understand what's going on, Tyler. I'm not sure yet. That's why I have to find out."

Understanding dawns on his face. "Find out what, Olive? What are you racing toward?"

I shake my head, tugging at the uncomfortably tight seat belt in my lap. "I don't know." I hope I won't end up running *from* something.

"Olive." Tyler's voice is steady as he reaches across the armrest and places the tips of his fingers on the inside of my wrist, rough skin against smooth. "Talk to me. As a . . . as a friend. Please."

As a friend. It's what I wanted, right? The place I'd hoped we'd get to after I blew everything up?

But now I'm not sure it's possible. Still, in this moment, trapped in the sky with the boy I once loved, I find myself telling him everything, from the start.

Chapter Nine

Though leaving Tyler felt like a necessary evil, and it hurt like absolute hell, I had no choice but to pick up and keep moving. With the rest of junior year still ahead of me and senior year looming on the horizon, I was ready to buckle down and at least focus on my academic future, since it felt like the only thing I had any control over at the time.

I was still reeling from the soul-shattering heartbreak of ending things with Tyler *and* swiftly losing Delia and all our mutual friends in the process. In that moment, all I really needed—or wanted—was a friend.

Jack filled that space, being kind and warm and friendly and funny at a time when it felt like I needed it most. We slipped into our rapport easily, and the fact that we seemed to be two of the most overly ambitious students at Becker High helped. We'd chat after school and sit together while he did his chemistry homework and I would ink my upcoming study schedule into my planner. He was always commenting about how neat my handwriting was, or how I always had a planner sticker for everything.

Soon we transitioned from library study sessions to

occasional coffee shop meetups, discussing the best interview prep strategies—which became weekly hangouts, and then talks over dinners.

By the time I was invited as a plus-one to a fundraiser his family was attending, we'd unofficially been "together" for a little over a month. I got to borrow one of his sister Isabelle's dresses, a deep green gown with a structured bodice beaded with delicate crystals that took my breath away and was easily the nicest garment I'd ever put on my body. She'd discarded it as *so last season* but it still made me feel like a princess, heart swooping and soaring every time the lush emerald hemline brushed the floor.

The feeling of self-confidence was so nice that it didn't even bother me that my lips didn't tingle with fireworks after our first kiss. Jack and I were standing outside of the venue waiting for the valet to bring back his car when he'd leaned forward, brushing his hand against the small of my back, splaying his fingers and pulling me closer. As he pressed his lips to mine gently, it *should've* felt perfect. It should've felt movie-worthy—him in his sharp tux, me in a gorgeous ball gown, the cold air of the night swirling around us and contraband champagne on our tongues and music floating out from the ballroom, the stars sparkling above our heads.

It definitely felt *nice*. I wouldn't lie about that—but I do remember feeling a quick surprise in my chest when I didn't experience the *zinging* my lips felt after Tyler first kissed me in his Jeep, his tongue tasting like Coke slushy and buttery popcorn.

Not long after Jack and I got together, I "officially" drifted out of my old friend group's orbit—mainly because they were still friends with Tyler, which made things extra awkward and painful—and into the bubble of Jack and his friends, who took me in, albeit with lukewarm acceptance.

The first time it really stood out to me was at the next senior house party, which I'd managed to score an invite to. The party was pretty much everything I expected—a lofty McMansion belonging to some other senior, packed to the gills with people pouring out of doorways and alcoves, making out in dark, smoky corners, spilling various punches on the carpets, and clinking giant handles of liquor on the kitchen island.

Jack had squeezed my hand and smiled at me confidently as we wove through the crowds, coming to a stop in the kitchen. I watched carefully as he poured a cup of Sprite, adding a light splash of vodka and holding it out to me.

"A little more, please," I said primly, and his eyebrows shot up in surprise. *Me too, buddy.* For someone who had never had vodka in their life up until that point, I was feeling pretty bold—and desperate to fit in.

"Will do." Jack nodded appreciatively as he poured some more into the cup. "Didn't strike you as a doubles kind of girl, Olive Austin." He held the cup out to me as an offering, and I took a generous sip, swallowing down the carbonated burn and doing my best not to choke in front of a room full of people.

"There's a lot you still don't know about me," I wheezed, blinking the tears out of my eyes before they had a chance to fall. Jack just looked impressed, nodding.

"Yeah," he murmured, eyeing me up and down with a newfound appreciation in his expression. "I'm looking forward to finding out."

The night was a weird push and pull that I wasn't quite used to, where I was invited into conversations between Jack and his friends but didn't understand the references or have anything to contribute. Eventually, some drunk guys swaying over at a Ping-Pong table challenged Jack to beer pong with his buddies, and after giving my hand a squeeze and giving me a quick kiss on the cheek with a "Just hang with Siena and Rio, okay? I'll be right back," I found myself on my own in a corner with two heavily made-up senior girls, eyeing me suspiciously. The taller one, who I assumed was Siena because someone called her name from across the room earlier, raised one perfectly plucked eyebrow in my direction, her shiny blond hair glistening in the strobe lights.

"Jack's new boo?" she asked, her tone sounding like she'd tasted something sour. Next to her, Rio's riot of dark curls shook as she snickered, bangles jangling as she (poorly) hid her laugh behind her hands.

"You're the one we've seen around with him in the library, right? The one with that super-big planner?" Rio's tone was just as rude, curling her lip in distaste. While I'd never particularly cared about what people thought of me before, somehow the way they were speaking about me—like being organized and hanging out with Jack even though I was a junior was something to be *ashamed* of—set me off.

Even though I was younger, I wasn't dumb. I clenched my jaw and raised my chin, a newfound determination raging hotly through me—or maybe it was just the vodka burning through my bloodstream. *Jack invited you here*, I reminded myself. *You're his girlfriend, and you have every right to be here.*

"Yeah," I heard myself saying, though everything sounded

a million miles away with the crowded room and the thumping music and the alcohol making everything fuzzy at the edges. *When did I almost get to the bottom of this cup?* "I'm his . . . I'm his girlfriend."

Siena's brow arched even higher, and Rio snickered again. "Really?" she mused, perplexed. "I don't think Jack Cameron's ever dated a freshman before."

White-hot rage and embarrassment blinded me temporarily, and all I could hear was the crinkle of the Solo cup as I pressed it deeper into my fist. "I'm a *junior*, and Jack and I have been together for—"

"Jesus, you two," a third voice interrupted us, and I turned to see a willowy girl with long, bright red hair down to her waist push into our semicircle. "You don't have to be so rude to the new girl all the time. It's a tired look." She turned her back on Siena and Rio, who stood gaping, and flashed me a warm smile. "Ignore them. I'm Mira. Also a senior, but way less likely to bite your head off."

I liked Mira instantly. She accepted me into the fold of her friends at the party, bringing me around and introducing me to some other seniors—all way less hostile than Siena and Rio, who were still standing in their corner whispering to each other furiously—and she even refilled my drink a few more times, eventually switching my vodka Sprite for water when it was becoming clear that the world was starting to tilt around the edges.

"So," she said as we sat on a bench in the backyard, the cool night air kissing our skin as we watched Jack and his buddies dominate the other team in beer pong. "Is this your first time at a senior party?"

"Yeah," I slurred, eyes struggling to follow the Ping-Pong ball as it dipped in and out of plastic cups of foamy beer. I couldn't help but think about the first time Jack had invited me to a senior party, back when I'd turned him down because I was with Tyler. Even though I'd felt jealous in the moment when I skipped the party for our movie night, wondering what was happening there, in this particular moment I realized that maybe I wasn't missing out on much at all.

Except for Mira, who seemed pretty okay.

Her eyes tracked my movements, and when our gazes locked, she gave me a sad smile. "It's hard trying to fit into Jack Cameron's world, isn't it?"

My cheeks immediately pinkened with the embarrassment of being seen. "It's all right. He's . . . he's really great, so it makes the rest of it worth it."

Mira just hummed, giving me an unimpressed shrug. "If you say so. Seems exhausting, if you ask me. I heard his family's rich and intense. Like I said, has to be tiring."

It is sometimes is what I didn't say, though I was surprised at how insistently the words pushed at my teeth, dying to get out.

But that was then, and this is the unfortunate now, crammed in a too-small seat on an airplane next to my ex for the next god knows how long (actually, the pilot knows how long, but the TV screen in front of me turned off and I'm too stressed right now to turn it on and check the map), so may as well let it all out, right?

"So, yeah," I sigh into the cramped space as I finish my recap. "That's how things have been going with me lately. Welcome to the unfortunate reality that is my life."

Tyler's silent next to me, mulling my words over until I get to my last sentence. When I do, his eyes snap to mine, sending a jolt of electricity down my spine that startles me. *What the heck was that?*

"Nothing about your life is unfortunate," he says seriously. "I mean it, Olive. You have an amazing mom. And you do really well in school. And you're setting yourself up for the future you want—those are all very admirable things." It's hard to miss the melancholy in his voice when he says it, though.

"Yeah," I whisper, almost to myself. I'm not even sure he can hear me over the dull roaring of the plane's engine.

Am I really setting myself up for the future I want? I wonder, keeping that one to myself. Because the future I wanted never included an unfaithful partner—or an inattentive one, either. And it seems like at the moment, that's the situation I'm presented with.

It also didn't include Tyler Ferris showing back up in my life, but that's another thing that's out of my control, even if I'm still flipping out internally about it, because *how did that happen?*

I give myself a hard mental shake. It's better to focus on Jack—whatever's going on there—than digging too deep into my existential crisis right now.

"Something just doesn't feel right," I say while fiddling with the cool metal of the seat's buckle. "I keep trying to tell myself I'm crazy, or I'm paranoid, or maybe he's busy with classes—"

"Bullshit." The warmth in Tyler's voice is gone, now hard as flint. "Anyone who knows even a single thing about you would know you're too great of a person to ignore. He's an idiot if he can't see that. When we were dating—" He stops there, jaw set in a hard line, but the rest of his sentence floats in my mind, as if he'd spoken it aloud, my heart filling in the blanks. *When we were dating, there was never a day where I wouldn't talk to you.*

Just because he's right doesn't mean that I can let us walk back into the past. Not when I know that road isn't leading to any sort of good future. "When we were dating was different, Tyler. We . . . we didn't work out."

He shakes his head vigorously, upset. "That's not true. *You* thought we wouldn't work out in the long-term. You never gave me the chance to even prove to you that I could change. That I could be better. That I could come up with a solid life plan that satisfied you—"

If my knees weren't crammed against the seat in front of me, this would be the perfect moment to stand up in frustration. "That's part of the problem!" My whisper-hissing must be loud, because the disgruntled father of two rowdy toddlers in front of me whips his head around and gives me a pleading look.

They just fell asleep, he mouths, motioning to the seats on either side of him, presumably containing the sleeping toddlers in question. Not wanting to be one of Those People™ on the plane, I slump back against my seat and sigh. "That's part of the problem, Tyler. I didn't *want* you to come up with a random career or a random life plan to keep me and to make me happy. I wanted *you* to want it. I wanted you to be more responsible. Because it's not a big deal now, but we're going to get older, and it's going to become a much bigger deal. I can't be with someone who isn't ready to face the future in the same way I am. And I didn't want to stay in a relationship where I saw the dead end coming from a mile away."

He looks like I've slapped him, leaning so far back over the armrest of his seat that he's practically in the aisle. "Is that what you saw us as, Olive? A dead end?" The hurt is written clear as day across his face, sharp and brutal.

And it makes me feel like a monster. My chest constricts so tight that I wish the oxygen masks would drop down from above our seats so I could push some cool, clean air into my lungs and revive myself after realizing that I said an awful, awful thing that I never should have.

"Bad choice of words," Cranky Lady mutters under her breath next to me, refreshed from her nap and now toying with her e-reader. And yeah, maybe they weren't the best words I could've used, but it doesn't make them any less true.

But, based on the way Tyler's looking at me with such a wounded expression, it doesn't make me any less monstrous, either.

A flight attendant comes by again with the drink cart, glancing at us as she scoots by, sensing we aren't in the mood for refreshments.

My voice is quiet. "We were just too different. Too different where it matters. The kind of different that can't be fixed."

Tyler won't have it. "Or you're afraid of ending up in a situation like your mom. A situation I swore I'd never put you in, and even up until our last day together, I never had any intentions of doing that. I had my own way of doing things, and you didn't like it." He's fidgeting around in his seat now, knuckles turning white as he grips the armrests, eyes darting to the air-conditioning vents, the screens, the other passengers—anything but my face.

I feel naked and cold, sliced clean through with his accusation about my mother. "That's not it, Tyler. We weren't a good match. Sometimes good things just run their course. It was never anything more sinister."

Tyler sighs, muttering something under his breath that I can't catch, only grasping the tail end: ". . . agree with that." Then he shakes his head, standing up abruptly and stepping into the aisle. A mix of anger and hurt is radiating across his face. "I'm sorry, Olive. I need a breather." He leaves me blinking in surprise, watching him take off down the crowded aisle.

Chapter Ten

At my first-ever sleepover—which was held at the embarrassing age of seventeen—Delia warned me about Tyler's tendency to retreat into himself.

"He just . . . gets like that sometimes." She shrugged, shoving a handful of popcorn in her mouth as we sprawled out on my bed. Mom had ordered us pizza for dinner and Delia had picked up ingredients for ice cream sundaes on her way over, and even after packing down all that food, we found ourselves tiptoeing into the kitchen at 2:00 a.m. for some microwave popcorn before we put on our next movie—a gory slasher that Delia was excited for and I was mildly dreading but still curious about.

"You don't feel weird that I'm practically poaching your best friend?" I'd asked Tyler earlier that afternoon, when Delia texted me to hang out and I decided to take the leap and extend the sleepover invitation. Tyler, however, wasn't bothered in the slightest.

"Of course not," he'd said, kissing the back of my hand that was threaded in his while we drove back from a slushy run. "It makes me happy to see my two favorite girls hanging out together."

I wonder if he'd say the same knowing that we were gossiping about him during said hangout, but alas.

"I guess that's true," I'd finally replied into my bowl of buttery goodness, unable to keep the frown from slipping into my expression. While things with Tyler had been generally great up until that point, he'd gotten into a particularly rough argument with his parents about college choices earlier that day and had been spotty over our text thread ever since. Even the slushy run didn't do much, other than give him a sugar high and me anxiety when I'd notice the strained way he smiled on the drive.

"I'm serious," Delia emphasized, leaning down until the indigo tendrils of her hair were brushing the edges of my popcorn bowl, her piercings glinting in the lamplight as she met my gaze. "It's nothing to take personally, Olive. When Tyler has something that he needs to work out, he just wants to slink off and do it in his own head. It doesn't mean he doesn't care about you—it just means that he needs a second to process things."

And while I knew, deep down, that she was right, it was still such a relief to hear it come out of her mouth. The relief must've been evident on my face, because in that moment, Delia Franklin did the one thing I'd never seen her do before. While I'd seen her break her wrist on a skateboard and get up laughing, or give herself a stick-and-poke tattoo in her cramped bathroom, or drive with only her knees, I'd never seen her give anyone a hug.

But that's exactly what she did—she placed her bowl of popcorn to the side and reached over to wrap her arms around my neck and squeeze me tight. After squeaking out a surprised little *oof,* I'd recognized the moment for the monumental occurrence that it was and squeezed back, breathing in the tangy scent of her perfume and feeling the tight pressure of her embrace.

I can't wait to text Tyler about this, I remember thinking. *He's going to go berserk when he finds out that Delia* voluntarily *gave someone a hug.*

When we pulled apart, Delia looked at me strangely.

"What's the matter?" I asked, running my tongue over my teeth to catch any stray popcorn kernels, suddenly self-conscious that I was making myself look like an idiot somehow at my first-ever sleepover. This is why the "first sleepover" milestone was meant to be for literal children with teddy bears and socially acceptable homesickness levels for their age, and yet here I was, almost a senior in high school and completely unaware of the social etiquette involved in having a friend stay over.

"Nothing," Delia replied slowly, chewing on her lip as she fell deeper in thought. "It's just . . . I think I just realized that you're kind of one of my closest friends now, and that's kind of weird, because I don't really make new friends."

"Oh my god." I clasped my hands to my chest in dramatic shock. "For real? I made the cut? Are we closer than you and Tyler?"

Delia blushed and threw a handful of popcorn in her mouth in a weak attempt to end the conversation. "Well, I never had a sleepover with Tyler, so."

"I *knew* it!" I squealed, tossing a few extra kernels in the air, buttery confetti raining back down on us. "I knew you were only pretending to have a cold, dead heart. It's all squishy and warm just like everyone else's." While Delia always tried to play the role of the tough, impenetrable fortress, it was becoming more and more clear that she was really anything but. She was actually a fantastic friend, and that night just proved it all the more.

This revelation gets a stray piece of popcorn-slash-confetti thrown back at me. "Yeah, yeah. Just shut up and accept the fact that we're besties, okay?"

I knew it, I knew it, I knew it, I continued to chant all throughout the movie, always at the most gory parts, just to make Delia laugh. And after two hours of needling her about admitting our best friendship, it wasn't until the credits were rolling and we were both dozing off on our respective pillows that I heard her speak.

"You're right," she sighed into the dark room. "Maybe you aren't half bad after all, Olive."

Thank you, I think I whispered back, or maybe I just thought it as sleep began to pull me under. But regardless, I distinctly remember the sweet glow in my heart at the thought of finally having another girl as a friend who wasn't forced to hang out with me because we happened to choose the same club or be on the same team. Delia liked me for *me*, outside of knowing me through my relationship with Tyler.

That was one of the first moments where I felt like I was really starting to belong.

Which makes me wonder why I thought it would ever be a good idea to torch it all.

Chapter Eleven

It doesn't mean that he doesn't care about you, past Delia's voice reminds me now as I stare down the empty aisle of the plane. *It just means that he needs a second to process things.*

The vinyl seat next to me rustles, Cranky Lady leaning over into my line of sight. "I don't mean to pry, dear, but it sounds like you've found yourself in quite the pickle." *Oh, now she suddenly wants to play nice.*

"Isn't that the truth." I jealously eye her plastic cup of champagne, wishing it was legal for me to chug a glass and succumb to the warm, bubbly feeling of *not being on this freaking plane right now.*

"To me," she sniffs in a voice that makes it clear she is offering her opinion whether I want it or not, "it sounds like that boy really cares about you."

"He does—did." Talking about my and Tyler's relationship in the past tense should be second nature by now, but some part of it still gets lodged in my throat. "Sometimes two people are too different and aren't a good match . . . right?" I look at my seatmate for validation, the irony of searching for it from a total stranger not lost on me.

She shrugs. "If that's what you think, sure."

I'm not convinced by her nonanswer, but I'm willing to take it anyway, until she flips open another magazine and continues speaking.

"But if two people are really meant to be together, no matter how different they may think they are, the relationship always finds a way. You see it all the time."

I chew this over, thinking back to the nights of Mom curled up on the couch with a glass of wine, crying like her heart was run over by a semitruck. "But sometimes it fails, too. Sometimes you're perfect for each other, until you realize there are parts that you can't compromise on. And that's where it ends."

We both glance over and watch Tyler emerge from the bathroom and head back down the aisle, cautious and sad-looking. Before he returns to his seat, she throws in one last remark. "The right relationships never fail, honey. Only the wrong ones." She tucks her head back into her edition of *Woman's World,* lost to the pages full of fad diets and book recommendations, but I'm still mulling over what she said.

Wait. Does that mean she thinks Tyler and I were the wrong relationship? Or that it's possible we aren't done yet?

Jack, my brain hisses at me, doling a mental slap upside the head. *You're sitting on this plane, next to Tyler, because you're on your way to see Jack.*

Tyler slides into his seat and turns to me, seeming less agitated than he was a few minutes ago. His skin looks a little shiny and the tips of his hair are all damp—he must've splashed some water on his face when he went in there to cool down. Still, even though he no longer looks hurt and angry, he does look a little bit bashful.

"Listen, Olive—I'm sorry about all of that, okay? All of what's been going on during the flight. Frankly, it's been a little . . . weird." He laughs nervously when I nod. "I want to start off on a better foot, okay? I haven't seen you in a while, and the past is the past, but that doesn't mean you weren't one of my best friends for the longest time. And we've still got a bunch of time left stuck next to each other, so we might as well make it a little better for the both of us."

"I'd like that." I turn so I'm facing him fully, on board with the idea. "How?"

His eyes sparkle with mischief. "How about a truce?"

I narrow my eyes and shift in my seat, the buckle sliding against my hip uncomfortably as I continue to scrutinize him. "What kind of truce are you talking?"

"One that will help us survive the remaining eight hours of this flight without killing each other." He leans in conspiratorially. "I have an idea of how we can level the playing field and then go back to being cordial seat neighbors who talk about nothing of substance. In-flight entertainment critiques and snack bag commentary all the way."

"I'm listening."

He grins wickedly. "Tell me a secret, one that you've never told me before. Preferably anyone, but just me is fine."

It's been a long time since I've shared any secrets with Tyler, but one comes to mind easily and spills out without warning. "The reason Jack is going to the University of Hawai'i is because he couldn't get into the Ivies."

Tyler's jaw drops. "No way—you've got to be kidding. Jack freaking *Cameron* didn't get into an Ivy League school? We all thought he was a shoo-in."

"So did he." I shake my head ruefully, my stomach starting to sour at the thought of revealing such a personal secret about someone else. Still, Tyler's magnetic pull, the one that charmed me all those years ago, keeps me talking. "But he still wanted to go somewhere that made people jealous, so that's how he ended up at UH. He told his friends that he rejected other offers."

"Didn't his dad go to Yale?"

"Yep, and that usually helps your chances, but it doesn't mean it's definite." I think back to the look of deflation on Jack's face, crushed and full of hurt, when his rejection letter came in the mail. I sympathized with him then, knowing what it feels like when something you've planned for yourself for so long ends up not working out. A good example is sitting right next to me, right now.

It's clear that my secret is satisfying enough for the truce, because Tyler looks dumbfounded. "I . . . Wow. I never thought I'd see the day that I'd have dirt on Jack Cameron, directly from a confidant." Something about the way he says it ignites a spark of panic in me, and I instinctively reach out and clasp his wrist in my shaking fingers.

"Don't," I hiss, "tell anybody. Other than his family, I'm the only one who knows. He'd know it was me." But my words seem to be falling on deaf ears, because Tyler's eyes are trained on my fingers, wrapped around his arm. There's a dull pulse between us, a once-bright spark that lost its magnetism, but only an idiot would deny that it's still there. Almost like it's lying in wait.

"Tyler." I squeeze his wrist for emphasis. "I'm serious. Please."

As soon as the *please* leaves my lips, his eyes snap up toward me, refocusing. He nods to himself, but I notice that he doesn't make any move to slide his arm out from under my grip. "Of course." His voice is a little bit hoarse. "You know I won't tell anyone."

With tension sizzling in the airplane's recycled air, I'm eager to pivot the conversation. I slowly pry my fingers from Tyler's arm and shake out my hand. "All right, enough about me and my supposedly groundbreaking secret. What about yours?"

"Are you sure you want to hear it?" There's an unmistakable challenge in his voice. "I'm not sure you want me to show you up with the World's Juiciest Secret Award right now."

This earns him a playful punch on the shoulder. "Just tell me, and then I'll be the judge of whether your secret is actually better."

"It definitely is."

"Then why are you not telling me?"

Tyler scrubs a hand over his face, cringing and clearly regretting his choice of truce activities already. "That fall"—again, he doesn't say it, but he doesn't have to—"before Lucas and Ella moved out to Hawaiʻi, they were living in his bedroom in the basement. You know, somewhere to stay while they were selling their old place and getting ready for the move out there. But I wasn't used to having a girl other than my mom living around the house, so I was a little . . . careless. With the closed doors situation."

"Oh no." The secondhand embarrassment is so bad that I find *myself* cringing, and Tyler hasn't even gotten to the end of the story yet. "You walked in on her changing?" I'm not sure what having a sister-in-law is like, but that definitely sounds like one way to ruin the whole family bonding thing.

He shakes his head solemnly. "I wish that was all it was. Would've been way less mortifying."

"Showering?"

"Also no. But you're getting close." He gives me a pointed look, akin to an English teacher trying to lead the class to the answer that's just out of reach. "I went into Lucas's room one night to find his spare game controller, but they were a little . . . occupied."

"No!" I cover my mouth with my sleeve to muffle my shriek of surprise. "They were, like, *busy*?"

Tyler's expression is grim, and if Cranky Lady didn't have her headphones in, snoring next to us while watching *Knives Out*, I'm sure she'd be contributing her two cents as well. "*Very* busy. And not under the sheets."

I shudder, horrified. Tyler looks like he's seriously considering picking up the barf bag wedged into the seat pouch in front of him.

"Oh my god." It takes a second to stop wheezing with laugher, trying my best not to cough so I don't wake up the sleeping toddlers in front of me. "Is that a secret only for me? Or does anyone else know?"

"I only told Delia, right after it happened." He looks positively mortified, and I bury the sting I feel at the mention of our formerly shared best friend. "I think I needed to get it off my chest so I didn't have to sit and stew in it anymore. I couldn't look Lucas or Ella in the eye for a solid month. And to make it worse, Mom thought we were avoiding each other because we had some sort of fight, so she ambushed us both one night at dinner and made us have this whole heart-to-heart about how we're brothers and will always need to be there for each other, blah blah blah. She thought we were in an argument over something stupid."

Keeping the laughter in is a full-time job now, and I'm dangerously close to letting out a snort that wakes up the whole plane. "Did you tell her the real reason you weren't talking?"

Tyler shoots me an *Are you kidding?* look. "Absolutely not. We let her think that he was mad that I dinged his car when I was trying to park. We came up with it on the fly and I'm surprised Mom didn't notice, given what terrible liars we both are."

"That's amazing." And so incredibly on-brand for both Tyler and his brother. It's the kind of story that, if it had happened while we were dating, would've had him driving over to my house in the middle of the night and taking me on a late-night slushy run so we could discuss the abject horror of it all. "I mean, it's definitely *not* amazing for you, but this story improved my day tenfold."

"It gets worse." He's grimacing now.

I can't help but gawk. "How on earth could it get worse?"

Tyler glances around the plane dramatically, even though nobody else here would even know the people we're talking about. Still, his voice is a hushed whisper when he continues. "A few weeks later . . . Ella announced she was pregnant."

"*No.*" My jaw drops to my lap. "You think . . . ?"

He answers with a grim nod. And even though he still looks like he's recovering from reliving his worst trauma, Tyler's smile breaks through. "I told you I had a good one."

"You did." I nod mock-solemnly, reaching under my seat and miming lifting a huge trophy out from my bag. "So I believe this belongs to you, the brand-new owner of the World's Juiciest Secret Award."

He reaches over and takes the invisible trophy from me, princess-waving at the other sleeping passengers on the plane.

"Thank you, thank you. I hope this will clear airport security on the way home."

"I got it on the plane," I point out. "I had to be prepared in case I wound up sitting next to my ex-boyfriend on a thirteen-hour flight, we got into some awkward conversations, and we patched it up with a secret-telling contest."

Tyler nods seriously. "Obviously. One can never be too prepared."

"Never."

"Like the time Delia showed up to the SATs with a huge deli sandwich in her bag, which they wouldn't even let her eat, but she insisted on keeping it in there for emergencies. And then the kid sitting next to her fainted ten minutes into the test, and the sandwich ended up helping him bring his glucose levels back up."

I snap my fingers in recognition. "Oh, that was Kenny Ploy! I remember hearing about that. I wasn't in the same room as you guys, though." I gesture between us, our A and F last names a canyon that separated me from Tyler Ferris and Delia Franklin, the two people I most wanted to be in the room with during SATs at the start of junior year. I remember jealously listening to the story in the cafeteria the next day, Delia's excited hand gestures drawing more attention to her shock of newly bright pink pigtails as she recounted the event.

"That reminds me." I pause as the flight attendants swoop by again, generously refilling Tyler and me up on Cokes and bags of chips. "How's Delia been doing?"

The crunching of the chip between Tyler's teeth is deafeningly loud on the quiet plane as people around us sleep and watch their movies in the darkness. Various overhead lights are on above different passengers, tiny pinpricks of warm beams. He seems to think for a second before speaking.

"D's been fine," he eventually offers. "She has a new girlfriend now, Cassie something or other. She's from a few towns away, but they actually met during one of those Science Olympiad competitions and hit it off right away. We all really like her."

I try not to let my brain snag on the *we* that I'm no longer a part of. I can still remember the day we were sitting in one of the booths at Suburban Slices, and in between bites of pizza, Delia casually mentioned that she may be questioning some aspects of her identity and who she was interested in at school, and then went back to eating like it was no big deal. Which, in true Delia fashion, it wasn't. She never wanted a big deal to be made out of *anything* in her life, and who she chose to date was no different.

"Good for her," I offer weakly, thinking back to the last few months of our friendship. "I'm glad that she's happy. Did her parents take it well? I didn't know she'd finally told them."

His silence is all the answer I need, a sharp reminder of her ultra-conservative parents who looked down on anyone who dared to "disrupt the status quo." A tiny fissure opens in my heart as I think about my best friend going through the grueling process of not being accepted by her family, and I wasn't there to be part of her support system. She has Tyler, and all of their mutual friends, but still . . . in the time I'd gotten to know Delia, we became something akin to sisters—something I never got to have growing up. And even a year and a half later, being without her still sometimes feels like I've lost an important limb and am just stumbling around off-balance.

Tyler, ever the mind-reader after all this time, catches on

quickly. "Delia wasn't, like, *alone* alone through the whole thing, Olive. She had the rest of us." *Even though it wasn't the same as it would've been if you were there,* he doesn't add. But it doesn't mean I'm not thinking it.

A sharp burst of sadness blooms in my chest, a painful reminder of how much I've missed in this past year and a half. Especially Delia.

Finally, I find the words to answer Tyler. "I'm glad she had you to be there for her. And the others." Tyler and all of our mutual friends, his Dungeons & Dragons and skating buddies, the fellow nerds who I used to spend time with, all melding together into a happy little blended family.

One I ejected myself from, on purpose.

Tyler claps his hands and interrupts my thoughts, while also startling one of the toddlers in the seat in front of him, who starts to wail. I can only imagine the eye-daggers their father is directing our way right about now. "No more reminiscing. Food's here!"

The nonstop flight on Hawaiian Airlines gives patrons the luxury—which is a generous word—of an in-flight dinner or breakfast. Since we're actually crawling back time zones as we zoom west, it's breakfast, although we've been in the sky for several hours already and my time-confused body is craving lunch.

"Damn it," Tyler mumbles under his breath, echoing my thoughts as he watches breakfast sandwiches being doled out to the passengers in front of us. "I was really hoping for the meat loaf. That was pretty good last time I flew out."

I lean over nosily as the flight attendant approaches our aisle and hands over the breakfast sandwiches. "What kind is it?" Next to me, Cranky Lady awakes from her nap with a yawn and gives us a curious look, as if she's checking to see the state of our awkwardness since she dozed off. Luckily, it seems like Tyler's secret-sharing idea was a good trick to break the ice, because while things aren't 100 percent back to the way they used to be when we were dating (which, admittedly, I don't think we could ever get back to), it feels like the early days of working together at Suburban Slices again. The easy banter, the flowing laughter, the gentle comfort of knowing that you're in the orbit of someone who isn't just kind and amazing, but also *gets* you.

He passes one of the breakfast sandwiches my way with a wink. "How about that airplane food, huh, Olive?" I glance down at the label and suppress a groan.

"Sausage egg and cheese on a croissant?" Cranky Lady exclaims in a huff when I pass her a sandwich. "I don't trust any sausage stored on a plane. I'd much rather have egg salad."

Tyler gives her a quizzical look. "You'd trust *egg salad* stored on a plane?"

She waves him away impatiently as she unwraps her sandwich and takes a tentative bite. "Better than I'd trust plane sausage, but this isn't too bad." She nods at us and speaks through a mouthful of breakfast sandwich. "My name's Ellen, by the way."

The three of us eat our breakfast sandwiches (two- to three-star rating at most, honestly) in relative silence, grateful for any kind of nourishment that isn't sugary soda or bags of candy or chips.

When he finishes, Tyler crumples up his wrapper and stores it in the pouch on the seat in front of him. "Well, that was positively mediocre," he comments, smoothing the creases in his jeans and looking at me. "What'd you think?"

I shove my wrapper in next to his. "When you're this high

in the air, food is food and you can't be too picky about it." Something—or rather, several somethings—on his hands catches my eye, and I lean in for a closer look. Tyler, understandably, is now looking at me like I have ten heads.

"Uh, Olive?" he hedges, and my eyes snap back up to his. "Not that I'm not flattered, but is there any particular reason you're staring at my crotch with such vested interest? I thought we've moved past that point of our lives."

"Oh my god." I rocket away from him, leaning so far back in my seat that I'm practically launching myself into Ellen's lap, much to her chagrin. "I *wasn't*. I was looking at your hands resting on your pants, I swear."

His cheeky grin makes me want to melt into a puddle on the spot. "*Suuuuure*. You *were* always obsessed with my hands."

"Ew, Tyler, enough!" As much as I want to punch him, I can't help the laugh that rolls out of my chest. When I glance over at Ellen, her eyes are wide with scandal, which just makes me laugh harder.

"But for real, everything okay there?" Tyler asks as I pick up one of his hands, running the tips of my fingers over the tiny pinprick scars on his. "Are you offering me a free palm reading? That also seems like something that would be out of bounds for exes."

I bat his joke away with my other hand, choosing not to dwell on the word *exes,* shaking my head and leaning in closer. "You still have the scars."

Catching on, his face morphs into something unreadable. "I do."

"But it looks like there are . . . more than last time?"

"Well"—he coughs and pulls his hand out of my grip, and

there's a rush of cold air where his warm palm used to be—"that's because there are."

That draws me up short.

Tyler Ferris, skateboarder and pizza slinger and all-around sarcastic, rough-around-the-edges guy, could *not* still be a cross-stitching aficionado.

It would upset the entire balance of the universe—a thought so outlandish that I can't help the squeak of laughter barreling out of my chest. If my eyebrows could shoot up any higher than my hairline, they'd be in the stratosphere right now. "You're not serious."

When Tyler came over to my house for the first time, he was in awe of the plastic tackle box on my desk organized neatly with various spools of colored threads and the stack of wooden hoops resting next to them. When I'd explained to him that I was into cross-stitching as a way to pass the time while watching TV with Mom, he didn't laugh at me like the field hockey girls had been prone to do whenever I mentioned it or when Mom was stitching on the sidelines of a match. Instead, he was impressed, telling me that he'd always wished he could be more artsy, and cross-stitching sounded pretty relaxing.

So, the first time he ever came over to my house, we didn't make out or watch movies or make awkward small talk with my mother. Instead, we sat side by side on my carpet, me walking him through the steps of stitching a tiny flower onto the Aida cloth, him following along dutifully and beaming at his clumsy attempt once it was done.

"I love this," he'd said to me, and I couldn't believe how lucky I was that this guy—this cool, funny, adventurous guy—thought that my little hobby was exciting. "It's not as hard as I thought it would be. Even though it *does* hurt like a bitch when the needle bites you."

For our first Valentine's Day together, Tyler had painstakingly cross-stitched me a piece of pizza and framed the cloth. It was touching and romantic and even if it wasn't stitched perfectly, it meant more to me than any fancy gift could've. And even though Tyler doesn't know it, that framed little slice is still hanging proudly (and crookedly) on the wall above my dresser, right where he'd left it when he put it up for me, while I sat on the bed and watched his bandaged fingers—ravaged from the sewing needle as he got used to cross-stitching, tiny white dots all over his hands—delicately hang it in its rightful place.

In that moment, I remember thinking that there was nothing our love couldn't overcome.

How naïve young Olive was.

Now, clearly no longer in a bantering mood, Tyler looks sullen as he shoves his hands in his hoodie pockets, out of my view. His tone is much cooler when he speaks.

"Believe it or not, Olive, parts of you stuck around even after you left me behind."

Chapter Twelve

Tyler looks at me, and I'm sure that the surprise is written all over my face as I study his pinprick scars. "You still stitch." It's not a question. I already have my answer.

"I still stitch," Tyler confirms, coughing awkwardly and then settling his hands in his lap. "I really did just try it for your Valentine's Day gift, but after I finished it and you loved it so much, I wanted to keep doing it. For me. It's a good brain-off activity while watching TV or listening to music when I need to relax." Just hearing him bring up his first clumsy attempt at a Valentine's gift for me all that time ago—that slice of pizza delicately woven into the Aida cloth—makes my heart squeeze fondly. I remember the belly-shaking laughter we shared when he showed me all the scars he got from his many failed attempts at getting the project right. It was a silly little trinket, but what Tyler gave me that Valentine's Day meant more to me than a crystal bracelet ever could.

Staring at his fingers, I say, "That's great, Ty. I'm happy for you."

A swirl of old feelings rises in my chest, and I tamp them down and lock them back in their box before they have a chance to make things complicated. Because no matter what I'm feeling on this plane—which is a bunch of melancholy nonsense—I'm on my way to see Jack. My current, very real, very dedicated boyfriend. The boy with the life plan sketched out to a T, the boy with the safety and security that I need, the safety and security that Mom never got.

Tyler Ferris was an excellent first love, and I wouldn't trade what we had for anything. But that doesn't mean it gets to continue into my current life. I won't let it. Not when he's a fly-by-the-seat-of-your-pants, go-where-the-wind-takes-you kind of guy. He isn't going to college and doesn't know where he'll even be next year, let alone ten years from now. At this point in my life, when it's just been me and Mom for so long, dealing with her whims and her rotating boyfriends, and all the chaos of not settling down . . . stepping into the carefully curated life plan with Jack is exactly what I need.

I just have to make my heart fall into step with my brain.

You're just confused. You're stuck in the sky for half a day with the boy whose heart you shattered, and you're getting caught up in old emotions. As much as I try to convince myself that that's true, the tiniest part of my brain is wondering what things would be like if they were different. If Tyler and I had stayed together, and instead of being two awkward exes on a plane, we'd be a couple heading out on a trip together to visit his family.

For a short, sharp second, I nearly lose my breath with how badly I would've wanted that in the past. But then the seat belt light dings on overhead, and I'm filled with a whole new sense of dread.

The pilot's voice crackles over the loudspeaker. "Morning,

folks. Please fasten your seat belts and return to your seats—we're about to fly through a few pressurized air patches, so there's going to be a little bit of turbulence, but we should pass through it quickly."

Tyler turns to me at the exact moment that I can feel all the blood draining from my face. "Relax, Olive. We're okay." It's clear that he hasn't forgotten my intense fear of turbulence, spurred by that particularly erratic flight to Las Vegas with Mom when I was a kid that I never got over and brought up to him often.

"I know we're okay," I force myself to say weakly. Suddenly, the already-small airplane feels too cramped, the air too thick, my breathing too tight. I managed to cram that anxiety in a box this entire morning, getting to the airport and through security and onto the plane, but now it's back with a vengeance, reminding me why exactly I hate to fly. The plane shudders as we hit the first pocket of bad air, and my stomach drops to the floor. "*Shit.*" Next to us, Ellen is back to snoring, undisturbed by the commotion on the plane. She seems to be well-traveled, completely calm as we potentially fall out of the sky. *Must be nice.*

Tyler squeezes my hand, running his thumb over the soft skin between my thumb and pointer finger. "Tell me something," he murmurs soothingly. "Anything." People around us have started white-knuckling their armrests, and a few are even taking out rosary beads and murmuring with their eyes closed. While that's all pretty standard fare for hitting patches of turbulence, it doesn't make it any less scary. It feels worse than normal, the plane making jerky movements as we dip in and out of air pockets. The meager contents of my stomach nearly rocket to the surface after a particularly stressful moment of free fall where it feels like I've somehow landed on the Tower of Terror—and I let out an involuntary yelp that gives away just how scared shitless I am.

Tyler's voice is gentle, cutting through the noise as his thumb sweeps over my hand. "Tell me a story. Or something that's weighing on you. Come up with your most creative list of curse words. Anything that'll take your mind off what's happening right now."

Jack! My brain is shrieking at me. *If this plane goes down, Jack won't even know I tried to come early.* But instead of voicing that, I turn to another thing that's been weighing on me. "I'm scared and I don't think I should be on this plane at all. Maybe this is karma for me trying to sneak up on Jack like this." Another shudder rips through the plane and I grip the armrest with my free hand so tightly that it's a miracle my fingernails don't start to bleed.

You know what? I think, not sure if my life is really flashing before my eyes or if that's just the severe flight anxiety talking. *Fuck it.* If this plane is about to go down, might as well get it all out in the open.

I take a deep breath and force the words out, one syllable at a time, while Tyler's thumb continues to stroke my hand in soothing circles. "I'm sorry for everything that happened between us, Ty. I . . . It was never about you. It was never about me not loving you." The tears are starting to prick the corners of my eyes now in panic. "And I know how stupid and cliché it sounds, but I really never meant to hurt you." I had to make the right decision for myself, even if it wasn't the easy one. And right in this second, it dawns on me that I never actually said these words to his face—they just lived in empty, unreturned texts.

Tyler's still squeezing my hand, but his eyes rake over my face carefully as he snags on one part of what I said. "So you never stopped loving me?"

It's different now, is what I want to say. But when the plane takes another steep jerk downward and I gasp involuntarily with panic, the truth slips out instead. "I don't think I could ever stop loving you, Tyler. Even if we aren't a good fit."

My words have an effect on him, because his face changes, morphing into an expression of pain. "You still think we aren't a good fit. It's just a different type of love now."

Another jerk of the plane, this time getting a surprised cry from a few of the passengers, which makes my heart beat even faster. Above us, the seat belt light dings ominously. I force myself to keep talking, the word vomit fully spewing now in a desperate attempt to keep myself distracted while also unloading the guilt I've carried for the past year. "You don't know what it's like to grow up without stability. You have both of your parents, who are so in love that it was sickeningly sweet to watch, and you don't have to worry about the next time you'll have to nurse your mom through a heartbreak." I force myself to look at Tyler, who is watching me intently. "I get that from your perspective, it's easy to take the chance. But it isn't that easy for me. Not when you aren't sure where you want your life to take you. That's a lot more stressful for me than it'll ever be for you, Ty."

His voice is low and full of hurt when he replies, but he doesn't stop stroking my hand soothingly. "I may not know what it's like from your perspective, but what I know is that I loved you more than anything, and I'd do whatever it took to make it work. But you didn't even give me the chance. You made the decision for me."

It feels like we're standing back in the hallway again, full of the stale air of gym socks and too much Axe spray, while I looked Tyler in the face and shattered his heart. "I didn't make the decision *for* you. But I knew that I didn't want to take the risk anymore." Almost as if the universe is punishing me for doing this to Tyler again, the plane shakes so violently that even the flight attendants moving the cart to the back have to kneel in place, and the two toddlers in front of us start crying in panic.

I think about Mom, about the nights spent primping herself for a date, painting her lips and spritzing perfume and insisting to me that *this guy is different, he's definitely the one, I can really see myself with him for the rest of my life.* And how, like the flip of a dime, those nights turn into the nights where she's curled up on the couch with a bowl of ice cream and a bottle of wine, sobbing like a broken animal, feeling used and heartbroken and kicked back to square one. Of how it's always been my job to pick up the pieces.

I think about her collection of chipped coffee mugs, of all the places she's been, of how many of those places are related to the men she followed and the heartbreak that inevitably came from it.

I think of all the times Jack has come over for dinner, to spend time with me, and the way I hurriedly shuffled him away from my mother before they could have more than a surface-level conversation. The last thing I need is for him to find out about my two-week-stand father, my mother's hopeless-romantic attitude, my turbulent life. Not while his life is filled with a gorgeous house, the perfect nuclear family, and everything he could ever want—everything that my and Mom's little family of two never had. While I let Tyler in full force (and felt the ramifications of that decision once he was gone), I worked extra hard to not repeat the same mistake the second time around.

When he senses that I'm not going to say anything more, Tyler nudges me with his shoulder. He opens his mouth to say something, but we go through another rocky patch of turbulence and he pivots to running his free hand up and down my arm soothingly. Even though I'm wearing a hoodie, I can feel the searing warmth of his touch through my sleeve. Squeezing my eyes shut, I try to ground myself in the sensation and forget the choppiness of the airplane slicing through the air.

After a few more agonizing minutes, the pilot's voice rejoins us. "Thanks for bearing with us, folks. Looks like we got through the rough patch. It should be smooth sailing from here." Sighs of relief echo around us, and Tyler takes that as his cue to slide his hand off my arm, the other still clasped around mine. My body is practically vibrating from the adrenaline comedown, and I can't help but realize that with Tyler by my side, surviving that scary moment of bad air didn't feel so impossible.

Still awful, but definitely not impossible. But I can't think about that right now.

Tyler continues speaking as if we didn't miss a beat. "I know you didn't do it to hurt me, but that doesn't mean it didn't hurt. And it doesn't mean I don't think we could've been something amazing if you'd given us the chance." Even though his expression is neutral, if not a little wistful, I can feel the frustration simmering beneath the surface.

"I'm sorry," I whisper into the hum of the engines, looking down at my lap instead of at his face. "It's just . . . it wasn't meant to be, Ty. Please leave it at that."

Now that the plane is coasting along smoothly and a general

air of peace is restored among the passengers, Tyler lets my hand go. I don't like the emptiness I feel when he does, but when I look up and lock eyes with him, his jaw is set and his eyes are sad.

"I guess we'll never know," he says quietly. He's closing himself off to me, leaning back in his seat and grabbing his headphones, plugging them into the armrest and scrolling through the screen's movie options. "I hope Jack realizes what a lucky man he is." With those parting words, he taps the play button on the latest blockbuster superhero film—the next one in our favorite series, which I still can't bring myself to watch—and effectively ends our conversation.

And I'm surprised by the pang of regret in my gut while I watch him do it. Left alone to my own thoughts, I pop in my earbuds, but instead of queuing up another podcast episode, I switch to a white noise video of a thunderstorm, closing my eyes.

My and Jack's relationship is stable, serious, and planned to a T—going to college, getting our degrees, moving in together, getting married, starting our lives, a family . . . all the things that feel so far down the road that they're not worth worrying about at seventeen. But if there's anything I've learned from Sherri Austin's life, it's that those years creep up on you faster than you expect them to, and the best possible thing you can do to save yourself is to be prepared. And while I do know that I love Jack, I also know that I don't get that same sparkly feeling in my chest that I got when I was with Tyler. Instead, I feel the warm, cozy feeling of a familiar security blanket, which is different—but does that necessarily mean it's worse?

Tyler made me feel brave and daring. Our relationship was filled with fun and love and adventure.

Jack makes me feel safe and secure. Our relationship is filled with comfort and stability.

Both, in their own ways, make (or made) me feel loved.

The realization dawns on me slowly but punches me in the chest all the same: My time with Tyler was *vastly* different from my time with Jack, yes.

But maybe not worse.

Which leaves a question floating through my mind as I drift off to sleep, my gut feeling like a yawning hole with no bottom—is it better to be loved with no life plan, or to have a comfortable life cut out for you, even if it lacks adventure?

A year ago, I thought I knew the answer. Now I'm not so sure.

Jack and I are growing distant, and even though I keep telling myself that we'll fix this, that I know we will, because he's my boyfriend and we have a *plan* and everything is going to be okay, the edges of the hole of panic in my stomach only stretch wider.

It's just some long-distance hiccups, I try to reason with myself. *It has to be.*

Because I shattered Tyler Ferris's heart for this. It has to be worth the cost, or I'll never, ever forgive myself.

Part Two

ARRIVAL

Chapter Thirteen

The flight eventually does what all flights do—land—and the next step in everyone's journey begins.

When the dinging of the seat belt sign stirs me out of my sleep, I rub my eyes and look at Tyler. He's carefully looping his headphones and putting them away, an unreadable expression on his face. Still feeling weird about how we left everything, and with the confusion swirling in my stomach, I opt to say nothing and put my tray up quietly instead and tuck my planner back into my backpack, zipping it up.

After an uneventful landing (during which several older passengers clapped, which I almost made a joke to Tyler about but saw his still-stoic expression and decided not to), we're suddenly standing, grabbing our bags from overhead, and shuffling single file out of the plane until we meet outside the gate and regroup. We walk side by side in awkward silence, following the crowd toward the exit, hovering in each other's vicinity but not speaking. At first, I think Tyler is going to jet off as soon as he's able to, getting as far away from me as possible, but he shortens his steps to match my stride. My heart blooms with a gushy warmth when I notice, the walking in tandem a familiar sensation from when we used to weave through the halls together at school.

See? my brain points out to me, rather unhelpfully. *Being around Tyler feels like muscle memory.*

No, I retort in my head, because I'm definitely delirious from traveling and starting to lose my mind a little bit. *It's just that he's like half a foot taller than me, and I have tiny legs and he knows it's rude to leave me behind.*

If you say so, my brain sighs. Or maybe I'm hallucinating that, too. Who's to say, after my emotions have been a jumbled mess for the last half day?

Tyler and I manage to make it the entire way to bag check without saying a word to each other, but once we're both standing there watching luggage spin on the carousel, he finally speaks.

"I hope you have a good time." It looks like every word coming out of his mouth pains him, and he doesn't take his eyes off the conveyor belt. "With Mr. Two—with Jack." He coughs into his fist awkwardly, not meeting my eyes.

"Thanks," I mumble, reaching out and grabbing my suitcase as it glides past. He helps me pick it up, setting it next to me and finally looking me in the eye as we straighten up. And maybe, just for a second, I believe that he doesn't actually mean it, that what I hear in his well-wishing isn't honesty but regret.

"It was nice to see you again, Olive. Even if just for thirteen hours." His smile is sad, and I awkwardly bump his shoulder with my fist for something to do. But once I make contact, Tyler shakes his head and wraps his arms around my shoulders, pulling me in for a hug. I make a little squeak of surprise before wrapping my arms around his waist and squeezing him back.

For a second, I feel like I've stepped into that alternate reality I was daydreaming about earlier—the one where Tyler and I are a couple on a trip together to visit his family, one where the bag check isn't where we're about to split up and likely not cross paths again until graduation. His hoodie smells like a mix of his spicy cologne, salt and vinegar chips, and stale airplane air.

"You have a good time, too," I mumble against his chest, slowly inhaling his scent, feeling thrown back in time. For a second, I close my eyes and let myself enjoy it. "Give Lucas and Ella my love, and give their daughter a kiss for me."

"Will do." He steps back and breaks our hug, my heart panging in disappointment, as he leans over and grabs his own bag. "Take care of yourself. And have a good time exploring the island. Still have my number if you need me?"

"I do." I think of his name sitting in the contacts list in my phone, the little pizza emoji next to it as an inside joke after all our time spent together at Suburban Slices. The emoji I never had the stomach to delete even long after I walked out of Tyler's life.

I do have it, but I won't need it.

Now he throws up a shaka, signalizing *hang loose*, and locks eyes with me as he takes a few steps backward, ready to head out. I stare back and feel my stomach drop just slightly, gripping the handle of my luggage tightly and not quite sure that I like the feeling of being the one walked away from this time. Tyler's eyes stay locked on mine for as long as he can, before he turns a corner and disappears out of sight. I'm surprised at how sad I feel watching him go, like I hadn't spent the last year not seeing, speaking, or talking to him. There's less time than that between now and graduation. *Relax, Olive. You've done this before, and you managed to pick up the pieces after.*

Tyler's disappearance is a shock to my system, dragging me back to the reality I'm in and not the daydream that I was thinking about. I'm now standing here alone, in an airport in Honolulu. A portion of it is open air, all dark wood with spinning fans lazily pushing around the warm island air, palm trees swaying in the breeze. It's a stark difference from New York, where everyone was cold and cranky and bitter. Here, airport staff walk around in brightly patterned Hawaiian shirts, arms adorned with fresh, fragrant leis, smiling and cheerfully making conversation with anyone they walk past. I admire the scene as I'm powering up my phone and deciding who I should call first—my mother or Jack.

I start with my mother, giving her a ring to let her know that I've landed safely.

"That's great, honey," she coos over the phone, pots and pans clinking in the background. It's 2:00 p.m. here, which means it's 8:00 p.m. on the East Coast. "I'm about to clean up dinner. How was the flight? Anything eventful?"

"Just some turbulence." *And an accidental run-in with the ex-boyfriend whose heart I shattered,* but she doesn't need to know that. My mother knowing that I spent the entire flight next to Tyler Ferris would open a can of worms that I'm not equipped to deal with when I'm this jet-lagged and stressed out. "Nothing eventful."

"Glad to hear it. Is Jack at the airport getting you now?"

"He's on his way." Another lie, because as much of a hopeless romantic as Mom is, I think even she would disapprove of my Surprising Jack plan. As far as she knows, he's expecting me and is excited that I'm coming. "I'm going to head to the exit and meet him out front. I'll call you later."

"Sounds good—love you, Ollie. Hope you have a great time out there."

"Love you too, Mom." I end the call before I cave and spill everything, staring at the dark screen and contemplating my next move. Wanting to put off calling Jack for a little longer, I order an Uber and wait out front. I take a second to admire the scenery around me—while the airport is the typical concrete hustle-and-bustle of a major transportation hub, it's still surrounded by impossibly tall palm trees that stretch toward the cornflower-blue sky. There's not a cloud smeared across it at all, just an endless expanse of blue, blue, blue and the gentle kiss of the breeze on my cheeks. It's paradise personified.

If this place is already taking my breath away at the exit from the *airport,* I can only imagine what the rest of the island has in store for me.

Once I'm settled into the back seat of the car and coasting along toward the University of Hawai'i, I decide that I can't put it off any longer. I pull up Jack's contact in my phone and hit the call button, heart hammering in my chest as it rings and rings.

And rings.

And rings.

And rings. And—

"Hi, you've reached Jack Cameron. Leave a message and I'll get back to you. Thanks!" The voicemail tone beeps, and I open and close my mouth a few times, wondering what the hell to say.

"H-hey, Jack," I stammer. *Already off to a crappy start.* "Not sure if you're busy right now or anything, but I have a surprise for you. Give me a call when you can, okay?" I end the call and lean back against the headrest, taking a few steadying breaths. *It's 2:00 p.m. Maybe he's still sleeping. Although Jack never sleeps late. Maybe he's studying, or he's in a class, or he's lost in the woods somewhere—*

Just to be safe, I also shoot him a text. *Hi. Have a surprise for you—call me when you can?*

The driver brakes sharply, startling me out of my mental spiral and nearly sending my phone skittering underneath the seat. "Sorry, Miss Olive," he apologizes empathetically. "The traffic on the Kamehameha Highway can be brutal this time of day." He continues to apologize at least three more times, which is four times more than a New York City cabdriver ever would.

Meanwhile, I'm still running through the address book on my phone, checking the dorm building and number of Jack's new school mailing address. As we near the campus and pull into the front entrance, I call one more time, hoping that this will finally be the one he picks up.

No such luck. *Hi, you've reached Jack Cameron. Leave a message—*

I don't even let the message finish this time, hitting end in frustration. *Guess this is going to be even more of a surprise than I bargained for.* The plan was to surprise Jack by telling him that I landed at the airport, but clearly things have changed. Now the new and improved plan seems to be that I'll knock on his dorm room door and surprise him that way.

Any other time, this would be the kind of surprise that excited me. Not the kind that filled me with dread, unsure of what I was going to find when—or if, honestly—he opens that door.

Enough, Olive, my brain chides me. *You're being crazy. Jack is in* college*—he has busy college things to do, like classes and projects and study groups. He's busy.*

But is he too busy for me?

Would I be too busy for him if the roles were reversed?

"It's just a snag that comes with long distance," I murmur to myself as I stare out the window, earning a concerned look from the driver up front. I pretend I don't see him and study the leafy green trees and lush mountains in the distance instead, approaching our destination with a mix of both excitement and a little bit of dread in my stomach. However, part of the dread is lessened by the beauty of the University of Hawai'i at Mānoa. Tall, leafy green trees stretch up toward the endless blue, making the entire campus look like the bottom level of a rainforest. All around me, students mill about, some in pajamas or hoodies, others in board shorts and flip-flops, all laughing and talking and joking and likely making plans for later that night. The curved stone pathways snake in and out of the various entrances to the stone-faced classroom buildings, many with tall stone columns snaking up toward the sky. It would take my breath away if I wasn't already short of breath from panicking about whatever the worst-case scenario is about to be.

I thank the Uber driver as we pull up to the dorm, one of a cluster of towers nestled on the campus and overlooking the volcano—Diamond Head, that sleeping giant keeping watch over the island of O'ahu. Around us, more tall tropical trees stretch into the sky, and there are even a few stray chickens clucking around on the street, pecking at crumbs on the ground and seemingly unbothered by all the students milling out. The air smells like salt and a freshness that we don't have on the East Coast, but no amount of beauty could cure the dread curdling in my stomach. Not even the warm beams of sun caressing my cheeks as I study my surroundings.

I check my phone for Jack's address again and look up at the corresponding tower, making sure I'm in the right place. Students are clustered everywhere, some with backpacks slung over their shoulders as they head off to class, others shuffling past in more pajama pants and hoodies, undoubtedly heading to a *very* late breakfast. There are even a few striding past in athletic gear, armed with water bottles or yoga mats, ready to get some sweat sessions in. The campus itself is its own tiny ecosystem of a million different personalities and voices and students.

And somewhere in that building in front of me, one of them may be about to break my heart.

The only snag I can see is that the front door looks like you have to scan in to enter. A student occasionally strides up to the door and taps a plastic card against the reader, the lobby door clicking open in response. I clutch my phone in my sweaty palm as another pajama-clad guy scans in and holds the door open for a petite girl with a messenger bag behind him. It strikes me that, if Jack ignores my final call, this is how I'll have to get into the building—trespassing.

I cross the fingers on my free hand as the line rings and rings and rings, feeling all sorts of awkward and embarrassed to be hanging around the front of the building but not going in, like a total weirdo.

Hi, you've reached Jack Cameron—

"Ugh!" I let out a frustrated shriek of annoyance and consider hurling my phone into the cluster of bushes across the path but think better of it in case Jack decides to call me back. I stamp the rubber sole of my sneaker on the pavement instead to expel the anger.

"Are you waiting for someone?" The inquiry comes from behind me.

I spin on my heel, mortification seeping into my pores. The tall, golden boy in front of me definitely witnessed my mini temper tantrum. He has long, loose curls, lit gold by the sun, and mossy green eyes that study me curiously. It takes me a second to register the large, waxy thing he has propped up against his cargo shorts and fitted white tank top—a surfboard.

"I . . ." My mouth opens and closes, refusing to form words. "Yes?"

The corners of his eyes crinkle playfully at my squeaky voice. "That sounds more like a question than an answer." He's noticeably taller than me, the surfboard only making him look more like a giant. Or a sea god. Or Poseidon himself.

While part of me can't stop ogling this golden boy right in front of me, I can practically hear Tyler's relentless teasing in my head. *You're on your way to reunite with Mr. Two First Names, crossing the entire continent with turbulence and your ex-boyfriend, and it's* Poseidon *that ends up being the roadblock?*

I fantasize about shoving Imaginary Tyler off the wing of an airplane before finding my words again. "Yeah, I'm, um . . . I'm waiting for my friend to come let me in so we can work on a project."

He nods and flexes his tanned fingers around the surfboard, seemingly accepting my answer. "I see. What dorm do you live in?"

Put on the spot, I try to run through the other dorm building names I saw etched into the signs on the drive in here, but I come up blank. "I—"

Poseidon seems to notice my discomfort, his tanned glow paling a little. Still, he laughs sheepishly. "Sorry, didn't mean to be a total weirdo. You looked like you had something going on."

"Nope, nothing," I shoot back in a voice that very clearly

screams, *Yes, everything*. He starts to turn away and lean down to shoulder the surfboard, but he eyes me warily.

"As long as you're sure."

Olive, you idiot, this is your chance. "Actually, well—it's kind of a long story, but my friend is taking a long time to come downstairs, and I really have to pee before we head to the library to work on this project, and I don't think I can wait—so I should probably meet her up there and use the bathroom before she comes all the way down here to meet me and we have to double back, you know—"

"Relax, dude." Poseidon chuckles and sets the surfboard against the wall, fishing around in his pocket until he produces his ID. "Don't have to make it a whole thing. Could've just asked."

I watch him tap the ID against the reader, which lights up green in sync with the click of the lock disengaging. "Thanks. Appreciate it." And then, because I'm a bumbling idiot with word vomit disease, the lie keeps going. "Girl stuff, you know? Periods wait for no woman."

His face screws up in disgust. "Er . . . yeah. Good luck with all of that." Clearly not in the mood to continue the conversation, he throws his surfboard over his shoulder and heads off down the path, stopping to give me another creeped-out look before he goes.

But none of that matters, because my sneaker is currently wedged in the lobby door, holding it open. Which means now there's nothing preventing me from getting inside and going up to find Jack.

And I still can't determine if my stomach full of butterflies is from excitement or dread.

"Three-five-three. Three-five-three." I keep muttering Jack's room number under my breath as the elevator coasts to the third floor, the butterflies building as I envision the details inked in my planner, poised and waiting for ease of reference: *353. Where my boyfriend lives, and hopefully is right now.*

I didn't even think of a backup plan for if he isn't here—that's how determined I am to fix this. Fix us.

But first, I have to know what I'm fixing.

As the doors ding open and release me, I can't help but think back to what Tyler said on the plane, his face morphing into an expression of anger when he found out about Jack's radio silence. *Anyone who knows even a single thing about you would know you're too great of a person to ignore. He's an idiot if he can't see that. When we were dating—*

I stop the replay right there. When Tyler and I were dating, things were fun but not permanent. This is the boy I'm aiming to be with long-term, and it's an entirely different situation.

Going down the hall, I see 349 . . . 351 . . . 353. I stop in front of the door, leaning my rolling suitcase up against the wall. The door to Jack's room is cracked open, and voices float out from inside.

". . . telling you, that's not the way he explained the formula." I recognize Jack's measured voice, a mix of friendly and frustrated. "I could've sworn he taught it to us differently."

"And I'm telling *you,*" another, noticeably higher, voice says, "that this is the way he explained it would be on the test, so this is the way we should practice it."

"Okay, Professor." There's a teasing lilt in Jack's tone that makes my stomach turn. "Whatever you say."

Even though the crack in the door isn't big enough for me to see through, the twinge in my gut confirms my fear—there's a girl in Jack's room. And to top it off, it sounds like they're bantering playfully, instantly sending my mind spinning in a million different directions of who this girl could be, her connection to Jack, what they've been doing together, if she even knows who I am.

Is she the reason Jack has been ignoring me?

I'm still standing outside the door like a creep, garnering strange glances from students who are making their way down the hall and observing the weirdo girl with the suitcase who very clearly is eavesdropping on whatever's going on inside room 353. It was one thing when an entire continent and the Pacific Ocean separated me and Jack, because at least then I could chalk up my worries to being paranoid or far away. Just not used to having a long-distance boyfriend, let alone one who is older than me and already in college.

The half-open door taunts me and I shift from foot to foot, wringing my hands and delaying the inevitable. Whatever waits behind that door, even if it's my worst fears come to life, is better than the anxious worry of the in-between.

At least, that's what I'm hoping for.

Unable to take the anticipation any longer, I squeeze my eyes shut, say a prayer to the gods I'm not sure I even believe in, and nudge the door open. It creaks loudly, announcing my arrival. I wait one second, then two, and then step directly into the doorway to see what waits for me on the other side.

Chapter Fourteen

At least my worst-case scenario isn't coming to life. Jack and the female I heard aren't tangled together in bed, naked with flushed faces. Or curled up together watching a movie, snuggling without shame. They're not locking lips over math homework banter, either.

They are, however, sprawled on his floor next to each other, books splayed out between them. They're both facing away from me, stretched out on the small square of space between Jack's bed and his absent roommate's, scattered pens and pencils and lecture notes piled around them. A quick glance at Jack's bedspread (thankfully unrumpled) shows the sleek rectangle of his phone, the screen black. *I wonder if the screen will still show my missed calls, if he really hasn't checked it yet*. They're deep in the throes of their studying session, not even turning to look at me.

"Hey, Leo," the girl says, still turned toward her textbook. "Sorry, I threw my stuff on your bed when I got here—I can move it if you want." I can't see her face, but a waterfall of auburn hair cascades down her back, and she's wearing petal-pink socks on her feet, which are kicked up behind her and gently nudging

Jack's own, almost absentmindedly, as they work together. They look like a couple—a much better fit of a couple than me and Jack, being that we've never played footsie with one another while working on homework, bantering lightly and laughing while doing so. Everything with Jack had always been strict, neat, stoic, and poised. It was just the way he was—how *we* were.

But not him and whoever this is.

Even if it hurts to admit, they look happy. Happy and at peace.

When whoever Leo is—probably Jack's roommate—doesn't answer them, they both turn and look at me. The girl frowns a little bit, eyebrows drawn, puzzling out who I am.

Jack, however, looks as shell-shocked as I feel, his bright blue eyes widening to match the popped-open O of his mouth. Almost instantly, his face drains of color, becoming even paler than he was before he left for school. I notice a new sprinkling of freckles on his cheeks and arms, no doubt brought out by the Hawaiian sun. His blond hair seems to have gotten even blonder, and it lost some of the perfect, close-cut trim it always had and looks a bit looser, a bit calmer, a bit more beachy.

"Olive." He doesn't say my name with any of the surprise or excitement that I was hoping he'd feel. He doesn't even look pleased to see me. What he looks like is a kid who's been caught doing something they shouldn't be doing—the expression of a child who knows they're out of places to hide and there's about to be hell to pay.

"I tried to call you." My voice comes out strangled, and I can't stop staring at the spot where their socks meet as they look at me over their shoulders. "I called you a few times, actually. Wanted to let you know that I was coming a week early as a surprise." I think of all the stickers in this week's planner page—the plane, the palm trees, the ocean, even a holographic shining sun. And it makes me think of that stupid diamond ring sticker from the morning Asher broke up with my mom before they went to Vegas—and how everything was ruined when I had to rip it out of the planner, to get rid of the cruel reminder.

I can only imagine how destroyed the pages will be if I have to lift up all these stickers.

Jack doesn't know what to say to any of this, his mouth set in a grim line. But he has the same calculating expression I've seen on him a million times before when I helped him practice for college interviews, or Yale alumni events with his dad, or when he was trying to nail a particular presentation during his senior year. It's his look of evaluating all options when he finds himself backed into a corner, figuring out what to do next.

The girl notices my discomfort, shifting subtly and stretching her legs out flat on the ground behind her, toes out of Jack's reach. "Hi, um . . . who are you?" She looks to Jack for an explanation, but he's still staring at me and blinking rapidly, as if he can't believe I'm really here.

"I'm Olive." I'm surprised I can hear my own voice over the sound of my warbling heart. A flare of rage spikes inside me, and I feel the venom on my tongue before I register what I'm saying, delivering what could possibly be a very devastating blow to this girl. "I'm Jack's girlfriend. From home." I think back to the disbelief on Siena's and Rio's faces when I told them that at the first senior party I went to. The way Mira—who I hadn't seen in the hallways of school since—came to my rescue.

It's hard trying to fit into Jack Cameron's world, isn't it?

But the g-word doesn't land like I expect it to. This girl's eyes don't widen, and her mouth doesn't drop open in shock. She doesn't turn to Jack, who is still sitting there looking shell-shocked, and demand clarification. Instead, she smiles warmly.

"It's nice to meet you." Her melodic voice is nothing but pleasant and welcoming. "I'm Lilly. I've heard a bit about you." I can't help but notice that she says *a bit* instead of *a lot*. Don't most people normally say they've heard a lot about someone's significant other? *Or does Jack not care enough to mention me much at all?* She spins the pen in her hand around her fingers casually, not at all stressed out by my presence. *Who the hell is this girl, then?*

"Olive." Jack starts to finally speak, seemingly spurred by the sound of Lilly's voice. He looks like he's chewing on glass as he flounders for what to say. "It's not what it looks like."

Lilly nods seriously, attempting to smooth over my worries. "It's really not, even though that was an absurdly cliché thing for him to say." She shoots him a look, and if we weren't in the situation we were in, I think I would've laughed at her comment, impressed by her wit. But even though she doesn't seem to be in a love triangle with me and my boyfriend, I still have no idea who this girl is, or why she's playing footsie with Jack. "We're friends from calculus class. We've been studying for the midterm coming up, nothing more." She holds her hands up in an *I come in peace* gesture, but it could just as easily mirror a look of surrender.

"I called you" is all I say in response, turning to Jack, hating how childish and hurt my voice sounds as I repeat myself. "And sent a bunch of texts. And plenty more in the past week, all that went unanswered." Lilly winces at this, eyes darting quickly over to Jack as if to chastise him for his stupidity.

Jack, to his credit, looks mortified. "I've been really busy, and things have been going on. You wouldn't get it. You're not in college—"

"Dude." Lilly's sharp laugh punctures his sentence and deflates it right in the middle. "Seriously? That's the excuse you're going with for being a shitty boyfriend to her?"

His eyes dart between the two of us now, even more cornered than he was a few seconds ago. And although I still don't trust the girl or know much about who she is, it's nice to feel like I'm not the only one who's unimpressed by Jack's answer.

But he just doubles down, digging the hole in my heart even deeper. "It's true, Lil. She doesn't get how much more stressful it is than high school, and all the studying, and how busy you wind up being all the time—"

"Oh, shut it, Jack." Lilly is standing now, gathering her books and notes and pens and pencils and shoving them into the backpack on Leo's bed. "I don't know what the hell is going on here, but at least don't feed her *that* shit." She zips up her bag and tosses it over her shoulder, giving me a look that could mean either *Men, right?* Or *I'm so sorry you have to deal with this, but I'm getting out of here,* before slipping out the door and down the hall. "Good luck," she whispers as she goes past, and I'm not sure if it's directed at me or him.

The interloper now gone, Jack has no respite from the hurt—and honestly, fury—that's roiling through me. The long hours on the plane, feeling gross from the stale air and sugary snacks, and the hurt swirling inside me all create a fiery combination that bubbles to the surface. "Really, Jack? You were too *busy*? I don't get it because I'm not in college? Give me a break." I've been annoyed at Jack sometimes, sure, and occasionally even hurt by him when his stupid, snobby friends didn't accept me with the warmth Tyler's friends once did, but I've never felt like this toward him—burning with an anger that is flirting dangerously close to hatred.

He runs his hands through his hair and then cups his head, leaning forward and staring at the floor. "Going radio silent definitely wasn't the best choice I've made lately, I'll give you that. But I can explain it all, Olive, I can. Please just give me the chance."

I didn't come this far to turn back now, so I cross my arms and do my best to channel my anger more than my hurt. "Why'd you ignore me, then?"

Hearing my concession, Jack looks up in surprise before scrambling to his feet. He stands awkwardly for a few seconds, unsure of what to do, before he crosses the room and wraps me up in a hug.

"It's so great to see you, Olive," he whispers into my hair, squeezing me tight. "Thanks for the surprise."

In any other moment, I'd melt happily into his embrace, but my arms are still crossed and now squished uncomfortably against our stomachs. "Why'd you ignore me, Jack?" I'm fully mumbling against his shoulder, and as soon as he notices, he steps back and drops his arms at his sides, looking sheepish.

"Okay," he begins, sitting on the edge of his bed. "First, let me be entirely clear—nothing's happened between me and Lilly. Not a *single* thing, Olive. I wouldn't lie to you about that." He looks so earnest and miserable that I know in my heart he's telling the truth. That may relieve one of my worries, but it sure as hell doesn't solve everything.

"You're still not giving me an answer." I've never been this sharp with him before, and I can see that I'm visibly rattling him, his expression more urgent now. He pats the space on the bed next to him, urging me to sit—and against my better judgment, I do. I've still had a long trip and am super exhausted, so even though I want to stick to my guns and stand, I don't.

I think back to Christmas break—when Jack was home for a few short weeks, and most of that time was spent catching up with friends and family, celebrating the holidays, and ultimately packing before going back. How our few date nights and dinners and hangouts felt more like he was ticking things off his to-do list versus actually looking forward to spending time with me. At the time, I chalked it up to busyness, that he had a lot to catch up on and a lot of people to see in the few short weeks he was home. I forced myself to be okay with it, to not overreact, to adjust and convince myself that this is what happens when someone goes away for college—their time home gets divvied up a lot more particularly and you can't have them to yourself anymore. I convinced myself that it was normal, just part of the regular growing pains we were bound to experience in a long-distance relationship.

But I'm not so sure anymore.

He sighs and picks up my hand, threading our fingers together. I'm still pissed off enough to want to yank my hand away, but my heart jumps at the feeling of his warm skin against mine. "It really *has* been busy," he admits sheepishly, giving my palm a gentle squeeze. "So at first, when I came back for the spring semester, I really was getting swept up in it all. Starting back up after the holiday break. It was chaotic, new professors, new classes, new textbooks to track down . . ." He trails off and sees my expression, which I'm sure is blindingly obvious in conveying that we're straying off the mark, so he rushes to course-correct.

"So it was getting really busy, particularly this calculus class, which has been a killer. And then I met Lilly in the class, and she's so skilled with this stuff, so we started studying together. And really, Olive, with the time difference between us, and the distance, and everything that's been going on, I just . . ." He takes a deep breath and my stomach tightens and I steel myself for the inevitable. "I thought it was best if I gave myself a little space from everything at home for a while, to focus on all of the craziness here."

Several things hit me in that moment.

One: Jack needed space from home.

Two: Jack needed space from *me*.

Three: Jack saw every message I sent and actively chose to ignore them.

Four: Jack is gravitating toward a woman who is a better fit for him.

"Oh my god." I can feel the pain inside settling on my chest, thick and heavy and hard. "You just promised that nothing happened between you and Lilly, but that doesn't mean you don't *want* it to. You want to break up, don't you?" I tear my gaze from the pilled carpet and risk a glance at his face, praying that I'm wrong, that he rushes to correct me.

He doesn't.

Instead, he keeps talking, each word digging like another razor blade deeper and deeper into my heart. "Lilly and I . . . we have a lot in common. A lot *more* in common. Nothing's happened between us, but the spark is there, and . . ." He doesn't fill in the blank, looking at me helplessly, so I'm the one who hammers the final nail into my own coffin.

"You want to see where it leads."

He coughs awkwardly into the floor, eyes skirting everywhere except toward me. "Yeah. I do. But Lilly has no idea I feel this way, that I want to act on anything at all. That wasn't some front she put on. And I haven't made any solid decisions yet—I wanted to talk to you about it when I came home for the summer."

I don't answer that, closing my eyes and seeing the image of pink and white socks dancing across the backs of my eyelids. *Was he going to let this weirdness go on for three more months before coming clean about it?*

Jack squeezes my hand again, drawing attention back to him. "I'm sorry I didn't go about it better." He looks like a kicked puppy, and in any other situation, maybe that would've made me feel bad. But instead, all I can think about is my mother, those nights on the couch, the ice cream and the wine and the crying.

Is this what it feels like? To put so much stock in a person and have them stomp on your heart anyway?

And then, a tinier voice, the quietest whisper in the back of my mind: *Did I make a mistake?*

Which decision was a mistake, though? Letting Tyler go? Letting myself get comfortable with Jack? Turning off my heart to side with my brain?

It's too much to process all at once, so I simply don't. I act.

I slowly detangle my fingers from Jack's and pull my hand away. It doesn't leave me feeling any sort of empty or cold, the way letting go of Tyler's hand felt on the plane. "I think I should go."

"Go where?" Jack echoes my own thoughts, frowning. "You just got here; where are you going to go?"

I'm already standing now, brushing off my hoodie. "I have to go, Jack. Somewhere that isn't here." I'm too paralyzed to think that far ahead, the only thought circling my brain being that I have to remove myself from this situation before I lose another piece of myself.

Jack rises to meet me, putting a hand gently on my shoulder. "Listen, Olive. I know it isn't ideal to stay here, but you shouldn't put yourself up in a hotel around here. They're outrageously expensive. I'll sleep on the floor all week if you want, and you can take my bed. Just . . . please don't leave."

I shrug his hand off my shoulder, the rage fully sparking and igniting now. "I'm not staying here so you can feel better about doing this to me after I flew all this way. I'm not your charity case." *I'm not his anything now.* Hurt and pain and embarrassment swirling in my brain, I step into the hallway and don't look back, even as Jack calls after me helplessly. I force my feet to keep going, one step in front of the other, away from the wreckage of yet another failed relationship.

Oh god, I think as I grip my suitcase handle and head toward the elevator. *Am I turning into my mother?* As much as she loves and protects and cares for me, my stomach churns at the thought.

For the second time in my life, I'm leaving someone I saw a future with behind. Only this time, the only heart breaking is mine.

Chapter Fifteen

I wish I could say that this was the first time Jack had chosen someone else over me, but that would be a lie.

Jack's graduation had been a weird experience for me, for several different reasons. First, my boyfriend was graduating *high school,* and I wasn't standing there beside him clad in my own scratchy graduation gown, because I still had another year to go.

Second, my ex-boyfriend, who also still had a year to go, was there.

I had been sitting in the bleachers with Jack's parents and his sister Isabelle, the hot metal scalding the backs of my thighs in the ruthless June sun. No amount of fanning yourself with a program leaflet would save you from the agony. Even Jack's mother, Missy, who normally looked like a porcelain doll right out of the box, had a dewy sheen on her upper lip. Isabelle sniffed loudly, her expression unreadable under the brim of her floppy white sun hat.

I saw a flash of Delia's hair—now eye-wateringly orange—first, followed by Tyler and a couple of their other friends all trailing after one another as they snaked through the crowd in the bleachers to find an open spot. I had no idea who they were here to see, but it looked like Tyler's friend group had acquired some new people in the last few months, so it could've been anyone. All I knew for sure was that they weren't there for Jack.

Throughout the entire ceremony, their group was all I could focus on. While the principal droned on, I stared at the pack of Skittles that Delia and Tyler were splitting between them. While the valedictorian gave their speech, I zeroed in on how the sun glinted off Ty's dark hair. And when everyone—including Jack—tossed up their caps in celebration out on the field, I didn't even see it. My eyes were open but my brain was lost, unable to stop thinking about the group of friends I'd managed to lose. The ones who made me feel like a puzzle piece that fit, not one that was fighting to be crammed into a picture that it sometimes felt like it didn't belong in.

But it didn't really matter, because my old group obviously didn't need me anymore. And it's not like I tried to stay in touch with them, either. I was no longer welcome among them.

By the time the ceremony ended and we were weaving through the crowds to get down to Jack, my brain was hopelessly lost in a spiral. It was supposed to be a good day, but all I could focus on was the negative, and it was so freaking *hot*. I was melty and cranky. The air smelled like sweat and hot dogs from the concession stand and a million different perfumes all mingling in the worst way, and I just wanted to go home.

We eventually found Jack, and I peppered him with

congratulatory kisses, trying to force myself back into the moment. We all took photos, and I said hi to some of his friends, who regarded me with lukewarm acceptance, as usual.

"So," I'd said to Jack once we broke off from his group of friends. "Where do you want to go out to eat to celebrate? My treat. Maybe that new steak house that opened by the highway?" I'd probably have to dip into a decent chunk of my savings to cover it, but you only graduate high school once, and I was determined to make it important.

Jack, however, had no such qualms about making the celebration special. Instead, he chewed on his bottom lip as his eyes drifted over to his friends, standing a few feet away and eyeing us curiously. "Actually, Olive, uh . . . I think the guys and I were going to go out to the diner. It's kind of been our post-graduation plans for a while."

"Oh," I'd replied, fighting to keep my voice bright even though it felt like a tiny piece of my heart chipped off at the dismissal. "That's fine, I'm good with the diner. You can never go wrong with disco fries."

The look on Jack's face got even more pained, and his friends started growing impatient, clearly waiting on him. "Well, I think we wanted it to just be a guys' night. No, uh, girls or flings or anything."

My skin had prickled at being thrown into the same category as *flings*, especially as his girlfriend of several months, but I was determined not to let it show and ruin the night further. "My bad. Totally get it." I took a step back, the harsh sun making my vision swim in tandem with the moisture welling up in my eyes. "Have fun with everyone!"

I expected Jack to call out after me, or give me an invite after all, but he just gave me a quick kiss on the cheek and bounded over to be with his friends.

He's a senior, and these have been his friends for years, I tried to reason with myself as I gathered up my things, said a quick goodbye to his family, and hurried to leave. *It's just a guys' night. It's nothing personal.*

It was when I was heading back to my car with a promise to meet up with Jack later that I bumped into Tyler and Delia again.

Or, rather, I bumped into a cranky-looking grandma who was squinting through the crowd looking for her grandson, and beyond her shoulder were Tyler and some of his friends, all clustered around a guy I didn't recognize, clad in a cap and gown. Tyler was in the middle of clapping the guy on the back when he almost turned and looked my way, and I ducked behind one of our physics teachers to avoid him. But I hadn't needed to, because a few seconds later, Tyler spun back around the other way and rejoined the conversation.

I have to talk to him. It was like I'd been possessed. I didn't want Tyler back, and I was standing firm in that decision—and, I reminded myself, I was happy with Jack—but I at least had to say something. Had to apologize for the shitty way I had ended things. I knew it was the right thing to do.

Just as I went to take a step forward, it was matched by Delia, who appeared out of thin air and was now eye to eye with me. We were so close that I could see the smudges of her winged eyeliner from the hot sun.

"Don't, Olive." It didn't sound like a warning—more like she was tired. I'd always been used to hearing the fight in her voice, that trademark Delia toughness, but in that moment, she just seemed drained. Whether it was from the scorching hot sun or the fact that she had to deal with me, I didn't know. "You've done enough. This is the first time in months that we were able to drag him out of his room for something other than a mandatory class." Her gaze locked on mine for a second before she tore it away. "He's just starting to come back to himself again after the pain you put him through. Don't be cruel enough to make him go through it twice."

Her words were a sharper sting across my cheek than the sunburn that was undoubtedly forming there. Tyler and his friends were still moving up ahead, not noticing me at all. Or maybe they did and were pretending they didn't. It's not like I didn't deserve it.

I stood there for a second, unable to say anything in response, watching her watching me with a guarded look in her eyes before she heaved another sigh.

And then she turned on her heel and they all disappeared into the crowd, and I went home, where I could quickly crawl back into bed and sleep away the anguish of the day in the coolness of modern air-conditioning.

Which is *probably* not how one should feel on their significant other's graduation day. Which just made the guilt worse, even if it was Jack who decided that he and his friends were going to hang out without their *flings*. Without me.

You're always with Jack, I stubbornly told myself, squeezing my eyes shut tighter and trying to let the hum of the air-conditioning lull me into the midafternoon nap I'd been craving. *You're his girlfriend, and he loves you, and he just wants to celebrate this achievement with his guy friends.*

You're literally going to see each other later. He's not choosing his friends over you.

Maybe if I repeated it to myself enough times throughout the never-ending afternoon, it would start to feel true.

That was the first time that everything felt like a charade, but it sure wasn't the last.

Chapter Sixteen

I don't feel the tears until I push out of the dorm building's lobby doors, the sunlight illuminating my wet cheeks. But I don't feel hurt—I just feel numb.

Every time I blink, I see those socked feet. The surprised look on Jack's face. The way his mouth moved when he admitted that yes, he wants to get to know Lilly better. I'm not sure whether to laugh or scream at my cosmic joke of a life, flying thirteen hours and thousands of miles across land and sea to surprise Jack, just to end up getting dumped. And it's not lost on me that he did a weak job of even trying to apologize, not even following me out to see where on earth I was going.

Frustrated and entirely too overwhelmed, I drag my suitcase over to the greenspace down the path, sinking into the grass against the trunk of a twisting, bending tree. For a few minutes, I don't do anything except sit there with tears streaming down my face, letting them fall into the mossy grass while I replay the events of the past hour over and over in my head. I keep it on loop until I don't feel it anymore, too desensitized, and then I wipe my cheeks and stare up at the branches above me, thinking.

I reach into my backpack and yank out my planner, opening to this week's spread and staring at the cheerful rainbow of stickers dotting the page, the bright ink declaring things like *finish packing* and *head to airport at 4AM* and *flight to Hawai'i*. All things that should be marks of an exciting vacation, making my stomach sour when I look at them now.

What I'm upset about more than anything else isn't that Jack wants to leave me—*did* leave me (or, more accurately, I left him, even though apparently he's been setting the stage for that for a while). What I'm really mourning is the loss of the white picket fence dream that I fought so hard for.

I left a boy who loved me because I was concerned about our future. And then put stock in another boy who left me anyway. The humiliation burns sharp and hot in my chest, nearly doubling me over. Still, I force myself to close my eyes and take a deep, slow breath of salty air, centering myself in the stillness.

That is, before the logistics questions kick in. I'm here for two weeks, with nowhere to go, nowhere to stay, nothing to do. I'm someone who thrives on planning, and my entire trip was essentially shredded up and tossed to the churning seas, leaving me feeling unmoored. The pain morphs to panic real fast, and I dig my phone out of my hoodie's pocket, poised to dial Mom. But once I think about the several issues with that—starting with the disappointment and worry she'll feel when she finds out what happened, and the fact that I lied to her about Jack knowing about this, for starters—I hesitate.

I'm well aware of the inevitable heartbreak that awaits me when I get home, but for now, all I want is to push it to the back of my mind. So instead, I stare blankly at the leaves dancing above my head, willing an answer out of thin air.

And while I don't quite get one, I *do* get the impulse to scroll through my contacts for the name that's been collecting dust. I glance down at the pizza emoji that's staring at me, taunting. Unable to stop the blink of surprise at the realization that I really never had the will to delete that stupid pizza icon, even after all this time, never feeling quite brave enough to edit Tyler's contact at all—a sharp mark of finality closing what, in retrospect, was one of the best chapters of my life thus far.

Not wanting to dwell on it any further, I press the button.

Tyler starts speaking after no more than two rings. "Olive? Missing me already?"

"H-hey." I suck in a deep breath, hating how shaky and cried-out I sound. "Just figured I'd check in and let you know that I got to campus."

"Uh, glad to hear it." His suspicion leaks through the receiver. "Why do you sound weird? Are you okay?" I hear the distant voices of other people in the background and the low gurgles of an infant. He's already at his brother's house.

"I'm fine," I say shakily. "I got here with no problems." *It's what came after that was the disaster.*

To his credit, Tyler doesn't buy it. He instead waits a beat before speaking again, softer this time. "You gonna tell me what's going on, or what?"

Unable to bear the weight of my heavy heart alone, I unload everything that happened in the past hour, Tyler listening intently without saying a word. When I finish my story, he takes a few seconds before he speaks, words tight and punctuated.

"Where are you?"

I look up at the leafy tree and my surroundings. "Still on campus. I'm sitting under a tree near his dorm building."

"I'll come get you." His answer is immediate, and I hear shuffling as he presumably gets up.

"Tyler, you don't have to do that."

"I know I don't have to," he says, voice stronger this time, rumbling with an intensity I haven't heard before. "I want to. This asshole stomps on your heart and emotionally cheats on you and leaves you hanging out to dry, all alone—"

Emotionally cheating? I didn't even consider that a thing before now. Is that what Jack did to me? "He didn't kick me out—he said I could stay there if I needed somewhere to go."

Tyler laughs without humor. "How generous. Breaks your heart and still offers for you to sleep in his bed."

"That's not what he meant." My voice is hot, surprising even myself. Jack may be a monumental asshole for what he did—no, he *is* a monumental asshole for what he did—but a small part of my heart still defends him, not yet coming to terms with the loss of the future I'd so carefully planned out.

"Anyway," Tyler's voice cuts through, filled with frustration. But no matter how angry he is, I know it's not directed at me, but in defense *of* me. "Regardless, I'm picking you up. Can you sit tight for another twenty minutes or so?"

"I can." My eyes scan the campus, looking for signs or a map post somewhere to orient myself. "Do you need me to wait for you at the main entrance?"

The jingling of keys comes in over the phone. "No, stay where you are. I'll come find you."

"You've never been on the campus before. How do you even know where I am?"

Some of the sharp anger in his voice dissipates, and he sighs. "It's you, Olive. I'll be there." He ends the call before I have a chance to question him. *It's you, Olive.* What is that even supposed to mean?

I scoot down further until my head is resting in the soft grass at the base of the tree trunk and look into the leaves, making myself comfortable. The stress of the crying, the broken sleep on the plane, and my heavy heart all blend together into a sudden and irresistible sleepiness—so, lured into calm by the warm ocean air and the gentle hush of tropical birds chirping in the tree above me, I let myself sleep.

It feels like I've only dozed off for a few seconds when the crunching of gravel snaps me out of a hazy dream filled with airplane bathrooms and pink socks. But when I open my eyes and sit up dizzily, there is Tyler, hopping out of a cherry-red Jeep and coming around to lean against the passenger door with his arms crossed. Even though he tries to look serious, a smile still fights its way onto his face.

"So, this is where you plan to stay for the whole trip, huh? Sleeping under this tree?"

I rub my bleary eyes and yawn. "Hey, don't knock it till you try it. It's the best ten-second nap I've ever had."

He chuckles at this. "Way more than ten seconds. I've been trying to reach you for the last fifteen minutes."

"You have?" I sit up straighter and fumble around in the grass until I find my phone, wedged under the wheel of my suitcase. I poke the screen and see that I have several missed calls and texts from Tyler trying to locate me on campus, and a few calls and voicemails from Jack. I swipe all of them away without investigating further.

Tyler watches me with interest, his gaze flicking between me in the grass and the tall dorm tower stretching up behind me.

Once his eyes get over there, he glowers. "I have half a mind to go in there and beat the shit out of him for that stunt he just pulled."

I stand shakily, getting my bearings and grabbing the handle of my suitcase, which Tyler swoops in to intercept and hoist over his shoulder as if it wasn't stuffed to its breaking point. "There's no reason to," I reply, trailing after him to the car. "He's not worth it. But more importantly, how the hell did you find me?"

Tyler loads the suitcase into the car and shakes his head like it's a silly question. "I told you, Olive, it's you. I know you." He ticks the bullet points off on his fingers as he talks. "Obviously I looked for you at the campus entrance first, because if there's anything you hate, it's being an inconvenience, so even though I told you to stay put, part of me fully anticipated you'd be there. But then when you weren't, I found my way to the freshman towers and knew you'd be out here." He points to the tree I was just napping against, pride on his face. "And I was right."

"You didn't think to try other places first?" It's my turn to tick off places that I could've been. "Maybe I was at the bookstore, or the library, or the dining hall."

Tyler smirks as he closes the trunk and follows me around to the passenger door, opening it with a flourish. "Nope. I know you hate being cooped up, and after all that time on the plane, the last place you'd want to be is inside."

If I hadn't loaned my heart to this boy all those years ago, I'd be shocked by the scary accuracy in how he reads me. But because it's Tyler, I nod and grab the handle of the car door, boosting myself into the seat. "Well, aren't you the detective. Have you become a *Law & Order* expert since we broke up?" Tyler closes my door and rounds to his own side, sliding into the driver's seat and grinning, seemingly unbothered by the mention of our breakup for the first time all day.

"Nah," he says casually. "I'm an Olive expert." He starts the engine and pulls out his phone, firing off a quick text before throwing it in the center console's cupholder.

My heart tickles excitedly at his comment, but I force myself to squash it down. *You're letting your emotions get the best of you. It's been a long day.* And it's also the first day I've seen Tyler and actually had a normal conversation with him since the breakup—I guess old habits die hard. Instead of responding to that, I force myself to redirect the conversation. "Where are we headed?"

"Just sit back and relax," Tyler replies, eyes on the road as he flicks on his blinker and pulls us toward the exit, the lush green mountains rising up around the paved highway. "Enjoy the scenery while I drive. We have some regrouping to do."

Chapter Seventeen

The sun is lowering in the sky when we show up to a small bungalow nestled on a quiet suburban street. I'd say it looks just like the regular rows upon rows of houses back at home, but these little homes have tall palm trees sticking up toward the sky, and there are even a few coconuts strewn around the lawn. As we near the front porch, I see a pile of beach toys and a few teeny-tiny bathing suits drying on the railing, and it feels as homey and chaotic as Tyler himself does. Without him even having to say it, I know that this is Lucas and Ella's house.

He doesn't have a chance to ring the bell before the front door swings open, Ella standing there to greet him. She looks like I remember, dark brown eyes and inky black hair in a neat braid down her back. Even though she's a few years older than Tyler, he has her beat with his height—but that doesn't stop her from reaching out and pulling him into a hug, which he stoops down to meet.

"You're back!" she says, ruffling his hair while still in their embrace. "I swear you've only been gone for an hour and it feels like you got taller. Do boys ever stop growing?"

Another voice chimes in behind Ella as she lets Tyler go. "Physically, no. Maturity-wise, I don't think any of us progress past the age of twelve." There's a teasing glint in Lucas's eye as he steps up behind Ella. While I'm standing there observing the whole exchange, I notice how much he looks like Tyler. But he's definitely more muscled—and tanned by the luscious Hawaiian sun—than I remember him being at the cookouts I'd been to.

Ella notices me first, eyes lighting up. "Olive! It's been so long. It's so good to see you, honey." She wastes no time stepping over the threshold onto the porch, wrapping me in a hug of my own. I squeeze her back, relishing in her familiar scent of coconut lotion and suntan oil. I guess everything those scientists say about smell being the most powerful trigger for memories is true, because being here, it feels like I've been thrown back in time, meeting her at a family dinner and finding solace in having a girl semi-close to my age to talk to about the Ferris boys.

Lucas gets to me next, folding me into a hug and giving me a polite kiss on the cheek. "Good to see you, Olive." While he's being kind—and more than generous enough by letting me visit their house—there's a slight layer of frostiness there. Tyler nudges his brother with a stern look, but Lucas just shrugs.

Duh, you idiot. You shattered his brother's heart. Of course you have some sucking up to do.

As if on cue, a piercing wail sounds from inside the house. Lucas grimaces and points at his brother. "Back to wake-up duty, kid."

It's exactly the kind of thing I'd expect Tyler to refuse to do—especially when being decreed by his older brother—but I guess he's changed in some ways since we were together, too, because his face lights up. "Oooh, she's awake!" He looks between his brother, Ella, and me for a second before stepping toward the doorway. "Want to come inside and meet Mele, Olive?"

"Yes, yes!" Ella waves us both inside and I step into the house, the smell of spicy stewed meat climbing into my nose and making my mouth water. "Dinner will be ready in a minute. We're so glad you could join us."

I follow Tyler into one of the back rooms in the house, the wallpaper adorned with little palm fronds, flamingos, and flowers. There's a wooden crib up against a wall, with a small pair of chubby hands gripping the railing, round brown eyes peeping over at us.

"Hi, Mele," Tyler coos, and my stomach flips. He crosses the room to the crib and lifts Mele from it, cradling her to his chest and snuggling her with a look of such adoration that it makes my heart squeeze.

He's a good-looking guy with a baby, Olive. They all look like that when they're around kids.

I try to visualize Jack in this same spot, cradling a baby that's ours. Once upon a time, that was a vision that soothed me, made me feel less stressed out about the future, knowing I was on my path there. But now it just makes me feel . . . empty. Something that I once thought would be shiny and exciting but now falls flat, a mirage that isn't as satisfying once you realize it's all an illusion.

Mele squeals gleefully at the sight of her uncle and flexes her chubby fingers toward his face. He catches her tiny fingernails against his lips and kisses them gingerly. "I've missed you so much," he murmurs. "You were going down for a nap when I got here, weren't you? So it's been a while since you've seen Uncle Ty.

Well, Mel, he is *so* glad to see you." He nuzzles her with a few more kisses, and I cross my arms tightly against my chest to contain my aching heart.

After another minute or two, he surfaces from his baby-induced stupor and looks up at me. Mele follows his gaze, blinking at me curiously. "Do you want to hold her?"

Panic grips my nerves and squeezes tightly, and I take a step toward the door. "That's okay. I've never . . . I've never actually held a baby." The thought of dropping sweet, squishy little Mele on the floor is too much, and my stomach bottoms out when I realize I'm semi-responsible for this tiny person's safety if I put her in my arms.

Tyler, however, is totally unconcerned. He stretches his arms out toward me, Mele dangling between his hands, kicking her little Michelin Man legs and gurgling gleefully. He wiggles her toward me, taking another step forward as I take one back to match him, before he sighs with a small smile.

"I'll show you what to do," he promises. "Just give it a chance." He notices my hesitation and rolls his eyes playfully. "You went on a plane across the entire US *and* the Pacific Ocean today, but *this* is what you're scared of? A cute baby?"

He's looking at me with a strange expression on his face, his eyes glazed over a little bit. And even though it's been so long since we've been connected, I'm able to tell exactly what he's thinking.

He's picturing exactly what I just tried to picture with Jack.

Which is why my body suddenly starts acting on its own accord, and I reach my arms out and accept the gurgling bundle from Tyler's waiting arms. Mele blinks at me curiously for a few seconds before seeming to accept her new fate, giggling happily and reaching out her chubby hand to wind a fist around my hair, tugging with abandon and making both Tyler and me burst out laughing.

"You know," I murmur to her, sniffing her sweet baby scent and letting it warm me from the inside out as she continues to tug on fistfuls of my hair. "I think I like you, Mele."

Tyler's watching us with his arms crossed, a thoughtful smile on his face. "It seems she likes you, too."

After a delicious dinner of a spicy local style of beef stew—and a lot of catching up on how we've all been since we've last seen each other, while all delicately avoiding any mention of the breakup—Ella is the one who finally brings up the conversation I've been dreading.

"Well, it's been lovely to see you again, Olive, but I *do* have to ask—" She narrows her eyes as she looks at me. "What exactly brought you here? My brother-in-law didn't give us any details other than that you were in town and he was bringing you over because you were having a rough day." She makes a dramatic show of playfully kicking Tyler's leg under the table, which makes him yelp and me laugh.

I take one last sip of the delicious passion-orange-guava juice that Lucas had given me before gathering my thoughts. "Well"—I look over at Tyler, who gestures for me to continue while Mele grabs at his ears—"it's kind of a long story." And I launch into the quickest explanation I can think of—that I came to visit Jack, who turned out to be a dick and broke up with me, and I called Tyler because I had nowhere to go.

"Well, obviously you can stay here for the rest of your trip." Ella looks over at Lucas, who nods, though his expression is unreadable. I want to say that I'm bothered by his uncertain reception of me turning back up in Tyler's life, but like I said, I can't fault him for being wary. Still, his and Ella's gesture tugs on my heartstrings.

"Thank you so much," I tell them both earnestly. "But I'm happy to find a hotel in the area. I'm going to look for a flight home tomorrow first thing in the morning, so I won't be in your hair for much longer."

Tyler scoffs at that, shaking his head and gesturing to his niece, who has moved onto poking his nose. "Please. You know Mele loves tugging on hair, so the longer you're around, the more she has to grab."

"Thank you," I say again, trying to keep my brain from anxiously spinning out of control at the thought of all the things I have to do later. *Find a flight, cancel that dinner reservation I made at the fancy outdoor steak house down in Waikiki . . .*

"Olive." Ella reaches across the table and squeezes my hand, her expression warm. "I'm serious. Please, don't sweat it. You can stay here as long as you like."

After eating, Tyler helps me bring in my luggage from the car and get set up in the guest room. I see that his own suitcase is already open in the corner, clothes and shoes littering the floor.

He follows my gaze as he sets my suitcase down. "Don't worry," he rushes to explain. "I'm going to take the couch for tonight. This room's all yours."

If I wasn't feeling guilty about intruding already, I certainly am now. "Don't be silly, Ty. You're doing me a favor by saving me an outrageous motel fee tonight. That's generous enough. I'm fine to take the couch."

He shakes his head defiantly. "You know I'm not going to let that happen, Olive."

I tap my finger to my chin, thinking dramatically. "I could always take up Jack on his offer and stay in his dorm room. He'll probably be kind enough to go stay with Lilly for the night. You know, make that sacrifice for my sake."

He chuckles. "She'd love that."

"Probably not, actually," I reply, thinking about the look on her face when she stormed out of his dorm room. "I have a feeling he's going to be in the doghouse with her for quite a bit."

This gets a snort out of Tyler as we flop belly-first onto the bed, pulling out his laptop to change my flight. Even though what's happening right now is totally platonic, the fact that we're on the *bed* together has my stomach swirling with nerves. I force myself to focus on the task at hand, logging into the airline website and scrolling to find a new flight to switch to.

"Perfect," I murmur, my eyes scanning the screen. "There's a three p.m. flight back to New York tomorrow." But Tyler is clearly having none of it, because he gives me a look.

"Stay one more day, Olive," he says, voice even. "You came all this way to see Hawai'i for the first time, and you're not even giving yourself a chance to enjoy it."

I'm already shaking my head before he finishes the sentence. "Nope. As beautiful as this place is, I'm not going to put your family out like that."

"It's not putting us out," he emphasizes, "because *we* offered. It's not a problem at all."

"It *is* a problem!" I protest, frustrated. "I don't want to be a nuisance."

"You're never a nuisance!" Tyler's answer explodes out of him so quickly that we both lean back from each other a little bit, startled into silence. He runs a hand through his hair and takes a slow breath before continuing. "You're always welcome here, Olive. Or anywhere I am. You know I'd never turn you out."

"But I'm not your girlfriend anymore, Tyler. It isn't your responsibility to take care of me." The words are like a sharp razor cut to our conversation, bleeding out silence.

He waits a beat before answering. "That doesn't mean I stopped caring about you. Or that I ever will, honestly. So do whatever you want, but all I'm going to say is that if you need somewhere to stay, or a ride to the airport, or help with anything else, I'm here. I'd do it for any of my friends, and we both know that. You deserve to enjoy the beautiful island that you traveled so far to see." With those final parting words, he pushes off the bed and stalks out of the room, a tidal wave of sadness following in his wake. I watch him go, feeling helpless.

I'd do it for any of my friends.

He confirmed what I wanted—that whatever happened between us in the past is dead and buried, that all we are now is friends. So then why does hearing it feel less like relief and more like a sucker punch?

But I don't have much time to dwell on it, because before I can stop myself, I launch off the bed and pad into the hallway.

Tyler's standing at the hall closet, riffling through the spare sheets and blankets. When he turns and spots me, his frown deepens.

"Fine," I blurt. "I'll stay."

Immediately, that frown tilts upward, and his eyes light up. "You will?"

"Yes, *but,*" I emphasize, holding up a finger. "For one day only. I'll let myself enjoy at least one day of this tropical paradise before I head back home." He *does* have a point. All I've managed to see of O'ahu so far were the lush rolling hills of the mountains by the highway, the dorm building on the University of Hawai'i campus, and the concrete and steel of the airport. I spent *way* too much time in the sky battling my fear of turbulence to not get at least one good vacation day out of it.

Tyler mulls it over for a second, shrugging before shoving the sheets he was holding back in the closet. "I can make do with one day. We'll have to squeeze a lot of stuff in, but we can still make it happen."

And as angry as I want to feel about my situation—everything with Jack, coming all this way just to have egg on my face—I can't help but feel a little zing of excitement at the thought of a Hawaiian adventure.

A Hawaiian adventure with Tyler, my brain tries to unhelpfully point out. But I bat the thought away and go back to helping him figure out which sheets to put on the couch.

The rest of the evening passes uneventfully—Tyler and I both agree that we'll head out tomorrow to start adventuring, but that this evening should be spent catching up with Lucas and Ella (and little baby Mele). I book a return flight, Lucas grills some chicken and pineapple skewers for an after-dinner treat, and Tyler and I follow Mele as she crawls around the backyard picking up sticks and marveling at bugs.

Eventually, the exhaustion of the day—and the fact that I've been awake for almost twenty-four hours—gets to me, and my body becomes so heavy that it feels like a Herculean feat just to get changed and brush my teeth. On my way back to the guest room to get into bed, I walk past Ella, who is cradling Mele on her hip in the hallway. She turns and looks at me with a gentle warmth in her eyes.

"Getting settled okay?" she asks me. "I heard that you'll be staying for an adventure day tomorrow."

I nod. "Seriously, I can't thank you enough for your hospitality. You *and* Lucas. You've both been so generous, especially with the extra day added on, and I really appreciate it." And I also desperately try to shove down the reminder of Tyler's plane story and Mele's conception, now that I'm face to face with Ella again after all of this time. *I'm going to strangle Tyler the next time I cross paths with him, I swear.*

"It's not a problem." She adjusts Mele on her hip, and the baby starts focusing on her mother's long braid. An obsession with hair, this one. "You're always welcome here, Olive. And Lucas . . ." She sighs and trails off, collecting her words.

"Don't worry about it." I totally understand his neutrality toward the whole thing. "It . . . Tyler and I have a past. I don't blame him for being a little wary of inviting me back here."

She waves her hand to swat away the thought. "Ah, don't worry about that. He'll be fine. And it's all in the past now—you and Tyler are getting your second chance, and that's what matters."

Her words stop me in my tracks, toothbrush hanging limply from my hand. "What?" It's so absurd that I have to laugh. "Tyler and I? No, that's not . . . that's not what happened. We're not . . ." I swallow the lump in my throat. "We're not back together. We're just friends."

Ella clucks her tongue and shakes her head. "Always oblivious, you two." She wishes me good night and trails off down the hallway, murmuring to her daughter as she goes. I catch snippets of my and Tyler's names, along with the repetition of *oblivious* a few times. Sheepishly, I scamper back into the guest room and flop onto the bed, my brain a tornado of confusing emotions.

My phone screen is alight with notifications, the missed texts and calls and voicemails from earlier today. All from Jack. Seeing his name on my screen ignites a new angry fire in me, so I delete every single one without opening or reading any of them.

Instead, I do one of the things I've been putting off all day: I call Mom.

"Olive?" She sounds slightly panicked when she picks up, and I check the time on my phone, mentally kicking myself for forgetting that it's 4:00 a.m. there. "Everything okay?"

"Yeah, Mom, everything's fine." It's not a *total* lie, because I *am* fine in the sense that I'm not physically harmed. But that doesn't mean everything's really *okay*. "I'm not hurt or in trouble, if that's what you're wondering."

She reads me like a book, as she always does, taking no time to beat around the bush. "But something's wrong in another way, isn't it?"

For a few seconds, it feels like time slows down, like we're swimming in molasses. It's the last few seconds before I have to find my voice and force the words out of my mouth, and join my mother in the pit of shattered hearts.

"Kinda," I hedge. "Something happened with Jack." And then, not wanting to let the lies fester inside of me any longer, I spit them out—everything about the flight in, sitting next to Tyler, going to see Jack, the Lilly incident, being left in the dust, where I am now . . . all of it. I come clean about every last thing. Mom listens intently without saying a single word, to the point that I have to look at my phone screen several times to confirm that the call didn't drop. When I'm done, it's silent for a few more seconds, and I swear I've lost her again, before she finally speaks.

"Of all the people in the world to run into on the plane," she muses, interrupted by a yawn. "Tyler Ferris."

I immediately sense where she's going with this, and my hackles rise. "Mom, *no*."

"I'm just saying, that's too good to be a coincidence. Maybe it's—"

"It's not fate," I interrupt, at the same time she finishes her sentence with "fate." "It's literally two people having the same place to go. And somehow getting the same seats next to each other on the plane. It's not a big deal. It doesn't mean we're going to get back together or anything."

She sounds amused when she responds. "I didn't say anything about you two getting back together. I said that it sounds like fate is bringing you two back together for something." I feel a burning sensation in my chest at being called out, but she continues. "I'm just saying, pea, it seems like you lucked out by having him as your seatmate. At least you aren't stuck in some last-minute motel nursing a broken heart on an island in the middle of the ocean."

"I *am* still nursing a broken heart," I remind her, even though it suddenly hits me that I don't quite feel that way. I'm pissed at Jack and want to punt him off the top of a volcano, sure, but I'm not sure if *heartbroken* is the way to describe how I'm feeling.

I should probably look into that further, but it's late, I'm exhausted, and all I want to do after this shitstorm of a day is go to bed.

It actually wasn't a total *shitstorm of a day,* I muse. *It was just a shitty bump in the road, but the rest of the afternoon turned out pretty okay.*

"Well, I'm glad to hear that." Mom's voice coming through the receiver startles me and points out that I actually said that last part out loud. "So go to sleep, honey, and then try to let yourself enjoy your adventure tomorrow."

"I'll try." Though I suspect that with Tyler involved, it won't be very hard. He was always the best at planning our adventure days. "I love you, Mom. I'll talk to you tomorrow."

"I love you too, pea." She yawns. "Be safe, and have fun." She wishes me good night and by the time we hang up, I'm staring at the dark ceiling with my phone pressed against my chest, my thoughts swirling at a million miles per hour.

Jack.

Jack and *Lilly*.

Tyler.

Tyler's family taking me in.

Our adventure day tomorrow.

Jack.

Things failing with Jack.

What the fuck am I going to do now?

"What I'm going to do is try to keep it together," I sigh into the dark, feeling the edges of my vision get fuzzy as I drift off to sleep.

As if that's ever worked out for me in the past.

Chapter Eighteen

When I wake up the next morning, I decide that it's more than literally the dawn of a new day. It's the dawn of a new Olive—one who doesn't let herself mourn stupid guys like Jack Cameron.

New Olive is brave, I remind myself as I slip out of bed, brush my teeth, and yank on a T-shirt and shorts for the day. *New Olive is a badass.*

I even decide to leave my planner tucked in my suitcase before I head into the kitchen for breakfast. *New Olive sometimes hands things to the universe to decide her fate.*

That last one is a bit scary, so I have to give myself a few calming breaths as I walk down the hall, but I do it. I slide onto a stool at the breakfast bar and grab a box of cereal that Ella left out, along with a carton of milk. Getting myself set up, I take out my phone to idly scroll social media while I start eating, patiently waiting for my sleepy brain to turn on for the day.

"All right." Tyler claps his hands, causing me to lift my head from where I'm sitting devouring my Lucky Charms. "Let's get a move on."

"What exactly is on our agenda today?" I ask as we clean

up and then meander down the driveway. I boost myself into the Jeep. Tyler starts the engine. Even though I'm a bit wary of spending time just the two of us after so many months apart, I can't help the excitement bubbling in my stomach at the day that lies ahead.

"We, my dear Olive"—he winks at me as he pulls out of the driveway—"are going to explore the island of O'ahu."

"Exploring?" I can't help the playful laugh bursting from my chest as Tyler eases us down the sloped road and toward the main highway. "What do you know about Hawai'i? We got here at literally the same time."

He scoffs as he makes a turn and picks up speed. The sunroof is open and the windows are rolled down, so the wind whips through the car and swirls my hair around, making it hard to see him. "Give me a little more credit than that. This isn't the first time I've been here."

I do the math in my head of when his brother and sister-in-law moved to the island. "They've only been here a little over a year, Ty."

Through the floating tendrils of hair coating my face, I see his expression turn sheepish. "Okay, this is my *second* time here. But I'm still not a total newbie like you are." He shoots me a triumphant smirk and then starts to roll up the windows when he sees the messy state of my hair.

I dart my arm out and rest it on his bicep, stalling him. Tiny pinpricks of electricity sprout up where the pads of my fingers rest against his smooth skin, making me shiver involuntarily. "No, leave it. The air feels nice." He nods at my request but looks straight ahead at the road, looking as if he's swallowed a bug. "Is . . . is everything okay?"

"Everything's fine." His voice sounds off, but the playfulness is gone, leaving me with an emotion that I'm not really able to process. Tyler shifts his arm out of my reach, scratching his temple, and I sit back in my seat and watch the tall green mountains and puffy clouds float by as we whip down the highway. We meander for a while, admiring the sights and the hypnotic blend of modern concrete and steel buildings mingling with the palm fronds and lush hills, the air smelling like both seawater and sunshine.

Finally, after driving around and a lot of window-gazing, my anticipation reaches a boiling point. "Where are we going, seriously?"

The mention of our itinerary seems to bring Tyler right back on track. "First, I figured you'd want to get something to eat." He licks his lips, igniting a fresh wave of chills up my spine.

The mere mention of food has my stomach rumbling, even though it hasn't been long since I finished my cereal. "Sounds great." Emotional whiplash can do that to a person, I guess. "What'd you have in mind?"

He *tsks* and takes his eyes off the road to point a finger at me accusingly. "Nope, I'm not telling you. It's going to be a surprise."

"Oh god." I slump in my seat and roll my head toward him. "Why can't you just tell me?"

Now it's Tyler's turn to look surprised, and a little indignant. "You don't trust me?"

My answer comes easily. "Of course I trust you. I'm just not a fan of the anticipation."

Tyler clicks his tongue at me again and shakes his head in mock disappointment, humming for a second as he thinks.

“Well, I’m still not going to tell you where we’re going, because I’m not ruining the surprise. But I can give you a hint.” His eyes sparkle with mischief. “We’re going to try a true local delicacy.”

Horror overtakes me at the first thing that comes to mind. “Oh god, please don’t say you’re taking me to eat Spam.” Just the thought of the canned, salty meat is making any notions of hunger dissipate into thin air. It’s some people’s jam, but not mine, even though Hawai‘i is all over it.

Tyler throws his head back and laughs, a full, deep belly laugh that I haven’t heard from him since we were together. “First of all, that’s offensive—Spam is delicious and you are a hater. But second of all, no, I’m not making you eat Spam for lunch. I definitely wouldn’t live to see the end of the day if I tried that with you.”

I nod in agreement. “You’re right. You wouldn’t.” I rack my brain for other popular local dishes that I know but come up empty. So I let myself sit back and enjoy the rest of the trip while Tyler queues up some indie music—some things never change—and we coast down the tropical highway toward our secret destination.

After what feels like forever (but was probably only twenty minutes tops; hunger has a way of making seconds feel like hours), Tyler pulls the Jeep off the road into a concrete parking lot littered with cars and a small building. The giant neon sign on the building front stretching up toward the sky illuminates two words: Rainbow Drive-In. The face of the building is painted in a wide array of colors to match the name, and I immediately find it charming.

I peek my head out the window and study the line of people

snaking from the ordering counter into the parking lot, which Tyler tries to avoid as he navigates to find us a spot. It's surprising how urban Honolulu feels—how much like home. Especially with the boy sitting next to me. Even though I'm in a brand-new place, so many things still feel familiar.

"Okay," he says as he puts the car in park and we hop down, shaking out our car-cramped limbs. "This is the Rainbow Drive-In."

I study the tables of happy, sun-kissed people enjoying their lunches and chatting. Everyone here already seems so much more smiley and pleasant than they do back at home—but it's hard to make out what's on their trays from this far away. "What do they have here that's supposedly a local delicacy?"

Tyler's practically vibrating with excitement. "Loco moco."

"Loco *what*?" I'd think he was kidding about the name if he didn't look so excited about it. Not deterred by my skepticism, Tyler locks the car and we weave through the crowd. He waves me over toward the end of the line and we perch there in the sun, waiting for our turn to order. While we do, he fills me in on what we're about to eat.

"It's a classic lunch—or breakfast, or anything, really—combo of white rice, a hamburger patty, a fried egg, and brown gravy. It's all served stacked on top of each other, and I know it sounds a bit heavy, but it's truly the *best* blend of flavors." He licks his lips as if he's already drooling and we take another step toward the counter, closer to our turn. "I was pretty suspicious when Lucas took me here for the first time last year, but I'm telling you, once I tried it, I was a convert." He makes a motion with his hands next to his ears as if his mind is blown by the conception of this mishmash of food items.

I'm still trying to make sense of it all, distracted by the heavenly smells of grilling meat and sunshine wafting around us. "And this is something that people just . . . eat often? And it's supposed to be good?" I screw my nose up in confusion, puzzling it out in my head.

Tyler looks scandalized by my distaste, and so do the people in the line around us eavesdropping on our conversation. Already, there are almost ten more people in line behind us—this place is clearly popular. "Don't you like hamburgers, Olive?"

"You know I do." Our million midnight McDonald's runs when we were dating can attest to that.

"And fried eggs?"

"There's no other acceptable way that you can put them on a bacon egg and cheese, so yes."

"And rice?"

"Who doesn't like rice?" Honestly, why would he even ask that question?

"And brown gravy?"

"Obviously." I'm not above admitting that now my mouth is starting to water a little bit, both excited by the descriptions and by the fact that it's been a very, very long time since I've eaten at an actual food stand—something Tyler and I haven't done since we were together and would drive to check out new food trucks in town.

Tyler levels me with a stare. "So then, by that logic, you like all of the ingredients in a loco moco."

"Okay, but"—I wave my hand around the long line of people standing in front of the drive-in's window—"putting a hamburger patty on a bed of rice and topping it with a fried egg and gravy sounds like a heart attack waiting to happen." All of the starch and meat and grease and . . . *Mmm. That actually sounds delicious.* Who am I to question what Hawai'i has declared a delicacy?

Tyler simply shrugs as the line moves forward, unperturbed by that prospect. "Then it's a great way to go."

My eyes track the guy in front of us in line, receiving his steaming plate and walking toward some of the picnic tables set up in the shade. When he turns around, I find myself blinking in surprise, staring at none other than Poseidon himself, looking just as at home in his casual surfing attire in this atmosphere as he did back at the campus dorms. For a second, I think he doesn't recognize me—or worse, is ignoring me after the weird spectacle from yesterday—but he shoots me a wink as he breezes past with his tray, calling out to a group of friends at a nearby picnic table.

The loco moco heaped in front of him looks monstrously large, but at the same time, I can't deny that the scent wafting our way is making my mouth water.

Ty nudges my shoulder with a satisfied smirk. "Told you."

I cross my arms and sniff, trying to pull off indignant but actually trying to breathe in more of the salty, meaty, hearty smell that—yes, I'll admit it—seems pretty dang good. "I have no idea what you're talking about, Ty. I didn't say anything."

"You didn't have to." His answer is immediate as we move up to the register and he slips his wallet out of his back pocket. "You forget that I know you, Olive. I don't need you to tell me what you're thinking."

His words hit like the shock of the plane dipping during turbulence, low in my belly. And the stinging chaser is the unwanted thought in the back of my mind.

Jack doesn't know me like that. He never did.

I sneak another glance at Tyler, who is beaming excitedly at the cashier as he hands over some bills and orders us two plates of loco moco and bottles of Coke. This boy who's taking me to try new foods and knows what's on my mind without me even having to open my mouth. While the boy I'm *supposed* to be with is back in his dorm room, nudging socks with a girl who isn't his girlfriend, probably making plans for a future with her, too cowardly to tell me.

That thought is too much to process after an already exhausting day and a half, so I turn and follow Tyler to an empty picnic table instead, mind swirling.

Could it have always been like this?

And if so, then why did I ever think it was a good idea to screw it up?

Chapter Nineteen

"Oh my *god,*" I groan, clutching my stomach and nearly doubling over on the picnic table. "That was absolutely phenomenal. No notes." The loco moco was a perfect mix of a starchy, salty, meaty meal to fill me up after an entire flight yesterday of Coke and candy and bags of chips, and my eyelids start to get heavy. A post-Thanksgiving feeling in the springtime. Unlike Jack, Tyler clearly knows how to order for me.

He smirks proudly as he scoops up the last bit of rice and runny egg on his plate and pops it into his mouth. "I told you. It's going to be a long day of exploring if you plan on doubting everything I take you to."

I wipe my face with a napkin and tip it up to soak in the sunshine, soaking it in and giving my stomach a chance to breathe. "Okay, I won't doubt *everything.* But you have to admit, loco moco *does* sound a little strange when you describe it to someone at first." Tyler laughs at this and picks up our plates, throwing them away before joining me back at the table. He rests his chin on his hand and looks at me curiously, his dark eyes scanning my face.

"All right, tour guide." I swallow back a burp, cheeks reddening. "Where to next?"

To my surprise, he hesitates. "We should probably digest for a little while before we go to the next spot I had in mind. Do you want to talk about what happened yesterday?"

I can feel the walls of my heart closing off with every word that comes out of his mouth. "I already told you what happened," I mumble, chest tightening. Tyler shakes his head, looking a little exasperated at my response.

"You told me what *happened,* Olive. You didn't tell me how you *feel.*"

How I feel is embarrassed. Heartbroken. Ashamed. But I don't say any of those things to Tyler, because I long since lost the right to tell him those things about me. "Stupid. I feel stupid." I can't meet his eyes, so instead I trace the grooves in the wood on the picnic table, running my fingernail over a heart with a hastily scrawled *J + M* carved into the wood. I briefly wonder where J and M are now. If they're still together. If they're happy. I'd like to think at least someone is, if it can't be me.

"Stupid?" Tyler's face screws up in confusion, and he leans forward as if he didn't hear me correctly. "Why would that asshole make you feel stupid?"

I shake my head, rushing to correct him. "Not because of what he did. I'm not taking the blame for that—I'm sad about it, sure, but that was Jack's own asshole decision to make. But I'm feeling stupid, because . . ." I trail off, the words getting lodged in the base of my throat, refusing to come out.

They don't have to, though, because like Tyler so rightfully declared earlier, he knows me. "You feel stupid because you feel like your mom." He doesn't phrase it as a question, and I nod slowly in response, eyes burning a hole into the picnic table's wood, into the tiny carved heart.

Tyler reaches out and dips a finger under my chin, urging me to look up at him. When I do, there's a fire blazing in his eyes, but it doesn't look like anger—it looks like something more.

"Olive Austin," he whispers, his voice hoarse and nearly impossible to hear among the chatter of the customers around us. "You are anything but stupid. And, as much as I love Sherri, you are nothing like your mother."

My heart squeezes at the sincerity in his voice, but I force myself to turn my head out of his grip, focusing on the mountains rising behind us instead. "Are we really sure about that, though? My mom goes through a million men, each time swearing they're the one, letting herself fall and then getting hurt. Again and again. You've seen it, Ty. You know what it's like." Heat rushes to my face as I feel the hot prick of tears in the corners of my eyes. "I never had any doubts that she loved me, or that she loved every single one of the men that she swore was going to give her the fairy tale she's always wanted. But she ended up broken every time." All the nights on the couch. All the weeks where she moved through the house like a zombie. Is that what waits for me? Sometimes, I can't help but wonder.

"Olive." Tyler's voice is gentle as he reaches out and swipes an errant tear off my cheek with the pad of his thumb, making me shiver. "Not everyone gets the fairy-tale first-try romance."

"Not even us."

He looks sad as he smiles ruefully. "Not even us. But that doesn't mean every heartbreak you have will be a prophecy for the rest of your life. You're only eighteen and you've only had one heartbreak. I'd say that's well below average."

My mind snags on the *one* in his sentence. "What do you mean, one heartbreak? This is my second." Although it feels noticeably different than the first—it's not lost on me that this time, I'm more concerned about how *I* feel about my future, and less about what Jack did to me. The thought twists uncomfortably in my stomach, the same way it did when I was on the phone with Mom last night.

Tyler looks impossibly sadder but still smiles, bordering on a grimace. "Nah, you were the one that left our relationship. It's not the same thing as being dumped." Hearing him put the words out there so harshly stings, but I force myself to suck in a breath and sit up straighter, this conversation long overdue.

"Tyler Ferris." I steel myself to push the words out, the ones that didn't come that day in the hallway when I broke *both* of our hearts. "First of all, I know I've said this before, but I feel like I need to reiterate it. Our breakup was never, not ever, about something *you* did. It wasn't because I didn't love you—it was because I loved you so much that I wanted to end things before they got too serious, so it would hurt less."

His face falls slightly when I say *loved* in the past tense, but I force myself to carry on, the words thickening painfully in my throat.

"We weren't a good fit. It doesn't mean you're not a good person. It doesn't mean you're not a *great* person. It doesn't even mean you're wrong for feeling the way you do. Not everyone has to have a ten-step life plan, and they aren't lesser people if they don't. But that's something *I've* always needed, and that's why I walked away." The tears that were falling for my breakup with Jack are now falling for him. "That doesn't mean that it didn't hurt like hell. That doesn't mean that it didn't *break* me. I regret hurting you every single day. I never stopped feeling that way."

I'm full-on crying now, getting concerned glances from patrons walking by with plates stacked high with loco mocos. "I can never truly tell you how sorry I am for how it went down, but the one thing I can say for certain is that it *never* had anything to do with how much I loved you."

Tyler is silent, processing. His jaw tightens and he looks away from me for a second, taking a slow, steady breath through his nose and releasing it with his eyes closed. When he turns to me, he's a boy who's breaking inside. "Just tell me one thing, Olive." He seems so shattered that all I can do is nod, wiping away my tears. His voice breaks when he continues. "If I had gotten it together a little bit more for you, would we still be together?"

I chew on his question. *Would we still be together?* Would we be on this trip to Hawai'i to visit his brother *together,* a couple on a lunch date exploring the island? Would we be getting ready to walk across the stage at graduation as a couple, ready for what's ahead? "No." My answer surprises us both. "Because you'd only be doing it for me. I think eventually, we would've realized that we're two totally different people and that it wouldn't work in the long-term. It has to be a choice you make for yourself, not for me or for anyone else."

Several agonizing seconds pass while Tyler processes this, before he clears his throat and stands up, his eyes glassy. It's hard to get a read on him right now, but he doesn't look angry. He looks impossibly sad as he speaks woodenly. "I . . . I need a second. I'm going to head to the bathroom, and then I'll meet you in the car?"

I nod wordlessly, and he places the car keys on the table next to the little carved heart as he walks away, nervously running his fingers through his hair. All I can do is stare at the little heart until my vision swims, whether from tears or not blinking or both, I'm not really sure. All I know is that on top of the shitty day I had yesterday, now there's another emotion swirling through my stomach and making me feel sick. I can't help but question why I called Tyler in the first place—because somewhere deep in my gut, I knew the road would lead us back to the blockage we never got over.

I don't want to acknowledge it; it's been so long since I've really sat with this feeling. But I know the feeling of regret knocking against my rib cage, and it's not something that I can easily shake. Even if I'm confident in my answer—Tyler changing himself for me isn't really changing himself at all. And would I really want him to change?

I sit baking in the sun for a few minutes, thinking about moving into the shade but staying put to punish myself for everything that just went down. All the while, my thoughts swirl around Tyler and the conversation we had—but nothing about Jack. Life is funny that way: When I broke up with Tyler, it was all I could focus on for weeks, until the sting finally subsided. But Jack broke up with me less than twenty-four hours ago, and here I am thinking about something totally different.

After a few minutes, the heat starts to make me feel dizzy, so I grab the car keys, wish J + M's scribbled heart good luck, and head to the car, sliding into the passenger seat and starting the air-conditioning. I fiddle with the controls and the radio for a few seconds until Tyler approaches.

He's looking significantly less hurt but still a little withdrawn as he opens the driver's-side door and slides in, cooling his cheeks against the blowing AC, even with the sunroof open above us. "Sorry about that." He clears his throat and looks away from me, staring at the snaking line of customers ready for lunch as his fingers flex against the steering wheel. "It's . . . it's a lot to think about sometimes. Even though it was so long ago."

I force myself to be nonchalant, if for nothing else than to salvage the rest of the day. I shrug as I buckle my seat belt. "A year and a half is nothing in the grand scheme of things. Sometimes it still feels like yesterday to me, too."

He startles at this admission, looking over at me in surprise. His mouth opens like he's about to say something, but then he clamps it shut and turns his eyes back to the road, heading toward our next adventure spot of the day. I let him think in silence for a few seconds until he's ready to speak again. "Any guesses on where our next destination is?"

I study the highway we've pulled back onto, the same tall green mountains and palm trees and cornflower-blue skies, thinking—or at least trying to, but continuously getting distracted by the gorgeous view. O'ahu already seems to be a fascinating blend of tropical and modern—lush green mountains and leafy palm trees, bracketed by the concrete and steel of downtown Honolulu and the highway full of cars whizzing past. "Um . . . maybe the beach? A volcano?"

Tyler shakes his head. "No, but I hadn't thought of Diamond Head. That's a good one to add to the list." He studies the road signs as we drive, explaining that he's taking me somewhere that Lucas showed him last time he visited.

"That's not a hint!" I protest, fully twisting in my seat to make sure he sees my look of betrayal. "I have no idea where you went when you visited your brother last year. I didn't even know you *came* to Hawai'i. How can that be a hint?"

He sweeps his arm out, indicating the open road and the ocean to the side of us, frothy waves churning as if anticipating our gaze. "Think, Olive. What's something I'd be interested in doing in Hawai'i? Knowing everything you know about me?"

"Surfing?" I guess. Even as I say it, I know it's not quite right. Tyler likes adventure, but like most everyone else, he has a healthy fear of sharks after watching *Soul Surfer.* What else would Tyler want to do out here that isn't hiking the volcano, going to the beach, or surfing? *Maybe it's—*

I can feel the color draining from my face as I put two and two together. *Please, please, tell me I'm wrong.* "Oh no." We can't be going where I think we're going.

Despite all our time apart, I guess I do still know Tyler as well as I used to, because I watch his profile as his lips curl up into a satisfied smirk, reading my mind the way he always used to, like no time has ever passed between us. "Oh yes."

Chapter Twenty

"Please, Tyler." I'm not above begging. The car continues down the road, leading me to the one place I don't want to go right now. "Don't make me do this." My heart starts jackhammering in my chest, violent thumps that roar in my ears. At the next bend in the road, my vision swims, and I grab on to the passenger door handle like a lifeline, the greenery and blue skies blurring.

Tyler must underestimate the true panic I'm feeling, because he throws his head back and laughs good-naturedly. "Relax, Olive. I wouldn't take you anywhere I thought you'd get hurt." He gives me a pointed stare, raising one eyebrow. "But it would do you some good to learn to relax and take a risk or two every now and then."

I tactfully choose to ignore the dig about me not taking any risks in my life, the truth hitting a bit too close to home. Still, I focus on the matter at hand, and what Tyler is about to sign us up to do. "What if something goes wrong? I could *die*!" Tyler wouldn't really let me die in Hawai'i, would he? He can't be harboring *that* much resentment over our breakup. No teenage boy's revenge plan could be that cruel.

At least, I sincerely hope not.

He shoots me a mock hurt look. "Give me a little more credit than that. I told you I've done it with Lucas before, haven't I? And here I am, driving to go do it again. So clearly, everything is going to turn out just fine. You need to trust me, Olive. You used to—just do it one more time for me, okay?"

Tyler admitting to doing something stupid and then being willing to repeat that stupidity isn't reassuring. But it's so like him. It's so very . . . Tyler. *You need to trust me, Olive. You used to.* And he's right. I *did* used to trust Tyler—with our plans, with surprises, with my heart. But now . . . I'm not really sure how I feel.

Can I trust him again, just this once?

I guess it's time to try and find out.

I groan and flop my head against the headrest as he pulls us into a quiet residential neighborhood and puts the car in park. I glance around but don't see anything other than small, quaint houses and well-manicured lawns. It looks like any other American suburb, except for the tall palm trees dotting a few front yards and the gigantic mountain range rising up behind us, the ocean crashing against the rocks just down the street.

And it's definitely not where I was expecting Tyler to take me, so maybe our mind-reading skills *are* a little rusty. "Are we . . . not going to do what I think we are?" Even though I don't have a specific destination in mind—since I've never been to Hawaiʻi before—I thought I had a good grip on the type of activity Tyler was taking us to. But now I have no clue.

He swings the door open and hops out, flashing me another cheeky grin. "Oh, we are. We just have to take a little walk to the cliffs."

I slide out of my seat with a grumble and follow Tyler down the paved road until we come to a grassy clearing with a trail in front of it, a small sign posted at the trailhead declaring the entrance to Koko Kai Beach Mini Park. I make one last-ditch attempt to grab Tyler's arm and tug him back toward the car, but he chuckles and gently clasps my hand, leading me down the path and toward another, rockier clearing. Steep, sharp shelves of stone, meticulously layered lava rock from back in the island's infancy, jut out and kiss the frothing ocean, creating a multi-layered cliff face that makes the ocean in front of us feel like it could go on for miles. Like we're perched at the end of the world. Like this place where rock was poured from the sea hundreds of thousands of years ago is the quiet lip of the edge of the planet.

The sun is bright in the sky, illuminating the sturdy cliff of lava rock jutting out at various distances toward the churning ocean below. All around us are people, what looks like tourists and locals alike—spread out on picnic blankets on the higher rock shelves with sandwiches and sweating drinks, surfers out in the frothy waves, and people screaming gleefully as they catapult themselves off the lip of the rocky shelf and down to the water below.

"China Walls," Tyler declares. "One of the most well-known cliff-jumping spots on O'ahu. And a gorgeous place to come watch the sunset, if you're ever in the market for a romantic place to go." He practically chokes on the world *romantic,* cheeks flaming red.

I'm too busy taking in everything around me to fully think about what Tyler's saying, staring in wide-eyed shock as a girl in a bright yellow string bikini shrieks for her life, leaping off the edge. The air whooshes out of my lungs as her arms flail in weightlessness before she disappears and I assume crashes into the frothy water below. The guy with her—I'm guessing her boyfriend—leans over the lip to watch her descent, cheering and clapping when her head presumably pops above the surface with a happy shout. My staccato heartbeat slows only slightly with relief that she's alive, but the unease still lingers at what could've happened. "There's no way," I tell Tyler, my teeth already beginning to chatter from fear. "There is absolutely *no* way in hell you're expecting me to jump off this giant cliff into the ocean. No way whatsoever."

Tyler's hand is still clasped in mine, and he squeezes it gently over the sounds of the ocean, the shrieking, and the music coming from people's speakers. "Of course there's a way, Olive. You *jump*."

I take a step back, farther away from the edge and closer to the rock shelf behind me, where people are leisurely enjoying their lunches and staying as far from the cliff's churning edge as possible—exactly where I should be. "There is *no* way."

And yet, Tyler and I still stand at the end of a smattering of rocks jutting out toward the choppy ocean, and looking down, all I can imagine is the resonating *crack* of my skull against the stone.

"You do this for *fun*?" It's hard to keep the shriek out of my voice, which rises an octave higher when Tyler lets go of my hand, whips off his shirt, and presents his tan, rippling muscles to the warm sun. On his right shoulder blade is a small tattoo of a funky-looking fishhook—which was *not* there when we were together. I knew all his tattoos like constellations etched into my core memories, but not this one.

Surely my mouth is watering because I'm still hungry even after lunch, not because my outrageously ripped ex is standing right in front of me. He turns around and notices me staring, so I point at his shoulder in a weak attempt to justify my creepiness. "What's the tattoo of?"

"Oh, that?" He glances over his shoulder as if he could possibly see it, surprised by my question. "It's a Hawaiian fishhook. It's called the makau. It's supposed to bring good fortune and luck." He taps his collarbone. "Lucas got me a necklace of it last time I was here, but the string broke back home. I've been meaning to replace it. Our mom was actually really stoked when I showed it to her, you know?" And I do know. Tyler and Lucas's mother was born and raised on Maui but met Mr. Ferris when she went to Boston for college, and the rest was history. As far as I'd known from talking to them at Ferris family events, she'd gone back a handful of times before to see family, but never with the boys in tow. She was always promising them a big Hawaiian family vacation to help them learn their culture and get back to their roots, but up until now, it hadn't happened.

Maybe now, with Lucas and Ella being stationed here, they'd finally get to discover that part of themselves again. Tyler already seems gung ho to do so.

I force myself to swallow and focus on the conversation at hand, throat dry from the thirstiness that has nothing to do with the sun as I study the sharp slopes of Tyler's chest. "Uh-huh."

He keeps strolling toward the end of the cliff, unperturbed by my ogling. "It's really not as bad as it looks."

"The tattoo?"

He gives me a playful *keep up* look as I take a few hesitant steps toward him. "The cliff."

I keep my eyes trained on the churning water below. "Has anyone ever died here?"

No response. Tyler is staring at the ocean, too, his jaw working tightly to keep in the secret that he knows I probably assumed. If I wasn't already shaking with panic, I'd fumble into the back pocket of my shorts for my phone. "Ty?" I prompt him again, more cautiously this time.

He shrugs like it's no big deal before taking a few steps back to prepare for his running jump. "Don't Google it."

"Great," I moan, dropping my head into my hands. "So we're definitely going to die."

"We're not *definitely* doing anything, other than walking away from this with a really good story." He sighs and flexes his shoulders, preparing for the jump, and I find myself fascinated by watching the ink move on his tanned skin. "I told you to trust me, remember? Look at all the people who are here and having the time of their lives, and they're fine. It'll be an awesome memory of an adventure to look back on years from now."

I catch what he doesn't quite say. *When our adventure day is over and we go back to pretending we were never a part of each other's lives.*

It's hard to stop the squeak of panic from escaping my throat, especially after realizing that my disturbing vision of this all going wrong might not be so far-fetched. My fingers itch to take my phone out of my back pocket and Google China Walls and all the bad things that happen here. I instantly start spiraling, panicked by the risk, by the nonanswers, by the lack of a plan—

"Olive." Tyler's voice is suddenly stern as he takes another step, this time toward me, putting his hands on my shoulders and forcing me to lock eyes with him. I try to ignore the warmth of his palms seeping into me as he looks right into my soul, his usual Tyler mix of serious and playful. He smells like a blend of coconut sunscreen and boy sweat, musky and intoxicating. "Relax."

"I'm . . . I'm not even wearing a bathing suit," I stammer. Another weak attempt at putting a stop to this whole thing.

Tyler wiggles his eyebrows playfully. "You could always go in without one."

I slap him on the shoulder as a punishment. "Be serious. Also, there are like ten million children here." As if they hear us, a gaggle of them start shrieking behind me, one of them chasing another with a dead gecko they found nearby.

He sighs dramatically. "You know I'm kidding. Just jump in with what you're wearing. It's hot enough that you'll dry out in a second."

I break our gaze and look back at the foaming water, dotted with the tiny wet heads of jumpers who surface looking invigorated, reborn, alive.

What would it be like to feel that?

I've never taken a risk like that before—I barely take *any* risks, which Tyler knows. So why the hell he'd bring me here as part of our adventure day is beyond me.

"You only have to be brave for two seconds," he promises, reading my mind as he's squeezing my shoulders. "Just two. One second to step forward, one second to push off. Then you're in the air, then in the water, then it's done, and you *did it*." He gives me a little shake. "Think of how awesome it's going to feel when you finish doing it. Focus on that feeling and you're going to be fine. When I did it with Lucas, I honestly felt like I was on top of the entire *world* after."

"What if something happens to me?" Hysteria creeps into my voice. "I don't know what to expect with this. If I'll be okay. If something will go wrong. I don't *know* any of this, Ty." As someone who lives and dies by plans and controlled outcomes, this is going against the very fiber of my being. Every nerve ending in my body is practically screaming at me not to do it. To play things safe, like I always have.

Look where that got you, my brain whispers, but the dig is carried away with the sound of the wind from the ocean whipping against my ears.

Tyler lets go of my shoulders and takes a step back, the sunscreen smell drifting away with him and leaving my chest feeling strangely hollow. "I'm not going to force you to take a chance on something, Olive. That's all on you. Like you told me"—his eyes shine with something unreadable—"it has to be a choice you make for yourself, not for me or for anyone else."

Before I can process the subtle dig or the unreadable expression behind his eyes, he takes another step away from me and turns toward the cliff. My muscles move of their own accord, an invisible force tugging me toward him as I reach out for his shoulder, wanting to delay the disaster. Every cell in my body desperate to keep him on solid ground with me. "Ty—"

But he sidesteps my hand and takes a running leap, catapulting himself off the cliff. My panicked heart sails right over the edge with him, watching him fly toward the churning turquoise waters below.

My stomach feels like it's bottoming out as his body disappears out of sight, me shrieking Tyler's name and nearly jumping off after him. If I thought having to survive without Tyler after our *breakup* was hard, my brain nearly blacks out imagining having his entire existence wiped from the world.

Tyler. You have to save Tyler. It feels like I'm having a sensory overload, mind whirling with a million different possibilities. *Where is my phone? Why can't I reach my back pocket? Why isn't anyone around us helping me?* Instead of getting assistance from any Good Samaritans, I'm getting nothing but concerned stares as I struggle to suck in a breath, my limbs feeling numb. *Tyler. I have to save Tyler.* I almost don't want to look over the edge, scared I'll find blood or a cracked head or a severed limb or nothing—which would be much, much worse. Even the kids have stopped running around with the dead gecko, eyeing me with concern.

My brain scrabbles for purchase on any one idea when suddenly there's a peal of laughter coming from the churning ocean below, followed by a triumphant yell. I force myself to open an eye and peek over, where I spot Tyler, paddling without a care in the world.

"See?" he shouts up at me, waving one hand in greeting. "I told you it would be fine! Now it's your turn."

My knees buckle so hard that I practically sink to the ground with relief that he's safe. "You almost gave me a heart attack!"

"You almost gave *yourself* a heart attack," he clarifies as he starts swimming parallel to the rock face, toward the shore. "I told you from the beginning that it was going to be fine."

After a few more seconds of swimming, he's started climbing up the rocks toward me, and I have to step away and close my eyes to center myself. If the thought of Tyler careening into the churning ocean was scary, picturing him cracking his head open on the slippery, wet rocks on the way back up is even worse. Desperate for something to focus on to distract myself, I envision the small tattoo inked into Tyler's skin, flexing along with his muscles in the sunlight, crashing into the water alongside him . . . *Okay, maybe this isn't helping calm my heart rate much at all.*

Tyler's soft voice startles me out of my daydream when he meets me back at the top of the cliff, standing next to me again on the ledge as we stare at the water together. "You don't have to do it," he says gently, bumping my shoulder with his. "Not if you really don't want to."

"I really don't want to." My body still feels like it's buzzing from the adrenaline comedown of watching Tyler plummet off the rocks. Thinking of doing it myself seems totally out of the question. Tyler shrugs and heads over to his discarded pile of things, scooping up his wallet and car keys and T-shirt wordlessly.

"It was worth a shot," he chuckles as he turns away from me, heading back the way we came. "I thought you'd changed a little since we've been apart, but you're still the same old Olive." He says it with an affectionate warmth in his voice that definitely isn't meant to be insulting—I mean, he *liked* me that way—but it still makes me bristle.

I took a risk coming to surprise Jack, didn't I? I did something so uncharacteristic, going against my carefully thought-out plan and following my gut to Hawai'i instead. I'm five thousand miles from home, with nowhere to go and no place for me to be, but I'm here, I'm adventuring, I'm exploring. I left my coveted planner in my suitcase. I'm standing on a bunch of lava rocks on the edge of the ocean, tasting the salt in the air and feeling the spray on my cheeks and *living*.

I got my heart broken again and I'm still standing.

My feet move automatically, kicking off my flip-flops. I slide my phone out of my back pocket and hand it to Tyler, who is now staring at me suspiciously. "What are you doing?"

I fight the urge to roll my eyes. "What does it look like I'm doing? Might as well check off *gets heart broken* and *goes cliff-jumping* in the same trip, right?" Even though I'm now shaking with both fear and the urge to feel the wind against my skin, I try my best to hide it. Not that it works against the first love of my life.

Tyler's expression morphs from suspicion to concern. "I was only teasing you, Olive. You know you don't have to do this—you said you didn't *want* to do this. So please don't."

I cross my arms and stare at him, the ocean sending a salty spray up like little kisses against the back of my calves. "I thought you told me I should take a risk?"

"I did!" He pockets my phone and runs his fingers through his hair, looking as distressed as I felt earlier. "I did, and I do still think that. But exploring the island without following an itinerary is enough of a risk for you; I know that. You don't have to prove anything to me."

I tilt my chin up defiantly. "You're right. But I'm still going to do it." *Because while I may not have to prove anything to you, I have something I want to prove to myself.*

I'm more than a girl filled with checklists and plans. I'm more than the carefully thought-out life that I laid down for my-self. Sure, I still want those things—but I can still reach back into myself and pull out Old Olive every now and then, the one who loved midnight slushy runs and movie nights and slinging greasy pizza with the boy who once held her heart.

Tyler's bravado is gone, his expression fully worried now. "Olive. Think for a second. Do you really want to do this?"

"Absolutely not." My answer is immediate and from deep in my gut. Once he hears it, Tyler shakes his head and takes a step toward me on the rock, reaching his hand out to brush my shoulder.

But it doesn't connect. Because the second the muscles in his arm twitch to reach for me, I take off running in the other direction, just like he did a few minutes ago. I barely hear him call after me, or the music, or the chatter of voices around us. I barely hear the ocean. All I can focus on is my breathing and the slap of my bare feet against the lava stone as I run, run, run, bend my legs, catapult myself forward . . .

New Olive is brave. New Olive is braver than she's ever been.

And then I'm falling, but it's slower than I expect it to be. It feels like I'm floating in the air, my stomach swirling up through my throat and nearly in my head, as the glittering ocean rises to greet me. Only one thought goes through my mind before the shock wave of hitting the water. *Oh shit. Oh shit. Oh shit, oh shit, oh shit—*

The crash of colliding with the sea is such a deafening roar in my ears that for a second I can't hear anything. It's dark and cool and bubbly and salty and *which way is up and which way is down and oh my god I really hope I'm not smashed like a rag doll up against a rock and is that seaweed or a fish or a dolphin or a shark and and and and—*

My legs kick at the current and my arms pinwheel unhelpfully until finally, my head pops above the surface, sticky tendrils of hair covering my eyes. I choke on the salty water as I come up for air, catching my bearings, being lightly tossed around by the ocean as I adjust to the sunlight and look up at the cliff's ledge I just fell from.

Well . . . not exactly fell. More like a voluntary leap. As

much as the fear is still coursing through my veins, something else joins it there now, too—something almost like pride. Like maybe there's something to taking these risks that Tyler swears by every now and then. The thought of the triumph makes me grin proudly as I start to tread along with the churning tide.

Up on the cliff ledge, Tyler looks like a mirror image of what I'm sure I looked like minutes earlier, eyes wide in shock, mouth popped into a panicked O. When he finally catches sight of me and sees that I'm okay, he whoops and throws his fist in the air triumphantly.

"That's my girl, Olive!" he crows. "I knew you could do it!"

I let out my own shout of surprise, excitement rushing off my tongue like popping candy, feeling the familiar old rush of being called *his girl*. "I did it!"

He's still grinning as he points in the direction of how to get back up top. "I knew you could do it. Perfect form, too. Sailed right off the edge."

I slow my breathing as I paddle along with the current toward the shallower side of the cliffs, where Tyler climbed back to the shore after his own jump. The entire time, he's walking parallel to me, shouting words of encouragement and grinning as we make our way toward the cliff's entry point together, by both land and sea. I stay treading the water for a few extra seconds, relishing in the adrenaline high caused not by fear this time, but by accomplishment.

The water is cool against my sun-warmed skin, even in my soggy denim shorts and T-shirt. In a few minutes, I'll be filled with sand and dampness and discomfort and regret, but for now, I'm floating. "That was awesome. I feel totally different." And it isn't only an expression. I really *do*. My blood is humming with a new energy, and my mind feels as clear as the water I'm paddling in. A year ago—hell, even an *hour* ago—I would've never in my life considered jumping off a cliff. But I did it, and I'm alive, and I took a chance and I'm still *here*.

It feels like I'm buoyed by more than the salty ocean water.

Tyler's looking down at me with absolute wonder on his face as he sticks out a hand to boost me up. "Olive Austin, I think you've just been reborn."

"Tyler Ferris," I retort as our palms lock. "I think I just became a different person entirely."

Chapter Twenty-One

After the emotional rush of cliff-jumping, Tyler and I both agree that we need something way more low stakes, which is when he asks me if I'm up for another drive. When I retort that we're already doing that, he shoots me a playfully stern look.

"A little bit farther this time," he explains, slipping on his sunglasses as we coast down the road after toweling off. "There's a cool little market I want to take you to."

As we drive, I can't help but take in the gorgeous scenery around me. Bordering the road are tall trees that Tyler explains are tropical pines that look like Christmas trees but a bit scragglier, their branches puffy with upright-standing needles. They wave to us in the ocean air as we drive by, the sun gently pulsing through the open roof, its warmth mixing with the slight chill of the wind rushing into the car.

This place is beautiful, I think in awe as my eyes catch on the various stop-off points with lookouts peering out over the vast, glittering turquoise ocean. I'd been on tropical vacations once or twice with Mom before, but the only places we'd ever gone were either in Florida or California—neither of which can hold a candle to the breathtaking beauty of Hawai'i. It's like a gorgeous tropical universe all its own, a shining gem in the middle of the Pacific. I can totally see why Lucas and Ella love it here.

It's well past lunchtime, dipping into late-afternoon territory, when Tyler and I show up at the little outdoor market on the northern shore of the island, which has noticeably less traffic and tourists milling around. The wooden sign arching above the entryway reads Hukilau Marketplace. All around us, there are tiny huts and some larger-scale buildings boasting different tourist memorabilia, clothes, snacks, and more.

"The North Shore is where more of the locals live, since downtown is so commercialized now," Tyler explains as we start walking. "And we're actually not far from the Hukilau Cafe—that place from *50 First Dates*. You know, where Adam Sandler meets Drew Barrymore while she's making those weird waffle houses? It wasn't actually filmed there—the physical diner in the movie was fake—but that place is where they got the name from."

"Really?" My heart soars excitedly at the thought, calling up the scene in my mind instantly. "We'll have to drive past. That's one of my favorite movies ever."

Tyler smiles softly, almost to himself. "I know," he says quietly. "I remember." Which would make sense, since we watched it together no less than ten times.

We head toward the first stand, passing stalls of brightly colored fruit, leis, koa wood items, jewelry—you name it. But the stand we stop in front of has none of those things, only a bored-looking teenager and a soda machine, a menu propped up behind him.

"What'll it be?" he asks in a monotone voice, so unlike the warm kindness of the other locals I've encountered so far that it throws me off guard. But I guess teenagers are teenagers, no matter where they are in the world.

Tyler steps forward and takes out his wallet, taking the liberty of ordering for the both of us. Which is totally fine with me. It's been a while since I jumped over that cliff, but I have a residual shakiness in all of my extremities, my heart still trembling from the impact. On the bright side, the trip over here with the sunroof and windows open dried off my damp clothes, so I'm already feeling much better.

"Two large Pepsis, please," Tyler requests, squinting at the menu. "With vanilla and raspberry." The teen nods wordlessly and spins around to grab the cups and get to work. While we wait, I watch tourists weave in and out of the other huts, arms laden with memorabilia to bring home. On their vacations without a care in the world. Not nursing a broken heart because of a lousy, emotionally cheating ex.

Although, as I think about it, my heart is feeling less broken today and more just . . . bruised.

Focus, Olive.

"Vanilla *and* raspberry?" I can't help but screw up my nose as Tyler pays and we grab our drinks, heading to a nearby picnic table and taking a tentative sniff. "That doesn't sound like it would be a good combo."

"You said the same thing about loco moco, but then you ended up eating so much of it that you felt sick." Tyler is unfazed by my skepticism, already popping his straw into his drink and taking a generous sip, eyes fluttering closed dramatically with a moan, making my own insides twist with surprise. "God, that's so freaking good."

I place my own straw into my cup and study the little soda

stand's red-and-white logo. *Sodabomb*. Deciding I have nothing left to lose (and yes, begrudgingly realizing Tyler *does* have a point about the loco moco thing), I take a tentative sip. And once I do, an explosion of delicious flavor coats my taste buds.

"Wow," I rasp, taken aback by how divine this drink tastes. "I have to hand it to you, Ty. You've been right about local cuisine twice in one day."

He snickers as he slurps his drink, winking at me over our cups. My belly does another nervous flip. "Second trip's the charm, I guess. I'm practically a local." That earns him a playful punch on the arm, and we enjoy the rest of our drinks in silence, listening to the wind and the birds before we stroll through the market and explore. I even find a hand-painted ceramic mug with gorgeous plumeria blossoms dotted all over it, *Hawaiʻi* carved into the center, and decide it's the perfect gift for Mom to add to her collection.

After shopping around for a little longer, we decide to keep the sweet-tooth run going and Tyler drives us to Leonard's, a famous bakery on the island. By the time we park the car and walk up to the front door to push through the crowds, he's already given me a full rundown of the place. It's a vintage-looking bakery—one of the oldest in Honolulu, apparently—with a line snaking out the door, people eagerly waiting for the sugar-dusted treats inside. There's a red-and-white-striped awning stretching over the building's face, a glowing neon sign with flashbulbs pointing a bright yellow arrow toward the door.

"Okay, so what Leonard's is most known for is their malasadas," he explains as we step inside, the yeasty-sweet smells of sugar and dough wrapping me in a warm hug that I practically sink into. "They're these Portuguese doughnuts that they fill with all sorts of custards and stuff."

I have to wipe the drool off my chin as I stare at the Nutella-stuffed doughnuts in the glass case by the register and the customers leaving with pink bakery boxes dotted with bright blue script boasting the bakery's name. "Oh my god, they smell *incredible*."

Tyler beams proudly as we walk up to the register. "They taste even better than they smell," he assures me as he orders for us—one Nutella malasada and one stuffed with a coconut pudding called *haupia*. "Ella told me that she and Lucas like to pick up a dozen for barbeques and stuff with friends. Talk about the ultimate hostess gift."

"Agreed." I can already picture an alternate universe where *I'm* the one who lives here, jotting down barbeque plans in a shiny planner and making a note to pick up some malasadas for guests before I go. Probably with a little doughnut sticker next to it, because I doubt they make malasada stickers and it's the closest thing, unless I ordered them custom . . .

I'm practically vibrating with excitement when we step back outside, the warm air mingling with the powdery scent of the doughnuts in our bag. We take them to the car, where Tyler rolls the windows down and we idle there, each grabbing our treats and taking a bite.

"Oh my *god*," I moan around a mouthful of sweet, Nutella-soaked dough. "And to think that I used to believe Dunkin' made the best doughnuts."

Tyler swallows and looks at me proudly. "I told you, nothing else compares. You can't come to Hawai'i without having at least *one* malasada, Olive. It would be a literal crime. I heard you have to do at least two years' jail time for it."

I salute him with the paltry remains of my doughnut. "Well, it's a good thing you helped me avoid that sentence, then."

We eat the remaining few bites in contented silence, sighing with full bellies after the treat. "Thanks for that," I say to Tyler, lolling my head to the side to look at him. "I don't think I'll ever be able to eat again, though."

He quirks up one eyebrow. "Not even another malasada?"

Which is how I reconsider my statement and we wind up back on line to order two more, the original and cinnamon sugar varieties, which are both equally—if not even more—delicious. This time, we sit on one of the vacated benches outside and watch the palm trees sway in the late-afternoon sun, a few streaks of bright, puffy clouds coasting across the never-ending blue.

Eventually, the sun sinks lower in the sky and Tyler checks his phone as we head to the car. He looks up at me with a strange expression on his face when he speaks. "Think you have time for one more stop?"

I can't help the laugh that bursts out of me, and I throw my hands up in the air, a little bit sugar-drunk. "Trust me, I have nothing but time. I'm supposed to be hanging out at the University of Hawai'i with a boy who claims to love me, but clearly that's out of the question. The bigger issue is whether you'll be able to roll me out of the car now that I'm stuffed full of all these malasadas."

Still, I force myself to focus on the positives, thinking back to the day we shared together. "Thanks for the adventure today, Ty. I had a really good time." And it's the truth. This trip may have started out shitty, but Tyler managed to turn it around so that for most of the day, Jack was the furthest thing from my mind.

Makes you think.

Tyler's voice brings me back to the present as he responds to my compliment, lip tilting up in that playful way of his. "No need to thank me, Olive. With us, it'll always be good."

Chapter Twenty-Two

After a whole summer of getting to know Tyler Ferris when we first started dating, I thought I'd found all the things that made me fall in love with him. But it turned out every new day was a surprise, a fresh discovery of something that made my heart flutter—and that particularly sweltering afternoon in July during our first year together was no different.

"God," Tyler groaned dramatically, a deep, guttural sound that felt like it was twining around my insides as we stepped into my house and into the cool air. I dropped my bag to the floor, so overheated that I didn't even care about my planner slipping out of it and skittering under the table, resigned to its fate and internally promising that I'd pick it up later. "I thought I'd never know what it felt like to be in a cold room ever again."

Tyler and I had picked up the earlier lunch shift at Suburban Slices that day so we could catch the release of the new superhero movie we were looking forward to later that night, but doing so meant we had to be out and about during the peak of the day, when the unforgiving sun was baking all of the little ant people living beneath it. After an afternoon of sliding pies in and out of the oven in the sweltering kitchen for the lunch rush and then having to trek home in the heat wave with the AC broken in the Jeep, we were practically puddle people by the time we walked through my front door.

"Amen to that," I echoed, closing my eyes in ecstasy as the cold air rushed against my sweaty skin. Tyler, always with more of a flair for the dramatic than me, sprawled out on the kitchen floor and pressed a cheek against the cool tile, moaning again.

Mom was out running errands (i.e., getting herself primped and pretty for her date later that night with Neil), leaving Tyler and me alone in the cold, empty house. I was still in the process of slipping off my shoes when he darted a flushed palm out and gently wrapped it around my ankle, motioning for me to join him on the floor.

"C'mon, Ol," he mumbled, eyes closed and nearly falling asleep at the immediate comfort of being cooled. "Lie with me."

"On the floor?" I questioned his antics but still I obliged, stretching myself out on the tile and feeling the rush of chills up my legs and arms when my skin made contact with the cold floor. As usual, Tyler was right, and now it was my turn to whimper as I snuggled into the crook of his arm, giggling at how ridiculous we probably looked, inhaling his scent—a mix of cologne, laundry detergent, and boy. But as soon as the noise of pleasure left my mouth, Tyler's spine stiffened.

I raised my head and looked at him curiously. "Everything okay?"

Tyler wasn't meeting my eyes, looking off to the side at the cracked leg of one of our kitchen table chairs. His voice sounded tight and scratchy when he spoke. "Yeah, everything's fine."

Even as he said it, I noticed his shorts, and it made me feel just as flushed and sweaty as I was ten seconds before coming into the house.

As if he could sense me watching him, Tyler turned his head and looked directly at me. But he didn't look embarrassed—his dark eyes were inky, swirling with desire. We hadn't had sex before, and it wasn't lost on me how monumental this moment felt.

I didn't even have to say what I was thinking, because it wasn't like he didn't already know. Tyler's always been able to read me like a book, and this moment was no different. Wordlessly, I pressed my lips to his.

The kiss was delicate at first, but it didn't stay that way for long. Tyler's tongue explored my mouth curiously, in a way that he hadn't ever done before. A way that sent electric currents zinging up my spine and into my fingertips, down to my toes.

"God, Olive," Tyler whispered against me, both of us growing feverish. "I love you so much. How did I land such a beautiful girl?" His words of praise sang through my heart and all its chambers, through my bloodstream, roaring in my ears. And there was a dull ache in my chest that I couldn't—and didn't want to—ignore.

He loves me. Tyler Ferris said he loves me.

I didn't think any sweeter words had ever existed in the history of all human language.

He broke our kiss to press his mouth up against the shell of my ear, his voice low and husky. "I'm ready if you are, Ol." Then he ran his hands down my sides, making me shiver all over.

After that, it didn't take long for us to scramble up from the floor and wind up on my bed, a blurry tangle of lips and fingers and discarded clothing and skin. Tyler was in the middle of searching through his tossed-aside pants for his wallet when I reached under my mattress and presented him with a thin foil square of my own.

He gave me a cheeky grin, standing there beautiful and so very, very mine in a way that I thought was forever. "Typical Olive. I'm not sure why I expected any different. I'm shocked this wasn't already penned into your planner."

I waggled the foil at him. "You know I'm always prepared." And while it was the truth, and I really did feel prepared, it didn't stop my spine from stiffening the moment right before it happened, with Tyler poised above me and looking down at me with such a tender look of concern that it felt like he squeezed my heart.

"What are you nervous about?" His voice was soft and concerned.

"I don't know." I buried my head in the crook of his shoulder to avoid looking at his face, even though I knew the last thing he'd do right now—or ever—was mock me for how I was feeling. "I just hope it's good. Not that, like, I'm worried about you being bad or anything, because you're *you,* so I don't really think it's going to be an issue . . ." I trailed off, sighing. "I hope I make you feel good enough, because I love you, too."

I'd remember every second of that moment for the rest of my life, but what stuck with me and shone brighter than anything else was the gentle way the tip of his nose brushed mine, and the soft feathering of his breath on my lips as he moved, comforting me through every second.

"With us, Ol, it'll always be good."

Chapter Twenty-Three

With us, it'll always be good.

The only sounds in the car are the rush of wind through the windows and the dull hum of the tires against the pavement as we coast along the highways of Hawai'i. My entire face feels like it's on fire, and I'm flushed from my head down to the tips of my toes, thinking about the night that Tyler first said those words to me. That perfect, awkward, amazing night. The one that led to several similar nights, the memories of which make my blood tingle and start up the surprising hammer of my pulse in the base of my throat.

I'll remember every second of that first night for the rest of my life. The gentle whisper of his voice soothing my nerves. *With us, Ol, it'll always be good.*

Always.

Always.

Always.

What happens when always eventually ends?

Right now, I'm feeling not only flustered, but there's also a distinct, cozy warmth nestled at the center of my chest. It's started raining outside, a gentle drizzle pattering against the windshield. We didn't think about putting the top back on the Jeep before we left Leonard's, so droplets land on our cheeks and arms and hair as Tyler drives, but with the accompanying warm breeze, it's kind of nice.

Tyler looks over at me curiously as we head to the next stop on our adventure—he revealed we're heading down to the island's famous Diamond Head dormant volcano for a small hike before going back for dinner. As we sail down the road, my brain traitorously focuses on a raindrop on the apple of his cheek, my fingers practically twitching in my lap, itching to brush it away. But I hold firm. "What's wrong?" he asks, frowning slightly.

"Nothing," I answer, a little too quickly. I force myself to clear my throat and get some more words out, watching the gray clouds swim by overhead. "Just thinking."

"About what?"

I'm a terrible liar and I'm certain Tyler sees right through it when I skirt my gaze away from him and say, "About how crazy it is that of all people I could have been stuck next to on that flight, it was you."

He hums in thought for a second while we drive. "You know," he says after a beat. "Part of me wants to agree about how nuts that is. But I can't shake the feeling . . ." He shrugs and keeps his eyes on the road, the windshield wipers gently *swooshing* in between our breaths. "I don't know. I just can't shake the feeling that there's nobody else *but* you that could've been assigned the spot next to me on that flight."

"And Ellen," I point out, thinking back to her disgruntled sniffs and rustling magazines. "That woman was something else."

He chuckles. "How could I forget? She's the final piece of our trio. Maybe we should start a band. What would we call it?"

I pretend to think it over for a second. "How about *Please Fasten Your Seat Belts*?"

Tyler's face brightens and he instantly launches into a debate about the most ridiculous names we could come up with for our fake band, a few other rejects including *The Flight Attendants, Turbulent Tunes,* and *Baggage Claim*. The whole time he talks, I sit there stewing in my own thoughts, and one rings louder than the others.

Despite the shitty start to my trip, I'm enjoying my time with Tyler more than I expected to. And while part of me relishes the glimmer of excitement that brings to my chest, the smarter part of me knows I need to snuff out that flame, immediately.

I loved Tyler. A part of me will always love Tyler. But it has to remain a *small* part. Because the things that broke us apart once will break us apart again, and that's not something I can do to either of us a second time.

It's already over. We had our chance.

I'm not going back.

Instead, I switch to talking about the fact that my phone is racking up an increasing number of missed calls and texts from Jack, all of which I'm ignoring, especially now that I don't want to take my phone out of my pocket in the rain. Tyler looks conflicted about it when I explain the morning's messages.

"I don't know, Olive. I get not wanting to give him the satisfaction, but as far as the guy knows, you left his dorm room and vanished. Even an ass like Mr. Two First Names deserves to hear that you're not dead in a ditch somewhere." He flashes me a wink as we drive through the entrance of the park, the rain starting to clear up and thick beams of sunshine beginning to poke through the scattering clouds. "Or dead in a volcanic crater, more likely."

"Oh, absolutely," I agree. "Much more fitting for me to be dead in a volcanic crater here on the island, you know? Fits the tropical Hawaiian theme."

But he isn't taking my nonanswer for an answer, pointing an accusing finger at me as he puts the car in park. "I get not wanting to talk to him, I really do. I wouldn't want to talk to him, either. And, if I'm being entirely honest, I'm very much loving that you're giving Jack Cameron the silent treatment. *But*, you've made him sweat a little bit. At least let him know you're okay."

"And then I can tell him to piss off and continue ignoring him?"

Tyler nods triumphantly. "And then you can tell him to piss off and continue ignoring him. In fact, please do. As your jilted ex-boyfriend, I highly recommend a little retribution."

My brain snags on the *jilted ex-boyfriend* part of his sentence, causing my heartbeat to stutter. I never really thought about it that way before—and it's a little funny to imagine Tyler as a jilted bride standing at the altar—but he's not entirely wrong. One day we were together with everything ahead of us, and then we just . . . weren't. It's too much to think about right now, the guilt already starting to gnaw at the corners of my mind, so I force myself to focus on the stunning view of the winding mountains and the task ahead instead.

Right as we hop out of the car to start the climb to the

lookout point, I slip my phone out of my pocket—now that the rain has pretty much stopped—and fire off one perfunctory text to Jack to get him off my back before putting it away and enjoying my last day on the island with Tyler: *Nothing's wrong and I'm safe. But that doesn't mean I want to talk to you. Heading home tomorrow morning—don't worry about where I am for now.*

To his credit, Tyler doesn't ask me what the message says, although the expression on his face makes it clear that he's burning with curiosity. Still, he watches me tighten the laces of my sneakers and slip one of Lucas's old baseball caps on my head as we head off down the trail toward the island's most famous volcano. The sun is melting in the sky, a breathtaking blend of pink and orange hues, and the clouds are rolling over the hills above our heads in delicate wisps that I almost feel I can touch.

"Olive," Tyler whispers in awe a few minutes after we begin, stopping me in my tracks and pointing out toward the ocean. "Look." And when I follow his line of sight, I can't help but gasp.

A gorgeous rainbow streaks across the whole sky, its colors vibrant and breathtaking. It seems to stretch from the heavens all the way down to the ocean, giving it a gentle kiss where it meets the horizon, the waves out in the distance lapping up to greet it.

I've seen rainbows before, but for some reason I can't tear my gaze away from this one, utterly transfixed. As if the rainbow could speak to me, it looks like its colors are wiggling a little bit. Whispering, *Don't worry, Olive. It's all going to be okay.*

"Now you can see why Hawai'i is called the rainbow capital

of the world," Tyler says quietly, as if it can hear us and we don't want to scare it away. "I don't think I've ever seen one that strong."

"I can definitely agree with that," I murmur, sending back my own mental wish to the rainbow. *I hope you're right. Please let everything turn out okay.*

We continue to hike in silence for a good stretch, nothing but the sound of the chirping birds and the wind and the ocean crashing nearby to distract us. It's the perfect time to stew in my thoughts about everything that's happened over the past twenty-four hours—and a quick glance at my watch reminds me that it's been over a full day since I walked in on Jack and Lilly.

Once we've gotten about half of the journey under our belt, Tyler finally speaks, slightly out of breath. He's hiking ahead of me, so all I get is a view of his backpack bobbing up and down while he talks. "He didn't deserve you, you know. And before you claim I'm just saying that because I used to date you, I'll have you know that it was Delia who started calling him Jackass first. I was merely an accomplice."

Sounds totally like her, to be honest. "Okay," I wheeze in response, chugging a cold sip from the water bottle he picked up for me before we got here. "We are *not* having this conversation. Especially when we're on a journey where every gasp of air feels like a precious resource."

This gets a snicker out of him, but he takes a deep breath and continues speaking. "First of all, this is not supposed to be a strenuous hike, so I think we're just awfully out of shape. Second, I'm not trying to get into a whole big debate about it, Olive. I'm just saying—he didn't deserve you. Not when you flew all this way to surprise him, and then that's how he treated you." He coughs, whether because he feels awkward or from a lack of oxygen, I can't quite tell. "I know it probably hurts now, and it's definitely weird hearing it from me of all people, but the pain will pass, and you'll be better off for it."

"You're right," I agree, nodding even though Tyler can't see me struggling to walk behind him. "It is *definitely* weird hearing advice about my ex-boyfriend from another one of my ex-boyfriends. But I know what you mean." Even though all I feel for Jack Cameron now is a simmering rage and a desire to toss him into the ocean as far as I can throw him. It's been a day and I haven't had the urge to be on Lucas and Ella's couch with a pint of ice cream, nursing my heartbreak. Instead here I am, hiking in the sunset with the boy whose heart I really *did* shatter. Having witnessed a beautiful rainbow and tried loco moco and malasadas and even raspberry-vanilla Pepsi. Having jumped off a cliff and swum in the ocean and packed more once-in-a-lifetime experiences into a single day than I have had in my entire existence beforehand.

When I blink, behind my eyelids, I see Tyler's broken expression in our school hallway after the damage I'd done. And Delia's dark glare at me during Jack's graduation, reading right into my intention to go up and talk to Tyler. *Don't be cruel enough to make him go through it twice,* she'd said then, her voice abrasive and cold. While she has never been someone I'd necessarily classify as *warm,* I'd still never heard her voice reach such chilly depths before.

I won't, I promise Delia in my head now, as if she could really hear me. *I promise.*

Tyler hums in agreement and we keep walking up the path,

passing other sunburned tourists and joggers as we make our way toward the top. From here, you can spot all of O'ahu's various aspects—its stunning beaches, its stretching cityscapes, its quaint suburbs, its lush jungles.

It's a view so striking that I can barely find my breath, and it has nothing to do with exertion from the hike. This place is *beautiful,* in a way that I haven't really stopped and appreciated during this whirlwind trip. It's more than just a tropical paradise. It's a lush, breathing gem floating in the middle of the Pacific Ocean.

"Yeah," Tyler murmurs next to me, reading my mind as he adjusts his backpack straps and soaks in the view, bathed in the golden glow of the sunset. It seems like everything is coated in a warm, honey gold. The kind of comforting coziness that you feel snuggling up under a blanket. "It's stunning, right? That's how I felt the first time I came here, too."

"It's more than stunning," I whisper, feeling the need to lower my voice in the hushed reverence of this place. "It's absolutely perfect."

Tyler hums mildly in agreement, and when I turn to look at him, I see that his eyes are focused on me.

His attention catches me off guard and nearly knocks me off-balance—or maybe my weakening knees have something to do with the walk to get up here. All I can do is stare back at him, locking eyes until I feel a chill run up my spine. Right as I open my mouth to say something—what, I'm not quite sure—Tyler turns back toward the panoramic view of O'ahu spread out before us.

"It feels like a place that isn't real," he says gently, so quietly that the breeze practically whisks his words away. "A place that lives and breathes magic."

A place where anything can happen, I agree, but I keep that one to myself.

It's such a breathtaking view that we can't help but stop to take pictures, including a selfie with the sparkling expanse of the ocean behind us. The feeling of Tyler's stubbly cheek pressed to mine gives me tingles all over, my fingers still twitching as I send the photos to Mom, who responds with a suggestive winky face that gets promptly ignored.

After we admire the scene for a little while longer, the sun starts to kiss the churning waves of the horizon, the rainbow long gone, and the park is closing soon. We begin our walk back in silence, basking in the gentle birdsong and the sound of the wind whipping up the ocean below us.

Eventually, I find the courage to ask the question that is sticking in the back of my mind, demanding to be let out to play. "When did the pain pass for you?"

This stops Tyler in his tracks, but I don't notice at first, so I come up so fast behind him that I bump straight into his backpack with a little *oomph* of surprise. He turns to look at me, sweat dotting his upper lip and hairline, but his expression is incredulous. We're standing so close together that I can practically feel the heat radiating off his sun-kissed skin, even though the hottest part of the day is long behind us.

He echoes my own question back at me. "When did the pain pass for *you*?"

I have to think about my answer for a second, specific moments hard to pin down among the hazy fog of pain and despair that I tripped into headfirst. In some ways, it feels like yesterday that Tyler and I were a couple for the last remaining seconds before I shattered his heart in our high school hallway. But in others, it feels like that was a whole different lifetime. "It took a really long time, I guess. The whole not talking to each other thing made it extra hard, I think, because you were always the person I came to with the things that were bothering me . . . but that was obviously the one time where coming to you wasn't an option." All those nights spent clutching my phone and sobbing into my pillow like a broken animal, unable to reach out to Tyler because *I* was the one who broke *his* heart.

This is the exact moment that a sharp, painful thought hits me: If it hurt that badly for me and I was the one who made the decision under the assumption that I was doing the right thing, I have no idea how extra painful it must've been for Tyler, knowing that I completely blindsided him like this. "But don't dodge my question. When did it pass for you?"

Tyler studies the darkening horizon, chewing on his lower lip as he contemplates an answer. When he finally speaks, his voice is low and quiet. "In a lot of ways, I don't think it ever passed at all. I learned to live with it as a part of me. It made getting through the day-to-day a little bit easier."

Ouch. Hearing those words leave his lips is an extra painful twinge in my gut. A cold reminder of all the damage I caused in the past, the aftershocks still rippling through us all this time later. "I know it's definitely too little too late, but I'm really sorry about everything that happened, Ty." It's a paltry apology, but it still deserves to be said. It's the kind of thing that I should be apologizing for years from now, honestly.

Tyler licks his lips as his eyes trail over my face, and I feel a heat stirring in my heart that has nothing to do with the setting sun, and a chill on the back of my neck that has nothing to do with the breeze. He speaks slowly and deliberately, each word carefully thought out, his mixed scent of spicy deodorant and boy sweat making the hair on my arms stand on end. "Do you miss me at all, Olive?"

"Every day." My answer is immediate and impulsive and I want to kick myself for blurting my feelings out so recklessly, especially with this weird haziness between us. A haziness that Tyler seems to take as an invitation, stepping closer to me as the sky gets duskier behind him.

"Not only missing me as a person," he murmurs, reaching a hand up and gently grabbing a stray tendril of my hair, running it softly between his fingers. His face looks dreamy, but his eyes are hungry. "Do you miss me as your boyfriend?"

Don't say it. Whatever you do, don't say it. It's an answer that I hadn't considered in over a year. One I hadn't given any consideration to, until now. My lips and tongue betray me anyway, against my brain's better judgment. "Every day." If I'm being totally honest with myself, I've missed him every day since that moment in the sweaty gym sock–scented hallway. No matter how far down I tried to shove the regret, it always resurfaced, now more than ever.

My answers seem to be fueling whatever's happening here, because Tyler makes a low growl in his throat and drops my lock of hair, sliding his palm down to grip my waist instead. An embarrassing gasp of surprise slips out of my mouth, carried away on the wind. We haven't even made it to the bottom of the mountain yet, but luckily it seems all the other tourists who were up there with us have either already finished their hike or are still a decent pace behind us, nobody else in sight. "Tyler." I whisper his name into the universe like a question and a plea and a declaration all in one, which he accepts willingly, pulling me closer until my chest is pressed flush against his and I can feel his ribs expanding and contracting with every breath.

"What's the matter? Cat got your tongue?" He smirks devilishly and leans closer, until our foreheads are pressed together and I can feel his breath skimming my face. I close my eyes tightly, hoping I can bottle up this feeling and hang on to it forever, long after the moment passes. *Tyler. My Tyler.*

His lips brush against mine once, featherlight. I wouldn't even count it as a kiss. Still, I gasp. "What do you want right now, Olive?" He growls again, and I'm embarrassed by the chills visibly popping up on my arms, standing my hairs on end. There's also a low heat pooling in my belly that's impossible to ignore. "Anything. Tell me and I'll give it to you."

I want you to kiss me. I want you to carry me off this mountain and take me back to the guest room. I want to rewind the clocks and never track you down in that hallway to say what I did. I want so many things from our past to be different. I want I want I want I want . . .

I don't want to go back down a road that's only going to lead to hurt. To being my mother. To being brokenhearted and alone. That much I know.

"I want us to finish this hike." My answer is like a douse of cold water on whatever flame is sparking between us, fizzling it out in a sharp tang of smoke. Tyler steps back from me as if the wisps sting across his face, eyes flashing with hurt.

He shakes his head, defiant. "No." His voice comes out hoarse. "You want me to be more like Jack. More responsible, my life more thought out. I can do that, Ol. I can work on that—"

I fight the urge to reach out to him, my feet rooted in place. "I don't want you to be more like Jack. I don't want you to be like Jack at *all*." If there's one thing Tyler takes away from this conversation, I hope it's this. "I would never want you to change exactly who you are. And that's why it's not a good idea to jump back into something. Not now. Nothing has changed, and it *shouldn't* have to. You're not a bad person. Or a *wrong* person, for not wanting to do life the way I do."

He scoffs, bitterness lacing his words. "Let me guess. Just the wrong person for you, right?"

I guess I deserved that. "Tyler," I whisper, hearing the hurt cracking in my own voice. "You have no idea how I feel right now. But the facts are the facts—there are differences between us that we can't change." Differences that still feel like an ocean or a canyon that we won't ever be able to cross, no matter how much we may want to. No matter how many times we jump off cliffs together or hike volcanic mountains or try local delicacies, the core of who we are doesn't change. That can't be faked. There are so many glossy magazine articles about finding The One or taking a chance and going on dates, but the mainstream media has significantly less advice on what to do if the person who *feels* like The One is someone you can't actually be with, whose priorities don't align with yours.

Just like it's not easy for Tyler to suddenly shift his entire personality to be more responsible and future-oriented, how am I supposed to let go of the constant fear clawing at my throat of ending up alone? Of sitting on the same couch with my mother for the rest of my life, wallowing in our loneliness, getting our hopes up only to be let down again and again and again? It's a future so bleak that no fiber of my being thinks taking a chance on love is worth it. Not with someone whose philosophy on life is the total opposite of mine.

We were destined to fail from the beginning—but our hearts refuse to get the message.

Tyler's eyes are swimming in pain as he drops his hand from my waist and steps back, stung. "Why does it feel like we're doing this all over again?"

And he's right, I know he is. We're back in that hallway, two people with feelings for each other that can't surmount the circumstances surrounding them. But *shit*, I severely underestimated how badly it would hurt the second time around. "I'm sorry. I don't know what else to say other than I'm sorry." And this is exactly why I wanted to continue the hike. To escape any chance of having to feel this brokenhearted misery again, and to know that it's all my fault for setting it into motion.

Tyler shakes his head and runs his hand through his hair, thinking. After a second, he sighs in defeat and looks back up at me, eyes still hurting but a new determination shining in them. "Listen. It's no secret that I still want to be with you, but . . . I respect your decision." The words are like shards of glass piercing his mouth as he says them. "I lost you once, and I'm not going to lose you again. I'd rather have you here as my friend than not have you here at all."

It doesn't quite sound like he believes it.

"Thank you." My voice is as shaky as my legs and heart feel, but I force myself to take my own step back and gather my thoughts. A few seconds pass with nothing but the sound of the wind whipping down the hills and my heart slowing to a semi-normal rhythm. Tyler stands there for another second, visibly collecting himself, before the light slightly returns to his eyes and he slides his backpack strap up higher on his shoulder.

"Ready to head back?" His voice is chipper again, if a little hoarse, but my heart floods with gratitude at his effort to keep things comfortable. Which is why I find myself straightening my back and doing the same.

And I smile at that, even though I know it doesn't quite reach my eyes. "Sounds good. Let's do it."

Chapter Twenty-Four

By the time we get back to the house after our adventure day, I'm exhausted, sweaty, mildly sunburned, and emotionally wrung out.

Ella makes a face as we come through the kitchen and she sets plates of shredded pork and mini slider buns on the table. "Looks like you two had a long day."

Tyler laughs good-naturedly, but I seem like the only one who's able to notice the lack of warmth in his tone. "That doesn't even begin to cover it, El."

Lucas comes around the bend to join us in the kitchen, Mele squealing happily on his hip and reaching out her chubby fists as soon as she catches sight of her uncle. Even with the exhaustion lining his features, Tyler beams at her and takes her from his brother, immediately peppering her with kisses.

"What a perfect girl," he coos against her cheeks as he blows raspberries on them. "How was your day, Mele?"

"Certainly not as eventful as yours," Ella murmurs as she glances between the two of us. "You guys look like you were stuck in a blender for an hour and then spit back out."

"Just a long day," I reply, glossing over the emotional turmoil of the last hour and instead recapping our loco moco, cliff-diving, and hiking adventures. Ella and Lucas soak it all in, offering commentary here and there—with Lucas giving Tyler a playful smack upside the head when we start talking about our adventure at China Walls, telling him that it was a boneheaded thing to do again after almost breaking his leg last time, which was conveniently left out of the narrative when we were there. The whole time we're talking, Tyler and I carefully avoid looking at each other, the awkwardness still radiating between us. Luckily, Lucas and Ella don't seem to notice.

"Sounds like you two had a good day after all." Ella smiles when we finish dinner, rocking Mele to sleep on her lap. "Are you all packed for your flight tomorrow?"

I expected to feel more relieved to be heading home, being able to process my heartbreak in my own bed and next to Mom on the couch. So I'm definitely taken by surprise when I feel a sharp sting of sadness in the center of my chest.

"Almost," I finally answer, my throat feeling rough and scratchy with emotion. "I'm glad that I got to spend at least one awesome day here, though." My eyes meet Tyler's across the table, and he gives me a weak smile, the hurt still simmering behind his eyes with an intensity that makes my stomach wrench with guilt.

But if I needed any reminder of why I made the decision I did, I get it when I call Mom later that night, freshly showered and nestled in bed in the guest room, finishing packing up my suitcase and getting ready for tomorrow's flight home. My mother is chatting happily on the other line as she sits in her own bed with her mug of tea, making time for our conversation even though it's well past 4:00 a.m. at home again. I have my planner open in my lap, jotting down our plans for pickup tomorrow. As I'm writing, I can't help but think about how I didn't have it on me all day and I managed to survive just fine—thrive, even, until the disastrous end to our great day.

"I'll pick you up tomorrow at the airport," she promises. "And then I can tell you all about this guy I went on a date with tonight. His name is Connor, and he's a total doll."

My heart sinks at the mention of her next love interest. "New guy?" I ask weakly, trying to sound excited. *Already?* is what I don't add.

But Mom continues the conversation, totally unfazed. "Well, nothing's set in stone yet, but we ran into each other at the grocery store last week and went on two dates already, and he's so charming and sweet. You're going to love him, pea. He's way sweeter than Neil ever was. You seemed so preoccupied with packing and getting ready to see Jack that I thought I'd wait for a good time to tell you, you know? And now that I know things are going to work out between us, it couldn't be better."

"I'll bet." *This is exactly the same thing you've said about every guy who came before him. Someone's always better than the one who broke your heart.* "Does he make you happy?"

She stops and takes a slurp of her tea before sighing dreamily, and I can picture her sitting up in bed, pulling the blanket up to her chest with her tea-free hand and swooning. "He makes me very happy. I'm excited to see where it goes."

I pick at a loose thread on the guest room comforter, trying not to let my emotions get the better of me. She's always excited to see how things go with a guy, and sometimes they do go great for a while, until the honeymoon phase ends and shit gets real and she's left curled up on the couch, broken and being consoled by her teenage daughter. It's a tale as old as time—not that it ever stops her. "I'm happy for you, Mom. I hope it goes well."

"Thank you, pea." There's some rustling as she sets her mug on the nightstand and shifts her covers, yawning and clearly ready for bed. "How did things go with Tyler today? Any developments there? I saw your selfie from your hike—it looked like you two were back to being thick as thieves, hmm?" There's an excited edge to her voice, the hopeless romantic in her dying to be let out.

It's moments like these that I wish I wasn't an only child, so I wasn't the sole focus of my mother's attention. I opt for the lie anyway, both because it's less awkward and because I'm tired and not in the mood to discuss my lack of love life or what happened on the hiking trail today. "It was fine. We saw the dormant volcano on the island. Went to lunch and to see the ocean. Typical touristy stuff." *With a side of failed professions of love, no big deal.* I'm also smart enough to leave out the China Walls excursion from my story, lest I want to get an earful. "I'm excited to come home and see you tomorrow, though."

"Me too, sweetheart." She pauses, hesitating with what she's about to say. "Any word from Jack today?"

It's another thing not worth getting into the drama of, not when I'm in no mood to be talking about it. I give her a semi-truth. "Nothing crazy, just a few texts and voicemails, but I haven't been answering them. It's not worth my time."

She hums in thought but keeps her opinion to herself, opting to wish me good night instead. "Well, that's good that he isn't bothering you. Men that would do that to you aren't worth it—and they're hardly even men, they're just boys. But never mind him. I'll see you tomorrow, okay? I love you."

"I love you too, Mom." I grip my phone a little tighter, my eyes getting hot with the oncoming rush of tears. Thinking about everything that's happened and all the emotional confusion I've been feeling lately, plus on top of that being five thousand miles and an entire ocean away from home, I've never felt so much like a little girl needing her mom the way I do right now.

She must sense my hesitation to end the call, because she speaks again, carefully this time. "You had a good day with Tyler today, did you not?"

"I did." *The best.*

"He even convinced you to break out of your shell a little bit and try new things?"

"He did." *And I loved every single one.*

Mom's voice is soft through the receiver, getting heavier with sleep. "You have to follow your heart, pea. It's the only way you're ever going to be happy."

Like that's ever made you happy more than temporarily? "I know how to listen to my heart, Mom. I'm telling you, it's not saying anything of value."

Another yawn. "Well, as long as you're sure, Ollie."

"I am sure." I force myself to say it with more conviction than I feel. And then I tell my mother good night and get ready for bed, shutting the lights and crawling under the covers, getting accustomed to a guest room in the house of the boy who feels like anything but a stranger to me.

But that's when I hear the voices, stirring my curiosity.

The first voice I hear is Tyler's, which is interesting since we both went to bed half an hour ago, wanting to be well-rested before having to get up early in the morning to eat breakfast with Ella and Mele before I head to the airport. I quietly sneak out of the room and tiptoe down the hall, following the sound of his voice, until I peer around the doorway and see him slumped at the kitchen table with his brother. They look like they're having some sort of manly conference that intuition tells me I definitely shouldn't disturb.

"I don't know what to do, man," Tyler sighs, looking lost. He traces his fingertip around the place mat in front of him, and I know him well enough to tell that he's mentally laying out his options. Lucas sits across from him sipping a beer, clearly lost in his own train of thought. It's been so long since I've seen them together like this, so long since Tyler's had a conversation like this with Lucas, that it's fascinating to observe.

"What are your options, Ty?" Lucas asks his brother, staring at him long and hard. "She said she didn't want a relationship. That you two aren't compatible. There isn't really much room for negotiation there." Okay, so clearly Tyler spilled everything to his brother and now I'm being a weird Peeping Tom on an advice session that seems to have something to do with me. My cheeks immediately flame with embarrassment in the dark hallway.

"Getting back together isn't an option." Tyler groans and puts his head in his hands, shaking it for a few seconds. "I know that. She doesn't want us to be together, no matter how much *I* may want it. I think the thing I'm struggling with is whether to stay friends after she gets on that plane." And even though he's putting a voice to a personal fear that's been rattling me since that conversation on the trail, hearing it out loud feels new and fresh and even scarier.

It feels like I just got Tyler back in my life—but does it really only have to be for a few more hours?

There's one second of silence while Lucas swallows another sip of his beer, looking thoughtful. After a minute, he clears his throat and lobs one careful question at his brother. "Do you still love her?"

Tyler doesn't even hesitate with his answer, shrugging helplessly. "I never stopped loving her, Lucas. I love her as much now as I did when we were younger, if not more. I even tried to take that stupid online accounting course that you helped me with last year, but even your genius skills couldn't keep me from flunking. It's not going to work." His words hit me like a snowball aimed right at my chest, a shock of cold followed by a dull warmth in the muscles from the impact. *He never stopped loving me. And he tried to change. He tried to win me back.*

He even took a damn accounting course for me. Last *year.* Which is exactly the type of selfless thing that Tyler would do, and Jack never would. The revelation stops me cold, and it feels like every cell in my body is hanging on the precipice of the China Walls cliffs, waiting for my next move.

And they're going to have to wait a whole lot longer, because I'm not even sure of the answer myself.

Did I ever stop loving Tyler? Maybe a few days ago I'd say yes, but I don't really think that's the case now. Not that I'd know—the past day has been such an emotional whirlwind that it feels a little difficult to tell up from down right about now.

A chair creaking breaks me out of my thoughts and I look at the brothers, where Lucas is leaning his chair back on two legs in the same way their mother used to scold them for whenever I was over for dinner. "Love is a big factor here, for sure.

But it isn't the *only* factor. That's not something you can really ignore."

"She doesn't think I'm good enough. There's a reason she doesn't think we're compatible, and I'm pretty sure that's it." The glumness in Tyler's voice hits me so hard that my knees nearly buckle.

Lucas sighs. "That's not true. She doesn't think you're mature or stable enough. That's not the same thing."

"But don't opposites attract?" There's a hope in Tyler's voice that makes my own heart feel a little sad. "You and Ella aren't the same person at all, and look at your marriage. Your family. Your life." He sweeps his hand around the kitchen to indicate everything Lucas has that he wants. Everything I want more than anything else in the whole world. *Love. Safety. Security. A family. A steady job.*

Lucas chews on this for a moment before presenting his answer. "I guess you have to decide if your differences are something that brings out the best in each other, or something that brings out the worst. I think that's why some people who are majorly different survive in their relationships and others don't."

"But what if I make the changes she wants from me? I can try again. I can think of something better this time." Tyler's practically pleading now, fingers tracing fast routes on the place mats and begging his brother for the easy answer that nobody has. "She says she doesn't want me to change for her, but maybe that's what we need to be together. Maybe if I take a different class, or find an online tutor—"

At least on this Lucas and I seem to agree, because he sighs again. "You know that isn't the right answer, Ty. I *know* you know that. You may be eager, but you're certainly not dumb."

"You're right," he grumbles in defeat. "I don't know if I'll be able to stomach only being friends with her, even if it's just for a few more months before we graduate and go off on our own. But I also don't know if I can go back to existing like I did when she wasn't a part of my life."

"Only you know what the right decision is. None of the rest of us can give that to you. But the most important thing is you have to let her take the lead, because whatever will happen will either happen or not, but not if you force it." He socks him on the arm. "But first things first, you have to get to bed so you can drive that ex-girlfriend of yours back to the airport so she can fly away from you."

Tyler stands up and gives Lucas one of those signature bro hugs where they pat each other on the back, before heading off to the den to crash on the couch (which I still feel guilty about). I turn on my heel and am about to tiptoe quietly back down the carpeted hallway toward the guest room when Lucas's low voice rings out behind me, deep and quiet, and I just *feel* that it's directed solely at me.

"Just go easy on him, okay? It feels like he's just now starting to adjust to life without you in the center of his orbit. Just . . . please. Don't make him go through that again." For a second, I think he sounds a little choked up, but he masks it with a cough and another sip of beer. Face burning red even though I'm still in the hallway, I feel the pressure and embarrassment of being seen, and so I scurry back to the guest room and bury my head in the pillow, begging sleep to come to end the mortification. *Oh god.* He totally knew I was there the whole time—clearly I can't add sleuth as a potential career path of mine.

Tyler Ferris still loves me, despite everything that happened in our past. Despite everything that happened today. And sure, maybe he hasn't changed, and maybe he's still that funny, adventurous boy who first caught my eye in Suburban Slices on a hot summer day all those years ago.

But, I think, mind swirling with the possibility of another future, *is that really a bad thing?* My heart, still fluttering with excited butterflies upon hearing Tyler's declaration of love for me, is trying to tell me that it isn't. That maybe Tyler as he is now is the Tyler I'm meant to be with after all.

But my brain believes it knows better, as always. So as much as I want to go race down the hall and into the den and fling myself into Tyler's arms, I resign myself to the sinking feeling that it just isn't in the cards for us. That I have to be practical, and not only think with my heart. Because if there's anything I've learned from my mother, it's that thinking with your heart only gets you hurt.

If Delia and I were still friends, she'd tell me I was being a coward or a chickenshit or a dummy. If she were here right now, she'd probably knock me upside the head with a pillow and reiterate that I was acting like all three.

The dark haze of sleep is threatening to blur my vision, but all I can think about is my conversation with my mother.

You have to follow your heart, pea. It's the only way you're ever going to be happy.

What if my heart wants what my brain has been going against all this time? What if it's the worst idea in the cosmic universe, because Tyler and I were never destined to be a match? What if I get my heart broken again?

Staring up at the ceiling in the inky black room, I'm startled more by that question than anything else. And not because I'm worried about getting my heart broken—but because there's a feeling stirring in my gut that I can't deny, no matter how hard I try to. If I get my heart broken by Tyler, I won't even care. I'll be grateful for every single second leading up to that moment.

Oh no. This is bad. I squeeze my eyes shut and try to force sleep to come, but all that's playing on the undersides of my eyelids is a highlight reel of our day together. Tyler's cheeky grin at the Rainbow Drive-In, a smear of loco moco egg yolk in the corner of his mouth. The feeling of the ocean rushing up to greet me at China Walls, and the cool tingle of the water as we meet. The taste of raspberry-and-vanilla-flavored carbonation dancing on my tongue at the soda stand on the North Shore. Holding Mele. Watching *Tyler* hold Mele. The Hawaiian pulled pork sliders still warming my belly. The breathtaking awe of Diamond Head's summit.

Tyler, Tyler, Tyler. All of the best parts of this day surrounding Tyler. Not a single thought to Jack or any of what came before that Jeep pulled up next to the sprawling tree on the University of Hawaiʻi campus. My heart knowing something that my brain hasn't quite caught up to yet, trying to give me signs with the butterflies and stomach swoops and all of the relentless blushing. Unplanned as it might be, maybe Tyler really was the right fit for me after all, even after all this time.

Well, shit.

I think I'm falling in love with Tyler Ferris again.

If I'm truly honest with myself, I don't think I ever stopped.

Chapter Twenty-Five

After the day I've had, I don't even dream. Instead, I fall into an inky, black sleep where it feels like my body is melting straight into the mattress from exhaustion, and I don't even move around until the incessant pinging of my phone forces me to blearily return to the land of the living.

With only one eye open (and half open at that), I reach for my phone on the nightstand and look at the screen.

15 missed calls: Jack Cameron
6 voicemails: Jack Cameron
32 unread texts: Jack Cameron

It takes a second for my brain to adjust to the fact that I spitefully changed his name back to his full name in my contacts before bed last night, not giving him the satisfaction and stripping away all of his emoji hearts and swoony faces. But seeing his name there, dull and blank and plain, makes me feel hollow inside.

I look at the time: It's only 9:00 a.m. and most of these calls and messages came through within the last hour. Unable to put it off any longer, I open the string of messages.

Jack: Olive?

Jack: You awake?

Jack: Listen, can we talk about what happened the other day? I feel like I didn't explain myself well enough.

Jack: Where are you, anyway? I know you said not to text, but I'm worried.

Jack: Olive?? Hello???

Too annoyed to read through the rest, I delete the thread and press play on the first voicemail.

"Heeeey, Olive." Jack sounds out of breath, and the pounding shoes on the pavement in the background indicate that he made this call while on his morning jog. Something about that makes the bile rise in my throat. *First he shatters your heart; then he can't even be bothered to fully dedicate his time and effort to a call without multitasking.* Still, I keep listening out of sheer curiosity. *"Listen, I think we really got off on the wrong foot when you got here. Seeing you leave like that . . . it made me realize what a shitty thing I'd done, and I don't ever want to be the one who hurts you."* He grunts and it sounds like he's stumbling over a rock. Hopefully it was a big one. *"Is there any chance we can meet up today and talk about what happened? I totally understand if you're not willing to do that, but please at*

least let me know you're safe. I have no idea where you ran off to after you left . . . Okay, talk to you soon, I hope. I lo— Bye." He ends the call before he can reflexively say those three little words, and I hate him all the more for it. I delete the remaining five voicemails without listening to a single one.

I sit and stew for a few more minutes, staring at the ceiling, before I drag myself out of bed and pad down the hall to brush my teeth and get my day started. Ella murmurs softly to Mele in the kitchen, and while it's still early, it's definitely late enough that Lucas is off doing drills or working or whatever it is you're supposed to do when you live and work on a military base (it's not like I'd know). The smell of eggs wafts down the hallway, and it makes my stomach grumble loudly.

I still haven't seen or heard from Tyler since overhearing his conversation with Lucas last night. I'm running through a mental game plan of the apology I'm going to give—*I'm sorry, I know I'm not your girlfriend anymore but I know that doesn't mean you and your family don't care about me; I feel the same way*—when the bathroom door swings open right as I'm stepping toward it and I run smack dab into Tyler's chest.

"Oof," he grunts, stumbling backward a little bit. And I, genius that I am, lose my own balance and continue to trip forward, placing both palms flat on the thin material of his sleep shirt to keep myself upright. We both pause for a second, my fingertips buzzing with an electric heat as they connect with the smooth, taut muscle underneath his shirt.

"You good, Olive?" Any tension from last night seems to be long forgotten, as Tyler looks down at me with one eyebrow quirked and his telltale smirk playing at the corners of his mouth.

His eyes are still a little bit hazy with sleep, but his breath smells minty fresh.

I take a deep breath, ready to launch into my spiel. "I'm sorry." My well-thought-out apology rushes to the emergency exit as the words blurt from my mouth. *So much for eloquence.* "I . . . yeah. I'm sorry. About . . . you know. Yesterday. I didn't want our adventure day to end that way." I peer around Tyler toward the toilet bowl, wondering if it's possible to flush myself down it and into the sewer pipes and far, far away from this conversation. But then I remember that I'm still awkwardly feeling him up in the doorway, and I step back as if his chest muscles are searing hot.

Tyler, thankfully, doesn't act like anything's weird about the awkward display, and he nods and leans against the doorframe. "You have nothing to apologize for. I'm the one who's sorry for coming on too strong like that and stepping back those few times when I needed a second. I just . . . It sucks to think that because of everything that happened between us, you still think we wouldn't be able to work out."

I think back to yesterday and the day before, on the plane and at the Rainbow Drive-In, both times that Tyler had to take a step away for a second. "I know you feel differently, and I get it. And you don't have anything to apologize for, either. I actually appreciate that you take a step away when you're feeling frustrated, you know?"

He nods thoughtfully. "I know. Learned the trick from my parents when I was pretty young. They always told Lucas and me that it keeps disagreements from getting ugly, if people excuse themselves when they feel their emotions running hot. Gives them a chance to come back to the conversation when they're calmer." He lifts a shoulder like it's no big deal and he didn't say one of the most profoundly introspective and mature things to ever come out of an eighteen-year-old's mouth. I tell him as much, which gets him to chuckle—and it sounds extra low and deep with his husky morning voice, sending a shiver through me.

"Fresh start?" he offers, pushing off the doorframe and stepping aside to let me into the bathroom.

I nod in agreement. "Fresh start." He pulls me into a quick hug, resting his chin on top of my head and breathing deeply before letting me go, the warmth of his body already gone before I have a chance to absorb it.

Ella's voice floats down the hall from behind me, and we both follow the sound to see her standing there, spatula in hand and looking at us curiously as we break from our hug. "Good," she says primly. "You're both up. I made some breakfast—anyone interested in some Spam and eggs before you head out?"

Tyler snorts from behind me, no doubt recounting our conversation from yesterday about the salty canned meat. Still, Ella and Lucas are gracious enough to let me stay in their home, and the last thing I'd ever want to be is rude, so I force myself to smile at her warmly.

"Of course," I reply, lacing my words with as much enthusiasm as I can muster. "I'd love some." Ella nods at my response, pleased, before taking off back toward the kitchen to make us some plates of food. As soon as she's out of sight, I turn around and see Tyler doubled over laughing, tears leaking out of the corners of his eyes.

I sock him playfully on the shoulder for good measure before stepping into the bathroom and pushing him out so I can close the door. "Scratch that," I tell him as I swing the door shut. "The fresh start begins after breakfast."

After a breakfast that consists of a lot of water drinking to mask the sounds of gagging (which is nothing against Ella's cooking, but *everything* against my renewed—and intense—hatred for Spam), Tyler and I get ready to leave. It's also a great excuse to stay busy and not look at my phone and the text messages and calls that continue to pop up from Jack throughout the morning, which all remain ignored.

As we zip up my suitcase and scan the room for any forgotten items like my phone charger or headphones, we don't talk about what I overheard in the hallway last night. Being that Tyler doesn't mention it while he brings my suitcase out to the car, I take it that Lucas didn't tell him about our little exchange—if that's what you can even call it. He also doesn't bring it up when we all gather in the living room to say goodbye after Lucas's training ends, Mele yawning sleepily and clinging to Ella's shirt as we all exchange hugs.

Ella squeezes me extra tight with her free arm while Mele tugs on my hair. "You be safe, okay? Let Tyler know when you land so I can make sure he tells us." She pats my shoulder affectionately, and we lock eyes before we let go. "It was really good to see you again, Olive. Don't be a stranger."

"I won't," I lie, because neither of us knows what's going to happen with me and Tyler beyond here—we know we won't date, but the friendship thing feels a little more precarious. Especially after knowing how much it's tearing him up inside—it's very likely that our paths probably won't cross again, and I'm surprised at how hollow my chest feels at the thought of it. Thankfully, Ella doesn't call me out on this, instead kissing my cheek and giving me another pat on the shoulder before stepping back to let Lucas say goodbye, untangling her daughter's fingers from my hair.

Lucas and Tyler finish another one of their bro-hug, back-slapping man things before Tyler steps aside, leaving Lucas standing right in front of me. For a second, the awkward tension is ripe in the air, so thick it feels like I can choke on it. We both remember his parting words to me in the hallway last night, even if neither of us wants to acknowledge them. *Don't make him go through it again.*

I look him in the eye and hope I can convey the answer sitting inside my own brain, the one I won't speak aloud just in case Tyler or Ella overhears. *I won't.* For a second, I seriously doubt my telepathy skills, until Lucas nods in appreciation, a look of understanding on his face.

He pulls me into a quick, awkward hug, giving me a pat on the back. "It was nice seeing you again, Olive." His voice is gruff and maybe a little bit emotional, but it's hard to tell when he's mumbling into my shoulder. "Have a safe flight home. See you again soon?" He pulls back and locks eyes with me, a challenge there.

"Of course," I lie, pasting on a smile. "I'll be back before you guys know it."

Lucas looks pleased at this, nodding carefully.

As if that's the cue, Tyler and I say our final goodbyes, give Mele little kisses on her chubby cheeks, and head out to the car. Even Tyler looks glum as he waves goodbye to his niece, though his trip isn't over.

"It makes me a little sad," he explains as he turns the key in the ignition, as if he's reading my thoughts. "That the next time I come back to visit, she'll have grown so much. I wish I could live here."

"Why can't you?" My question shocks both of us, and Tyler turns to me in surprise. I rush to clarify. "I mean, you've always been about last-minute, spur-of-the-moment kinds of adventures. Moving to Hawai'i after graduation seems exactly like the type of thing you'd do. You know how your mom wants you guys to connect to your roots more." I don't mean it as an insult, more so that I'm jealous of Tyler's ability to be so carefree and spontaneous with everything, but my words still seem to sting him, shuttering his expression. He nods and we continue the drive to the airport in silence.

"I know you think I'm totally reckless," he says quietly after a few minutes, nothing but the hum of the tires taking up the sound in the car. "I know I don't have a ten-step life plan the way you do. But moving across the entire continent—hell, *off* the entire continent, without a job and leaving my parents—is a little reckless even for me, don't you think? Even if it meant connecting with my heritage."

I'm still in damage-control mode, but I surprise myself with the words that come straight from my heart, meaning every single one. "I don't think I'd call that reckless. You have family here, and a niece that you want to see grow up. A huge part of your ancestry comes from this beautiful place that you want to learn more about. It's not the same thing as if I decided to drop everything and come here, you know? I'd have nobody. But you'd be following your family. That . . . that seems like a pretty good life plan to me. And certainly more exciting than my riveting plans of an accounting degree from community college." I briefly wonder what life would've been like if Jack hadn't done what he did, and if we were still dating. I didn't have any plans to come out to the University of Hawai'i with him, but what if he'd decided to stay here after college? Would I have had to shift my entire life plan to accommodate him? Would I even *want* to?

I can't help but think that if Tyler was factored into the equation, maybe I'd at least *consider* the idea.

Tyler's still nodding along as I finish speaking, deep in his own thoughts. "You know," he finally says after a second, flicking on his blinker and merging into the lane that will lead us toward the airport departures. "You have a point. Maybe that isn't the worst idea."

My chest glows with pride at the compliment, and at finally being able to do the one thing I hadn't been able to do with Tyler in all the time we dated—convincing him to think about his life plan. But then my stomach practically bottoms out at the follow-up thought—that I may have convinced the boy I'm falling for to move five thousand miles away from me. *Again.*

How many people does that happen to twice? I mentally kick myself for even suggesting the idea, but I don't have much time to dwell on it, because soon we're pulling up to the airport and Tyler is swerving off into the parking garage, stopping the car and hopping out.

"What are you doing?" I ask, puzzled as he opens the trunk and takes out my suitcase. "I can get to my gate in one piece, I think."

He nods. "I know. Just wanted to walk you up to security, you know? Make sure you get there okay."

I eye him warily as we start walking in step with each other toward the airport entrance. “I can get to security just fine.” I take my suitcase from Tyler as we walk through the double doors into the lobby, the rush of cool air greeting us and making the hairs on my arms stand on end.

Tyler throws his hand up in a *You caught me* gesture. “Okay, fine, fine. I want to spend a little more time with you before you have to go. Is that such a crime?”

If I thought my chest was glowing before when Tyler complimented me, it’s a full-on sunbeam pouring out of me now. “No, that’s definitely not a crime.” And as excited and fizzy as my blood feels at the prospect of getting to spend a few more minutes with Tyler, I can’t get Lucas’s stern expression or pleading voice out of my head. *Don’t make him go through it again.*

Calm yourself, my brain hisses at me, finally delivering the mental pep talk I need. *You have to get your act together. He’s just a friend. We’re not going backward. We’ve come too damn far to go backward.* We weave through tourists at the airport as we head toward the security checkpoint, the tension growing thicker and thicker between us with every step we take.

Finally, we stop in front of the snaking line of people, and I check the board to make sure that I still have plenty of time until boarding my flight—which I do. With nothing left to stall us, I turn and face Tyler, who is looking at me with a strange expression on his face. We both turn at the excited groups of people coming out of the arrivals gate, laden with leis and sun hats and thrilled expressions on their faces.

It makes me smile, even if my heart sinks a little. “Wow,” I note to Tyler, catching his attention. “All of these people are so excited to be getting here and starting their adventures, but it's time for me to end my own."

He snorts. "That was entirely too profound." His sarcasm earns him a playful shove on the shoulder, and he catches my wrist in his grip, eyes sparkling playfully as he lays my palm over his chest so I can feel his heart thumping through his T-shirt.

"But that means it's time for a new one to begin, doesn't it?" He arches an eyebrow at me, a test I'm not sure how to pass. My insides are doing a million backflips while my face is heating up like the sun, and it seems like all of my brain power has zeroed in on the nerves at the ends of my fingertips, pressed against the thin cotton of his shirt, and the strong warmth of his fingers wrapped around the slender bones of my wrist.

I force myself to swallow and say some words. "I guess you have a point." They seem to be the assurance he needs, because he tugs me closer, the heat of his body suddenly much hotter and his musky, soapy boy scent even more intoxicating.

We're not going backward, I convince myself as Tyler loops his arm around my waist and pulls me against him. *It's just a goodbye.*

"Ol." Tyler's voice is low and husky, hard to hear over the continuous din of the airport gate announcements and the shuffling of people. But still, my ears are tuned to him just fine, and I even let the nickname slide off my back, forgiving it this once because of the warm, gooey feeling in my chest. "I know what you said about us being together, and I'm going to respect it, but you know I can't let you leave without doing this." His face inches closer to mine, his breath tickling my nose. Everything comes sharply into focus all at once.

Tyler Ferris is going to kiss me. It's an exciting and terrifying prospect all at once. Something I've done a million times before but holds so much more significance now. When we broke up, we had no idea that the kiss we shared that morning at my locker would be our last. But now this is it—our *real* last kiss. And judging by the way he's slowly inching toward my face and it feels like every nerve ending in my body is on fire, we're about to make this one count.

"Ol?" Tyler says again, tantalizingly close. "I'm only going to do it if you say I can."

"Y-you can." I'm not even embarrassed at the stammering, clammy idiot I've definitely transformed into. All I can think of is those lips on mine and how good it'll feel to have them there again and *oh my god he's kissing me he's kissing me and how did I go without this feeling for all this time and—*

He threads his free hand through my hair and tilts my mouth up to meet his, his tongue claiming me slowly, but with purpose. I forget where I am and loop my arms around his neck, a little moan of surprise escaping my lips and egging him on, encouraging him to kiss me harder and deeper and faster.

For a few seconds in the crowded airport, kissing Tyler feels like I've been transported straight to heaven.

That is, until a voice filled with hurt rings out, calling my name.

"Olive?"

Chapter Twenty-Six

I'm pretty sure that the betrayal on Jack's face mirrors my own from two days ago, when I walked into his dorm room and saw him cozied up with Lilly. He looks like he's been simultaneously punched in the face and seared with a hot iron, his expression an array of painful emotions.

"This is where you were the whole time, wasn't it?" His voice isn't angry, just quiet and hurt as I step away from Tyler with anger flaring deep in my belly. "You were with him?"

Tyler, choosing this moment to be territorial, juts his chin up defiantly and places an arm around my shoulder, always the protector. "What are you even doing here, man? She told you to piss off. So maybe you should go do that."

I'm still struggling to catch my breath, blown away by our kiss, but I inhale slowly and calm myself enough to speak, my pulse no longer jumping in my throat. "What are you doing here, Jack?"

He holds up his phone. "I've been texting and calling you, and I got no response other than that one text you sent me. I—" Now he's the one who looks out of breath, lowering his phone, his eyes nearly spilling over with tears. "I messed up, Olive. I was a complete ass. What happened with Lilly never should've happened, and as soon as you walked out of my dorm room, I knew that. It . . . it forced me to look at myself and think about a lot of things. And the conclusion I came to is that there's nobody else I'd rather be with in this world than you." His eyes are shining as he takes a step toward me, and Tyler's arm tightens around me, which releases a burst of warmth in my chest. "You're my partner in crime, Olive. You're the one who I planned my life with, who I dreamed all our big future dreams with. There's no other girl that could ever take your place, and I was a stupid asshole for even trying. Just give me one more chance, please. Please, Olive. *One* more chance." He swallows and turns his full-wattage puppy-dog gaze toward me, blinking pathetically. It's the same look he gave me for the first time in his dorm room when I caught him with Lilly, and whatever manipulative intention he has behind it, all it does now is turn my stomach as he keeps speaking. After a second, it's clear he realizes the begging look isn't working, so he wipes at his eyes with a dignified sniff.

"Jack," I plead, frustration rising. "Enough of this. Go back to school and go back to Lilly and go back to living the life I don't fit into anymore."

Tyler shifts beside me, and a quick glance in his direction shows his face change. As soon as the words leave my lips, I taste them—they taste just like the accusations he hurled at me when we broke up. About me accusing him of not fitting into the life I wanted.

I look between Jack and Tyler—the boy who abandoned me

and the boy who *I* abandoned, and the answer feels crystal clear, a sudden rush hitting me like a cool dousing of water. The unexpected wave of immediately knowing the right thing to do.

Tyler and I can't be together—there are too many reasons it won't work out—but that doesn't mean I should be with Jack, either.

"How did you even know I was here?" My question is short and sharp, startling him.

Jack only falters for a second before straightening his spine and putting on the air of confidence that I've seen him practice before a mock trial meet. "I know you, Olive. You said in your message that you were leaving today, and I looked up the flight schedules. I remember you saying you like to be an early flier, and I had to find you and get the chance to say all of this before you left . . ." He trails off, and in the awkward silence, the three of us stand there, shifting on our feet. Jack looks crestfallen, the corners of his mouth drooping pitifully when he realizes this is a court case that he can't win. Tyler looks and feels tense, his arm still protectively around my shoulder, ready to pounce in case Jack gets out of hand. And standing here in this airport, exhausted and not looking forward to a long flight and wrung out on the emotional whirlwind I experienced these last few days, I snap.

All of Jack's reasons for wanting another chance—that I'm the one he planned his life with, his partner in crime, that I'm the one who helped him figure out his future dreams—none of those things have to do with love, or soulmates, or wanting to be together because he *feels* for me.

It's because, looking back on it now, Jack and I have always been better friends than we were partners. Somewhere along the way in our relationship, we'd reverted back to the comfortable rapport of those early days of dating, of being friends who pushed and encouraged each other to chase their dreams . . . without the romance behind it. And it happened without us even realizing it.

My mind flashes back to him and Lilly sprawled out on the dorm room floor. *Or maybe he realized it already, but* I *hadn't.*

The realization is sharp and swift, and in that moment, I am *so* very done.

"You're out of chances," I say with finality, lifting my chin and struggling to remain calm. "You ghosted me and probably wouldn't have been upfront about your feelings for Lilly if I hadn't flown all the way here and caught you." I suck in a deep breath, channeling my heartbreak into anger as I continue. "I don't want that life with you anymore, Jack. And if I'm being honest with myself, this hasn't felt like a relationship for a while. You messed up with going behind my back, big-time, but as much as that sucks, it's not the only reason. For as long as we've been together, it feels like I've been more of a prop for you to check 'girlfriend' off your to-do list than someone who you actually love." *Which is never how Tyler made me feel.* My thoughts flash to him briefly, standing tall next to me and the muscles in his hands flexing, ready to come to my aid at a moment's notice. Always being the strong, steadfast Tyler that I remember.

I steel myself for the final dagger, turning my attention back to Jack. "And now we're done, for real. I meant it when I said I never want to see you again."

But Jack isn't taking no for an answer, anger and hurt warring on his face as he takes another step toward us. "Olive, please, give me one more chance to make it right and prove to you that I've changed—"

"How?" I interrupt, narrowing my eyes. "Please, enlighten me on how you've changed in the last two days."

I don't think Jack was expecting such a direct callout, because he flounders for a few seconds. "I, uh, I'm going to make more time for you, and call you more . . ." He trails off, looking lost and *very,* very cornered.

"Wrong answer." I jab my finger in the direction of the exit. "You need to go."

"You heard her, Jack." Tyler's voice is tight and clipped through his gritted teeth. "She said you're out of chances. I think it's time you leave her alone."

Now, in the year and a half that I've been with Jack, he's never had a mean streak. He was a bit cocky, and snobby at times, and he has some shitty friends, but the anger on his face now, nearly purpling his expression, is an entirely new phenomenon for me to witness. He speaks through tight teeth, his words sharp and precise as he narrows his eyes on Tyler's arm around me, seeming to register it for the first time. "What the fuck are you doing with my girlfriend, Tyler? Why are you even here?"

"*Ex*-girlfriend," Tyler points out smugly, a hint of glee in his voice. I sense the oncoming bro battle and extract myself from his embrace gently, stepping aside. "I guess she's both of our ex-girlfriend now, huh? Funny how things work out." He levels Jack with a stare that turns my blood cold with tension. "Even the guys who think they deserve everything in life find themselves losing in the end."

Jack clenches his jaw so tight that I'm surprised he doesn't crack a molar.

"Oo*okaaaay,*" I interject, stepping between both boys and raising my hands in an *I come in peace* gesture. "This is getting way out of hand, and we aren't a pack of lions in the savanna. I don't need someone to stake their claim on me. In *fact*"—I turn and look at both Tyler and Jack individually—"I don't belong to either of you. So cut this out."

Tyler at least has the decency to look chastened. But Jack is still splotchy with rage.

"This is what you've been doing the past two days, Olive? Rebounding with Tyler Ferris? That loser you left behind?" He spits Tyler's name out like it's a dirty wad of gum stuck under his shoe, and I see Tyler wince in response. And there's something about that, after everything that's gone on the past few days, that sets me off. I take a step away from Tyler and toward Jack, jabbing a finger directly into the center of his chest and making him startle with surprise.

"First of all, how *dare* you say his name like he's beneath you. Just because he wasn't born with a silver spoon in his mouth doesn't mean he's any less of a person than you are. In fact, he's probably better. He's *definitely* better." I take a shaky breath, the words threatening to break me, but I force them out anyway, saying all the things that need to be said. "And second of all, you have *no* right to show up here after I told you to leave me alone—which you probably thought was romantic but is definitely a little bit creepy—and then get angry at what you find. After you ignore me for weeks and then tell me that you're basically falling in love with someone else, you of all people know you're in *zero* position to have any opinions about me or my life choices. My life is not your business. You lost that privilege."

Jack swallows. His expression has dulled from a sharp anger to more of a surprised resentment. "I can't believe you'd do this to me."

The laugh is out of my mouth before I can stop it. "You can't believe *I* did this to *you*? First of all, I did nothing." *Except love you and show support for you and fly out here to surprise you like you surprised me now.* And okay, maybe it's not too creepy that he's here, but it doesn't mean I have to forgive him for wanting to hook up with another girl. And if I listen to my heart, I'm not even that upset about it, really, because it gave me a chance to connect with Tyler again—someone who is a real friend.

Or at least someone I hope becomes a real friend again.

Jack opens his mouth to retort, but before he can, I'm fueled with a rage to hurt him as badly as he hurt me. "Where's Lilly, anyway? She didn't want to accompany you for this?"

He rears back as if I've slapped him, and behind me, I hear Tyler murmur a quiet *damn*.

After gaping like a fish for a few seconds, Jack stumbles to find his words, wringing his hands nervously. "Lilly and I realized that maybe we aren't a good fit for each other after all. We both knew that my heart really lies with you."

I'm unimpressed and can't help but laugh dryly. "Which translates to her dumping you because she realized you're a sorry, slimy emotional cheater."

His silence is all I need to hear.

"Which leads me to my next point." I flick my wrist in Jack's direction, dismissing him. "It's time for you to go." Not wanting to hear another word from him, I grab my rolling suitcase and storm toward the airport security line. I don't stop to spin around and see if Jack is following us, but judging by the way Tyler is now loping next to me casually as if nothing strange happened back there, I'm assuming not.

He waits until I park my suitcase in front of the security line, preparing to go in, before he finally says something. "Okay, that was pretty badass."

"It was, wasn't it?" The aggravation's already started to dissipate from my bloodstream, replaced with a glowing pride as I play the conversation on repeat in my head. It's only magnified by Tyler's grin.

"Totally. I thought you were going to smack Mr. Two First Names right here in Hawai'i's biggest airport. You should've seen the look on his face when he left. He looked like he was on his way to find a brand-new litter of puppies to kick."

"Oh, please." I roll my eyes. "Jack isn't exactly known for his fighting skills." At this, we both laugh for a few seconds, until we quiet down and stare at the still-snaking security line that I need to get in soon if I have any hope of catching my flight. A small bit of sadness rolls in, though, too, thinking about another relationship I thought would last forever but instead is spinning down the drain.

"So." Tyler scuffs his shoe on the floor, looking bashful as he raises his eyes to meet mine and tugs at his hair nervously. "Before all of that back there . . . that kiss, huh?"

My stomach dips at the memory, already solidifying itself in my mind as something I'm sure I never want to forget as long as I live. Of all my moments with Jack, and even all of my previous moments with Tyler, nothing will ever top the toe-curling feeling of reconnecting after all that time. "Yeah . . . it was a pretty good kiss." One that already causes a deep ache in my chest, knowing I'll never get to experience it again. I'm surprised at the stinging in the corners of my eyes when I realize the loss of something that it feels like I just got back.

Now Tyler's expression morphs from bashful to wicked, and

he takes another step closer, back in my personal bubble. "Then let's repeat the performance, shall we?"

My body reacts, nerves standing on end. My heart hammers at the prospect of another kiss. Our *real* last kiss. Unfortunately, although my body is more than ready to be back in Tyler's arms, this time, my brain gets to have the say. I gently place my hand on Tyler's chest, and I don't even have to apply any pressure for him to get the hint.

His face falls and he takes a step back, voicing words that sound painful to get past his lips. "But you still don't want me."

I shake my head, chest sinking as I drop my hand. "It's not about wanting or not wanting you. It's that I'm still not able to be in a relationship with you, Ty. We're too different." Even though my mind will probably be replaying our kiss for the entire flight home, and likely the entire next day, and forever and ever on a loop after that. "If there's anything I learned from my mom, it's that wanting someone badly enough doesn't make you a good fit."

He opens his mouth like he's prepared to fight it, but then he clamps his jaw shut and shakes his head, eyes cloudy with sadness. "If that's how you really feel, I'll respect it."

"Yes." Every word of the lie coming out of my mouth tastes bitter. "It's how I really feel." Maybe it's not, but I know it's how I'm *supposed* to feel.

"That's it, then." His voice is resigned and overwhelmingly sad, like I feel inside. Here we are, in one of the sunniest and happiest and most beautiful places in the world, but all we can feel is sadness. I grab the handle of my suitcase, ready to make the exit I've been dreading. I think I feel more nervous now than I did in the airport security line three days ago, when I was headed to

O'ahu and had no idea what I was going to find there—or who I was going to bump into on that plane.

"How long are you still here in Hawai'i?" I'm suddenly unabashedly desperate to keep our conversation going, not wanting to say goodbye.

Tyler must feel the same, because he blows out a short puff of air as he thinks it over. "Until the end of spring break. Well, not totally—I get home a few days before classes start back up again."

That's too many days away. "I hope we can hang out again when you're back home. You know where to find me." It's a shot in the dark, especially knowing how conflicted Tyler feels about continuing our friendship, but the small, selfish part of me isn't ready to let him go.

His smile doesn't quite reach his eyes, but I can still feel the emotion radiating there. He presses his lips to my forehead one more time, slow and soft and sweet, before stepping back.

"I already told you, Olive. I'll always know how to find you."

Part Three

BAGGAGE CLAIM

Chapter Twenty-Seven

The entire flight home, I will myself to sleep. No podcasts, no movies, no bags of chips, and definitely no conversations with ex-boyfriends who wind up in the seat next to me. This time, my seatmate is a perfectly fine middle-aged woman who spends the entire journey watching movies with her headphones in and not creeping over to my side of the armrest, which should be a relief, but instead just feels like a painful reminder of the companion I had on my way here.

And Ellen. She wound up being pretty okay, too.

I didn't think it was possible to feel more shattered leaving Tyler now as friends than I did all that time ago when I broke his heart, but here I am—curled up in a window seat with a heart cracked into a million pieces, watching the island, with its glittering turquoise water and rich green mountains—and the boy I reluctantly miss—get smaller and smaller until I close my eyes and beg for the loss of consciousness.

Returning back to normal life at home isn't much easier. Mom picks me up from the airport with a beaming smile that immediately dims a few watts when she sees my face.

"What's the matter, pea?" She drops the Welcome Back sign she's been holding and pulls me into her arms, stroking my hair while I sigh into her shoulder. The tears that had been threatening to spill since I boarded the flight thirteen hours ago still won't fall, locked up inside my heart with all the hurt I feel. On the drive home, I shakily find my voice and come up with the best lie I can think of, half hidden in truth. I tell her that Tyler and I got into an argument before I came home, realizing that even being friends is hard after our history, and we should cut off contact. I don't tell her that Tyler's the one struggling with having a friendship with me. Or that I wish I could hop on a departing flight right back to that island and tell him that I'm not ready to leave.

None of those things happen, though. I get into Mom's car and we weave through traffic until we arrive back at home. I put down my bags, coming up with an excuse that I need a nap but really needing some time by myself. Mom gives me a concerned look but takes my suitcase from me and tells me she'll see me when I wake up. I nod woodenly and head upstairs to my room, stripping off my hoodie and leggings and tossing them in a crumpled ball in the corner, sliding on sweats and an oversized tee instead. A tee that, until right this second, I hadn't realized belonged to someone else before me, but the faded indie band logo gives it away and shocks me with a new form of clarity.

Has my favorite sleep shirt always been Tyler's? It's a punch to the gut, but I still haven't cried.

It's only after I'm nestled in my bed, curled up under the covers in the darkness of the shaded room, that the dam breaks, the fissures in my heart crack open, and all of the hurt that's been festering inside of me pours out.

I wake up from my nap a few hours later, the room dark and my eyes stinging and crusty in the corners from all the tears that dried on my face. Mom still hasn't come in to wake me up, but I can hear the clanging of pots and pans as she prepares dinner downstairs, and my hungry stomach growls in response. Doing the mental math, I realize I haven't eaten since dinner the night before. But before I head downstairs for something to eat, I pick up my phone, expecting at least some sort of message from Tyler.

But the screen is blank. Not one text from anyone in the whole world. Not even any stupid social media notifications. It makes the yawning emptiness in my chest feel even deeper, and the sting of tears in my throat is harsh and sudden. It's not unlike how I felt in that airport security line just a few short days ago when I was starting my trip.

I tap out a quick text—*Made it home okay.*

His answer is immediate. *Glad to hear it.*

That's it. No asking how the flight was, no jokes, not even any damn emojis. Maybe he's feeling as empty inside as I am right now, the physical distance between us like the roaring ocean, cold and fierce.

Or, my brain unhelpfully reminds me, *maybe he's thinking about what he said to Lucas last night, about how he isn't sure he can stay friends with you with feelings like that. So maybe he's trying to make a clean break.* The notion shouldn't scare me, since I eventually did the same thing to him a year and a half ago when it was clear that he didn't want to be friends, but karma is a swift bitch and I feel like someone took a razor blade to my chest and left my heart at airport security before I boarded the plane. Too overwhelmed to deal with the possibility of that right now, I throw off the covers and pad downstairs, where Mom has a pot of sauce simmering on the stove and pasta boiling, ready for dinner.

She turns at the sound of my footsteps, her face brightening. "Did you sleep well, pea?"

I shrug and drop into one of the kitchen chairs, eyes skimming over her cluttered collection of mugs and making a mental note to give her the one I got her later. Which of course has me thinking about the outdoor market on the North Shore again, sharing those sodas, and my day of exploration with Tyler. The crack in my heart fissures. "I slept fine, I guess. Jet lag."

It feels like I felt all that time ago, where it seemed like every single thing I did or saw reminded me of time I spent with the boy I loved so much. Mom is always talking about soulmates this and soulmates that, but what about when two soulmates' lifestyles don't line up? How are things supposed to work then?

Mom, thankfully, reads my sulkiness in a totally different way, abandoning her post at the stove to drop into the chair across from me. She reaches over and grabs one of my hands in hers, squeezing it gently. "Still upset about Jack?"

Hearing his name is like a jolt back to reality, a reminder of something I'm supposed to be upset about this whole time. Because I feel stupid for flying all that way even when I had a bad feeling in my gut, wanting to deny the inevitable. Because I was stubborn and thought I could just will things into being okay by hopping on a surprise flight, will someone into loving me.

Damn. I guess I should *be upset about that*. What does it say about me and what type of person does it make me that Jack—and everything he did—had totally slipped my mind up until this very second? Still, I lean into it, not wanting to tell Mom the truth. *Hey, Mom, I accidentally fell back in love with my ex-boyfriend who isn't a good match for me, and I'm feeling pretty heartbroken right now.*

"Yeah. It's a lot to process. I . . . I think I can definitely say I wasn't expecting the trip to turn out like that." And it's the truth, even if it isn't in the way Mom believes. I thought I'd find Jack buried in textbooks, stressed out beyond belief, but relieved to see me and ready to spend a week decompressing and catching up together. I certainly didn't expect to find him twirling socks with a girl from his class. Still, ever the empath, my mother's eyes well up with tears and she leans across the table to squeeze me in a tight hug of sympathy.

"Oh, pea," she murmurs gently, stroking my hair, and I'd be lying if I said her touch wasn't comforting. "Heartbreaks happen. It's part of life. But you'll find your person eventually."

"I know I will, Mom." *What if I already have, and I just can't have him?*

She leans back and looks at me, running her thumbs under my eyes. I guess I *have* been crying without even realizing it. "What does Tyler think about all of this?"

Hearing his name makes me look up, and I'm sure I seem startled enough to raise suspicion. "Why does Tyler's opinion on any of this matter?"

She hums and stands up straight, heading back to the stove to stir the sauce. Even with her back to me, I hear the curiosity in her voice, clear as day. "No reason. You've just been spending time with him for the past few days, after not seeing him for a while, and everything that happened with Jack. It's bound to make anyone a little emotional—maybe even bond over that." She turns to grab the salt, and I see the mischievous smirk on her face when her profile comes into view. Maybe she isn't reading the situation as wrong as I'd hoped.

Still, the last thing I want to do is discuss my lack of a love life. So instead, I deflect. "He thinks Jack is an asshole. Anyone with a pulse would know that after what he did to me. But enough about me—tell me more about Connor."

At the mention of my mother's beau of the week, her face lights up. "He's wonderful. I can't wait for you to meet him. I think we're going out again tomorrow, so when he picks me up, I'll have him stop in to say hi. Seriously, pea—he's nothing like Neil or any of the others. I don't want to get too ahead of myself, but . . ." She hums excitedly while finishing dinner, not even needing to complete her sentence.

I do it for her, heart sinking. "You think he might be the one."

She points her wooden spoon at me with a noise of confirmation and a wink. "I don't want to jinx it, but . . . I feel different this time. I hope it works out."

"I do too, Mom." If only so I don't have to take another period of her couch-mourning and brokenheartedness. She deserves to find happiness, and although Connor is not nearly the first man she swore was the one, I hope this one sticks—just like I did with all the others (minus Asher, because that guy sucked from the start). I guess only time will tell.

We eat dinner with less sadness and more of our usual chatter, me giving her the rundown of everything non-romance-related that happened in Hawaiʻi, from our adventures to seeing his family, the flight, and so on. Mom counters by filling me in on everything I missed while I left, including her date with Connor last night. By the time we're done eating, we've sufficiently caught up and I'm so stuffed with pasta that I pass up Mom's suggestion of ice cream and a movie and instead waddle upstairs to digest in peace.

I flop onto my bed and pull out my phone, tapping the screen to bring it to life and swiping to my and Tyler's text thread. His last message still sits there, cold and distant. *Glad to hear it.*

I miss you already, I type out, blood humming with the overwhelming emotions jackhammering in my chest. *Maybe we can hang out when you get home?* Just because Tyler and I aren't going to end up in a relationship doesn't mean we can't pick up our friendship where we left off in Hawai'i, right?

Even thinking it in my head seems like a colossally bad idea, so I backspace the message and close out of our thread before I can make a bad decision. But the thought of reconciling has me thinking, so I pull up a new thread and send a possibly riskier text, crossing my fingers and hoping it all works out.

Chapter Twenty-Eight

Delia's looking at me from across the table at Le Petit Café with a guarded expression, the various piercings in her face glinting in the light. She tucks a strand of electric-blue hair—her latest color that she's been testing out, apparently—behind her ear and leans back in her seat, crossing her arms. Before she even opens her mouth, I brace for impact—because if Delia Franklin is anything, it's a straight shooter.

"Soooo." She draws out the vowel for a second. "Forgive me for being a little bit confused about why you asked to meet after all this time. This feels like an apology I've been waiting on for a while." It's not exactly aggressive, but she isn't being warm and friendly, either. She's regarding me with a look of suspicion as the waiter brings us our salads, Delia's piled high with a rainbow assortment of veggies, beans, and chicken, mine a classic Caesar.

She's clearly still on guard around me after everything that happened—not that I blame her. But she must've also been curious, at least some part of her, because we're sitting at a local café in town over lunch, and she's giving me the grace of at least hearing me out. And even if her tone is as prickly as ever, it feels like a breath of fresh air to realize that maybe not *everything* about my life has completely and utterly changed.

"First of all," I say carefully, rearranging the salt and pepper shakers on the table as Delia's eyes track my every move. "I want to say that I'm sorry. For everything that's happened in the past year and a half." When she just nods silently, eyes scanning my face, I continue awkwardly. "So . . . how are things with your girlfriend?"

"We're jumping straight into it, are we?" Delia's eyebrows practically rise to her hairline. "You knew about that?"

"I did." But I don't tell her that I only found out recently, the shame eating me up whole in the middle of the restaurant. "How'd that . . . go? You know, with your parents?"

Delia sighs matter-of-factly. "They flipped out after I told them about Cassie, obviously." She shrugs, pretending like it's no big deal, although it clearly is. "I knew it wasn't going to go well when I told them, but I did it anyway, because she's a really great person and doesn't deserve to be hidden like that." And that, I totally understand. Delia is a lot of things, but she'll be damned if she ever has to be anybody's secret. Or make anyone else feel even remotely close to the same way.

Still, she can't resist the chance to throw in at least one barb, no matter how well-deserved. "But these are things you would've known if you didn't just ghost me after the drama between you and Tyler, you know." The crunch of the lettuce in her mouth punctuates the end of her sentence, and my face heats up in shame.

"It's a lot more complicated than that," I retort weakly,

although in my head, I can't help but think, *Is it?* "I . . . these last few days have showed me a lot of things about myself that I didn't really notice before."

She rolls her eyes again. "Of course you didn't, Ol. Most of the time, we *don't* see ourselves super clearly. That's why it's up to the people in our lives to keep us in check." She points her fork at me accusingly. "Like our best friends. Those who, when we ignore their warnings, usually turn out to be right."

I let myself cling to the small glimmer of joy at hearing my old nickname again, and I'm not quite sure when I stopped hating it. Maybe it was somewhere between stepping onto that flight a few days ago and kissing Tyler at the airport.

Yeah. It has to be somewhere in there.

"You're right," I say at last, shame heating up my face. "You're right about all of it, D. Every last bit."

Her voice is surprisingly choked up when she replies. "I wish I wasn't," she sighs, batting away a stray tear. "You know, Olive, I understand you've had a lot of shit going on in your life since the breakup, but so have I. And . . . and I thought you'd become one of my best friends, and then suddenly, when things with Tyler fell apart, you just vanished, too."

Her revelation turns me cold. I want to open my mouth and tell her that she's wrong, that no, it was *her* who turned her back on *me* after the breakup . . . but the more I think about it, the more I realize that maybe that isn't quite true.

As if she can read my mind (which I wouldn't put past her), Delia speaks again. "I stopped texting *you* because *you* stopped texting *me*. Stopped seeking you out in the hallways at school, because whenever you'd catch sight of me, you'd practically sprint in the other direction. Eventually I got tired of trying to chase you. So I stopped. I already deal with trying to convince my parents to like me for who I am—I'm not going to try to convince you, too." She grips her fork tightly, her knuckles turning white, and it suddenly becomes abundantly clear to me how much she's been hurting this past year and a half.

You're so stupid, Olive, my brain chides. *So stupid and selfish.*

I hate how meek I sound when I reply. "I was avoiding you because I was afraid you were going to rip me a new one for everything that happened with Tyler, so I figured it would be better to just keep my distance. I shouldn't have, and I'm realizing that now."

She's thoughtful for a minute. "I mean, you're probably right. I *would* have ripped you a new one for a minute or two, because even if you didn't want to hear it, you definitely deserved it." She takes a shaky breath and pushes on. "But then we would've moved past it and gone back to being best friends, because Tyler or no Tyler, you still mattered to me. You didn't matter to me *because* you were with him, you know."

I think back to that first sleepover we had, with the scary movies and the popcorn confetti. Of the warm—and surprised—look in Delia's eyes when she admitted that maybe I wasn't too bad. *I think I just realized that you're kind of one of my closest friends now, and that's kind of weird, because I don't really make new friends.*

And those are exactly the words I need to hear to lift my spirits and push me to say the words I know I need to.

I sigh down at my plate, gathering my nerve. "I've been a sucky best friend—a sucky friend in general, really. I totally understand why you chose Tyler after everything that went down. I'm sorry, D. I can't tell you how sorry I actually am."

"*Chose* Tyler?" Delia laughs incredulously, her choked-up nature gone and replaced with her usual prickly—yet still loveable in a tough-love way—self. "Ol, I didn't choose him. You *left* all of us to go be with your uppity new Jack*ass* boyfriend. I wasn't the one who made that choice." Her words are sharp, but what stings more is the realization that Tyler wasn't the only person who I made a decision for back then. It's clear the hurt is still festering, long after the actual events happened.

"You're right." I swallow the embarrassment of admitting it. "I know I was a shitty person who made a lot of shitty decisions back then. But after talking to Tyler about everything during the trip, I feel differently. About a lot of things."

Delia's eyes pop as wide as saucers as she leans forward, placing both hands on the table and rattling her glass of water. "Hang on, *what*? What trip? You talked to Tyler? *Recently?*"

I furrow my brow in confusion. "He didn't tell you?" Delia was always the person the two of us told everything to, unless that changed—not that I'd know, with how long I've been out of the picture.

She lets out a low whistle and leans back in her seat, crossing her arms again. "Damn. Shit must've gone down for him to have talked to you again and kept it away from me."

Understanding dawns on me—Delia really doesn't know *anything* of what went down this past week. "I didn't only talk to him. I was *with* him."

I didn't think it was possible for her eyes to pop any wider. "Okay, I think we need to backtrack, and you need to start from the beginning, right the fuck now. Because this sounds like a way juicier story than I was anticipating." She's sitting so far forward that our noses are practically touching, confusion radiating off her, an excited hunger glinting sharply in her eyes. She looks so much like the Delia that I remember that my heart squeezes painfully at the reminder.

You can have this again, my traitorous brain whispers in the back of my mind. *You can have all of this back. Your relationship with Tyler. Your friendship with Delia. All of it.*

Instead, I tell my brain to shut up. Because nothing good ever comes from wanting things that you know could be complicated.

Realizing that Tyler doesn't seem to have told his friends anything—and I'm not sure if I'm upset about that because it doesn't matter as much to him or thrilled because it feels like the two of us have our own little secret—I tell Delia everything, starting with the plane ride up until the kiss at the airport before I left (which is one detail I didn't plan on sharing, but reconnecting with your ex–best friend has a way of making you want to spill all that's happened to you since you were last together).

When I finish the story, Delia looks shell-shocked. She takes a tentative sip of her Diet Coke while she thinks it over for a second. "Wow," she finally says, slow and careful. "So clearly, Tyler has some explaining to do about why he's been keeping all this from me. All I got were a couple of pics of some pretty sunsets and a promise for a pizza night when he gets back."

"So he hasn't brought me up at all?" I'm aware of how needy and clingy I sound as soon as it leaves my mouth. Delia sobers and levels me with a stare, stabbing her fork into her salad.

"Not that you have earned any right to know this information yet," she says. "But no."

I cling to the *yet* in her sentence as I pick up my fork and move a few pieces of lettuce around my salad plate. "Maybe he's still processing it. It's been a lot for me to wrap my head around, too."

And it's the truth. After everything that's happened, it feels like the trip dropped a bomb on my life as I knew it, in more ways than one.

"So now what?" Delia's voice cuts through the noise in my head, and when I look up from my plate, she's peering at me curiously. "Are you guys getting back together?"

"Absolutely not." I shake my head vigorously to emphasize the point. "We may have had a good time together on the trip, but vacation always has a way of making you see everything in a more special light—"

"Yeah, yeah, rose-tinted glasses, I know." Annoyance creeps into Delia's voice. "But you're forgetting that this isn't some sort of random vacation fling. This is a boy you dated for a long time, *whose heart you broke,* and who—as you admitted to me *yourself* a second ago—you never stopped loving. And, just pointing out, he's *here*—he doesn't live on an island in the middle of the Pacific Ocean." She pauses. "Well, I mean, he's not here right this second, but he'll be back soon, and he lives here. The circumstances have never been more right for you two."

But he might leave, my spiteful brain reminds me. *He might end up living on an island in the middle of the Pacific Ocean because before you left, you tried to convince him that it wasn't the worst idea.*

I shove down the doubt creeping up in the back of my mind, saying that maybe Delia's onto something. But I have to stay practical. It's the only way I won't end up like my mother, on another date this afternoon with a man she swears is her everything and will probably shatter her heart in two weeks' time. "I get what you're saying, Delia, I really do. But it doesn't mean that the facts have changed. I need stability in my life—someone with more of a life plan. Tyler is a great guy, but his lifestyle and the way he approaches things just don't match up with mine. And if it's already a problem now, I can only imagine how big of a problem it's going to be down the line."

Delia groans and stands up from her chair, frustration on her face. "I love you both, I really do, but I swear to god, sometimes you're both so stupid."

Her insult hits me like a slap, fresh and stinging, coupled with the confusing lift of my spirits that knowing after everything that went down, she still loves me. "What the hell is that supposed to mean?"

She fishes around in her bag for her wallet, throwing a couple of bills down on the table before fixing me with a *You are so oblivious* look. "Haven't you two ever heard of compromising?"

"Of course I have," I respond, my face starting to heat up. "But there are some things in life you can't compromise on."

This earns me an undignified snort. "Yeah, like someone's stance on gay rights or whether they think murder is an acceptable pastime. But none of the shit you two are working through is unfixable."

My vision starts to get blurry, frustrated tears pricking at the corners of my eyes. "That's not true, Delia. You know nothing about it."

But she isn't hearing it, shaking her head. "Yeah, Tyler needs to get his shit together a little more and learn how to be a functioning adult person and learn that life is not an endless backpacking *let's see where this takes me* trip around the world. But *you*"—her gaze turns icy—"well, it wouldn't hurt you to learn to loosen up a little bit, either. You're so hell-bent on plans, but it looks like every single one you've made has failed on you so far.

"And you've still got your head in your ass—we haven't talked about what's going on with me *once* during this entire exchange except for the first obligatory two minutes. Or how my parents have been handling—or more like *not* handling—me coming out. Or about how hellish my life has been at home lately." She takes a shaky breath, visibly trying to compose herself.

"Maybe it would do you some good to get a breath of fresh air and notice the people that are standing right in front of you from time to time, Olive. Maybe then you'd finally realize that the boy who's loved you forever is still waiting hopelessly for you out there, and everyone just wants to see you both happy. And that there are other people in this world with struggles who aren't you. You're just stuck in this weird headspace of trying to force yourself to grow up so fast, like you can bypass all of the stupid mistakes we're supposed to make and try to fix as we become adults." *Like you can bypass all of the stupid mistakes your mom made,* is what she doesn't say, but it floats in the air between us all the same. "But newsflash for you, Olive. You *can't*. You're going to make those mistakes whether you want to or not. You don't even realize that you're so intent on building this 'structured' life that you cling to it so hard, and everyone notices."

With those parting daggers disguised as words, she storms out of the café, leaving me sitting there with a pile of crumpled bills and emotional whiplash.

But she's not wrong. I know she isn't. Every single life plan I've made for myself so far *has* failed. Both the thought of that *and* the fact that other patrons are staring at me quizzically after our scene has my cheeks reddening in mortification and shame. But it's not as scary as reevaluating my whole strategy.

I want nothing more right now than to pick up the phone and

call Tyler, but after the weirdness of the past few days, it's best I leave him alone, at least for now. Maybe he's still struggling with the thought of staying friends, like he talked to Lucas about. Maybe he's focusing on spending time with his family before he has to fly back home. Or maybe he realizes that I'm better off not being a part of his life.

For once, I don't really want to know what he's thinking. It feels like whatever the answer is, it's going to hurt.

Chapter Twenty-Nine

After that disaster of a lunch, I spend some time wandering around town and popping in and out of local shops before going back to my house. It feels weird to be alone for the first time in forever—I was with Tyler on the flight, then with Jack in his dorm (however short-lived that was), then started hanging out with Tyler again, and then Delia . . . but now I have nobody's dismal company except my own as I half-heartedly flip through new releases at the bookstore and try chocolate samples from the new sweets shop.

I get home (sans any new books or chocolate, which is a direct indicator of how dire my mood is) just as Connor is dropping Mom off after their date, and she's practically glowing as she floats through the front door. She even invites Connor in for introductions, which goes fine—he seems perfectly nice and friendly and has that same rosy lovesick glow on his cheeks as Mom—but I can't help the sour feeling curdling in my stomach. The introductions are usually the first step toward the end, because this is where things are going to pick up speed, and go way too fast, and go off the rails, and then I'll be left picking up the pieces, just like I always am.

Enough, Olive, my brain reminds me, as if it hasn't done enough mental torturing today. *Let her be happy. Not everyone's doomed to a life of miserable singledom the way that you are.*

As hard as I try to tamp those feelings deep down and not let them surface, I'm sure the emotions—paired with the fact that I can't shake having heard how Tyler feels about me—are showing on my face. Still, I push on through for my mother's sake, because I'm just going to be a people pleaser until the end, I guess.

I exchange pleasantries with Connor for a few minutes while Mom putters around the kitchen getting glasses of water, but once they both have their beverages, I make an excuse to slip off and settle in the living room armchair, scrolling through social media on my phone and trying my best not to open my text thread with Tyler, staring at our lack of messages. It feels eerily like it did back in junior year when I was staring down the barrel of radio silence after blowing everything up. And it hits me with a cold shock that, in a roundabout way, I've just made the same mistake again, a year and a half later.

Tyler and I were building something good, and I destroyed it. And even if in the moment it felt like the right thing to do, as I sit here now—and as I sat there in my bed after our initial breakup, heartsick and lonely—I can't really remember why.

Even with hearts in her eyes, Mom has always been able to focus on me and my needs—a bond we've developed being each other's only true companions for all these years. I can practically see her floating on air as she kisses Connor goodbye a while later, shuts the door, and turns to me. Before I can say anything, she wordlessly points to the couch, her *we need to talk* expression settled firmly on her face.

Once we're both seated, she places one of her warm hands in

mine and squeezes gently. "All right," she says, determination set in her jaw, "out with it."

Even though it's fruitless, I try for deflection. "Out with what?"

She answers me with another level stare, arching one eyebrow—the universal mother's code for daring me to lie to her again. With Sherri Austin, it's a warning you don't want to receive twice. So, I don't—instead, I take a deep breath and steel myself to get this over with.

"I'm fine," I say, willing myself to believe it's true. "Just been in a bit of a funk with everything after coming back from Hawai'i."

"Because of Jack?" The happy, rosy glow on her face dims a little bit, replaced with a cloudy expression of concern.

I shrug. "Yeah." *That's part of it, at least.*

She sits up straighter now, giving my hand another squeeze, her focus snapping to attention. "Then let's talk about it, pea. What's on your mind?"

"There's nothing to talk about," I mumble down into the couch cushions as I pull one of our throw pillows onto my lap. Which, of course, immediately clues her in to the fact that there is very much something to talk about, and that activates her mother Spidey senses in a way that makes it clear she is going to be persistent and *not* let this go.

"Olive Amelia Austin." Her tone is firm. "I understand that as a mother, I'm supposed to give my teenager a little bit of agency and privacy, but in this particular moment, I can tell that you've been bottling something up inside. So what you're going to do is tell me *right now,* or at the very least tell me that there's nothing I should be concerned about, and then I promise I'll let it lie. But you're not going to get off this couch until I hear an answer from you either way." She crosses her arms and narrows her eyes at me, pursing her lips in what I'm sure she thinks is an intimidating interrogation tactic, but coming from my usually so bubbly and sweet mother, is more comical than anything.

Still, I don't laugh, because I don't have a death wish. Instead, I just sigh. "You have nothing to worry about, Mom. Nothing's wrong like that. I promise."

Dissatisfaction crosses her face, but she's true to her word, shrugging and patting her knees as she moves to stand up. "Well, all right, then. You know where to find me if you need me and decide you want to talk."

But as she tries to get up and move into the kitchen, I don't find myself breathing the sigh of relief that I thought I would at her leaving me alone. Instead, I feel a tightness in my stomach, an urge to keep talking. After keeping things bottled up for *days*, the pressure is becoming unbearable. And while my mother is still my *mom*, it's been just the two of us for so long, so in a lot of ways, she really *is* one of my best friends. She really is someone that I feel like I can talk to.

"Wait," I hear myself saying, my voice sounding tinny and far away even to my own ears. *I guess we're doing this, then.* "I mean, there is, uh, kind of something that I wanted to talk about, if that's okay."

She pauses and sinks back into her seat, the delight written clearly on her face before she schools her expression into something more serious and motherly. "Of course, pea. What's going on in that brain of yours?"

Everything, I want to moan, but I simply settle for "This funk feels kind of bad, Mom. But I know you're happy with Connor and everything, so I don't want to be a downer, especially after it seems like you guys had a really good date. And he seems really nice."

She smiles warmly and reaches over to squeeze my hand, that lovesick glow still on her face. "Thank you, pea. I'm glad you think so. I like him a whole lot." She gets serious again. "But he's not the priority right now. What's going on with you?"

I shake my head, determined not to dim her glow even further. "Just because it feels like my life is in shambles right now doesn't mean that you have to stop feeling happy and in love, Mom. It's the same thing you used to tell me, whenever . . ." I trail off, not willing to finish the sentence. We both remember all of the couch-ridden days when she gave me the same speech when I was feeling guilty about going on a date with Tyler in the middle of her emotional turmoil. *Your life doesn't stop just because mine's having a bit of a hiccup.* Even though it felt like it always did.

"Don't be silly," she scoffs, waving her free hand like I said the most ridiculous thing in the world. "I'm your mother. Talking to you about what's going on in your life is my job, and it's *always* going to be my most important priority. So, what about the whole Jack situation are you finding so hard to get over? Let's talk through it."

In an effort to appease her and to get her off my case, I open my mouth and let the words start tumbling out, careful not to let the real problem—the feelings stirring in my heart for Tyler—slip. "With everything that happened, and the way Jack was lying to me . . . it hurt. A lot. And then the rest of the time I was in Hawai'i, I realized I didn't really miss him at all, and I'm not sure if that's because I'm trying to lock away the hurt so it doesn't crush me, or because it means we were never really a good match at all. And it's a lot to think about." Okay, so not a *total* lie—all valid things that I've definitely been feeling in the past few days.

But Sherri's mom-tuition is strong today, because she nods sagely and reads right through me. She opens and closes her mouth a few times, seemingly mulling over her response, before she speaks. "Do you think Tyler's the one?"

Her question takes me aback and I yank my hand from hers, feeling flushed. How could my own mother ask me that when she's been through upward of twenty instances of "the one" already, and everyone left her behind? How can *I* even believe in it after everything I've seen with both her and me?

I can't help but sputter out a response, my cheeks flaming with embarrassment. "What? The *one*? Isn't . . . isn't it a bit early to think that? We're not even out of high school yet! And he has *nothing* to do with any of this." The lie doesn't sound the slightest bit convincing as it falls out of my mouth. Not even to me.

To her credit, Mom takes my overreaction in stride, nodding calmly. "Listen, pea, I'm sorry for putting you on the spot and asking you that, and you don't have to give me an answer, but that's absolutely something you should think over and find an answer for in your own heart. Because if you know someone's the one, you should go for it, no matter what it takes."

One thing I've learned by growing up with Sherri Austin as my mother is that you have to know when to throw in the towel and realize you've been caught. "Okay, so let's say I *do* think Ty's the one—which I'm not actually saying, so don't get any ideas." At this, a smile quirks at the corner of her mouth. "What if . . . what if I'm wrong?" What I don't say hangs in the air between us—what if I end up chained to this very couch nursing my very own heartbreak, wallowing in the feeling that the greatest love of my life just walked away?

It only takes Mom a second for the realization to dawn on her face. "Oh, pea. Is that why you've spent your whole life pushing people away?" She reaches forward and envelops me in a hug that smells like vanilla perfume and the mint tea she always drinks.

"I don't push *everyone* away," I mumble into her shirt. "You're still here."

Her laugh vibrates against my ear. "That's because I'm your mother, silly. You are my greatest gift—you couldn't push me away if you tried." She squeezes me tighter. "And you better not try."

"I won't," I whisper, tears filling my eyes and soaking the fabric of her shirt.

Mom rocks me for a second, rubbing my back. "Your life isn't my life, Olive. Just because things don't work out for me sometimes doesn't mean they won't work out for you. It doesn't mean that you should push people away first because you're afraid of getting hurt, because that's the number one way to guarantee that you stay lonely. I don't think you even realize how shy and withdrawn you were before you met Tyler—I practically had to drag you out of the car to go to those silly team-bonding dinners that your field hockey team has." Her eyes crinkle in the corners at the memory. "But once you met him, that all just . . . melted away for a while. You let yourself be happy and outgoing. You made new friends. You let yourself be *seen*." She squeezes my hand for emphasis. "Pushing people away now to avoid the hurt is just going to ensure that you don't let yourself get back to that version of Olive again, and truthfully, that's a damn shame."

She's so right that I have to suck in a deep breath, surprised. *Is that what I've been doing this whole time?*

"And you listen to me." She pulls back until her eyes are locked with mine. "I know you've witnessed a lot of my own heartbreaks while you were growing up, and I can't tell you how sorry I am for that. Those were never your burdens to bear, and even though I know you really are my best friend, sometimes it's easy to forget that my first and most important role is being your mother. Sometimes there were things that I just shouldn't have dragged you into."

My eyes are already starting to sting with hot tears. "You were never a burden, Mom. And you didn't drag me into anything—you needed me, and I was happy to help."

She squeezes my shoulders with a small smile. "Thank you for saying that, pea. It's true, though—even though I'm eternally grateful that you were there for me during all of those low points, that was never your job. I'm sorry I made you feel like it was." She takes a deep, steeling breath, eyes locking on mine with determination. "But really listen to me here—even with all of those men I thought were the one and weren't, I don't regret trying things with a single one of them. Because even if it blows up, even if it doesn't last, I've *never* been with someone who didn't make me feel happy, at least while we were together." Her words sink in slowly, a thick molasses on my skin that settles into my bones.

And thinking back, she's right—it's easy to remember all of the heartbreak, but sprinkled in between those moments were fresh-cut flowers in vases, rosy cheeks, sweet dinners, and so many giggles while getting ready for nights out. While it may not have always ended in happiness, the journey to the end was at least enjoyable. She was, in her own way, having a good time.

Even if things didn't always work out in the long-term for Mom, in the short-term, she always felt loved. And maybe, for her, that was worth the risk.

Maybe it could be that way for me, too. But could it, really? After I've screwed everything up so badly?

Wiping one of my stray tears with the pad of her thumb, she continues. "You chase and you chase and you *chase* love until it sticks, Olive. That's how it works. And, honey, watching you with Tyler back then and hearing you now—you two are stuck like glue. It's just taken you two a little bit longer to understand it."

I don't answer, pulling her in for another tight hug and squeezing. I inhale her calming, familiar scent of vanilla and mint, and she pats my head before pulling away and getting up to head toward the kitchen.

"Whatever you decide, don't make that decision out of fear." She looks down at me seriously, but there's a lightness in her voice, that rosy glow still there from her date with Connor. *He's actually a really nice guy. I hope he lasts.* "Because if you take the leap and chase that feeling, you might surprise yourself with the results." At those parting words, she slips around the corner and out of sight, leaving me with a thought scarier than the one bouncing around my mind when I boarded the plane to Hawai'i and worried about Jack's weirdness. It hits me like a freight train, fast and ruthless and so forceful that it almost takes my breath away.

Olive Austin, you total idiot. You're such *an asshat.*

I spent all this time convincing myself that Tyler would bring an instability to my life that I'm not ready for—but I've been the one overcomplicating it this whole time.

Maybe I just needed to let myself fall. Because, as Delia hurtfully but so accurately pointed out at our lunch . . . where has all my meticulous planning gotten me?

You're so hell-bent on plans, but it looks like every single one you've made has failed on you so far.

The planner sitting unopened on my desk begs to agree—all those plans, so meticulously entered and tracked and managed, and yet I ended up here anyway. The stickers haven't even been removed, first because I didn't want to get rid of the reminder of the good parts of the trip, and then because I've just been feeling too sad to think about destroying the paper pages and feeling even sadder.

Here I am, alone, in the end. And with a whole lot less happiness now that I've lost both Tyler *and* Delia in the process.

Maybe letting myself fall in love doesn't have to be this hard.

I know it in my bones as soon as Mom leaves the room—that I'm ready. That hearing those words from the mouth of the woman who I miscategorized for so long were just the words I needed to hear to set me free.

Shit—can I do this? Am I actually ready to do this?

I think I'm ready to do this.

I'm ready to jump back into our relationship for real, consequences and potential life plans be damned. Those things will all wind up working out—or not. But worrying about it right now isn't going to make me any happier.

Finally, my brain triumphantly declares to no one in particular. Probably my heart. *She's finally listening.*

Tyler Ferris is my person. The feelings swirling in my chest feel the same as they did the summer before sophomore year. Being back together is what Tyler clearly wants.

And I think I've finally realized that this is what I want, too.

If only I hadn't made such a mess out of everything. Which means that this is going to be a *lot* harder than it had to be.

Chapter Thirty

Hey. The three letters stare at me accusingly, followed by my blinking cursor as I debate whether or not to hit send. The clock on my nightstand reads 4:45 a.m., which is 10:45 p.m. back in Hawai'i. The rest of this week has been a blur of sulking and stewing in my feelings, and I'm not quite sure I got the date of Tyler's return right, but I still take a deep breath and force myself to keep typing. *If I did the math right and you're coming back tonight, can you stop over on your way home?* Thumb shaking, I push myself to tap send, shooting my request out into the void.

I behaved like an absolute mess, and this whole time I made Tyler feel like he wasn't good enough when in reality it was me who wasn't ready to face the music and bend my plans a little. How did I expect Tyler to give a mile when I wouldn't even give an inch?

I need to make it up to him. But that requires getting him to talk to me first.

The little note under my text bubble indicates that the message is delivered, but although I stare at it until my eyes water, until the clock reads almost five, the tiny *delivered* never changes to *read*.

It's still the same accusing message when I wake up groggily the next morning, the smell of coffee and the clanging of Mom's pots and pans stirring me awake. Lured by the thought of some food and warm coffee, I slog down the stairs and sit at the kitchen table, blinking blearily until she gently places a plate of food in front of me. But it still feels like my arms are filled with lead as I pick up my fork and take a tentative bite of the fluffy eggs. I decide to go a tiny bit crazy and send another text—a simple *Hey, did you get my message?*

But that one loads and loads, and never delivers. *Good going, Olive,* my brain snaps at me, enraged at me realizing my true feelings too late. *Now he probably blocked your number for being crazy.*

Mom takes one look at my face and frowns. "Rough night?"

I shrug into my plate. "Didn't sleep well." Not exactly a lie, even if it isn't the full truth. If Mom picks up on it, she doesn't let on, instead setting her own plate down, forcing me to make small talk to ignore the whirling dread in my heart.

"Connor and I have another date this weekend," she begins, unable to keep the smitten smile from blooming on her face. "He originally told me it was a surprise, but then he got too excited so he told me anyway. We're going to the botanical gardens and having a picnic there. Isn't that sweet?"

The mere mention of a picnic has my mind flashing back to images of my day with Tyler at the Rainbow Drive-In. The carved wooden picnic tables, the smells of meat and rice and egg in the air. Still, I rally for my mother and do my best to paste on a pleased smile. "That sounds awesome, Mom. He seems like a really nice guy."

She beams back at me. "Thank you, pea. I have a feeling this one's going to stick. I don't know how, but . . . he just feels different than the others."

A few weeks ago, if my mother had said those exact same words to me, I would've internally rolled my eyes and started counting down the guy's days. Lord knows she's said that more than two dozen times in her life.

But this time . . . I can't help but agree that it feels different. While she still seems bubbly and excited and madly in love, she also seems grounded, in a way that she hasn't ever before. Almost like her soul's at peace. Almost like when you find the right person, you can just let yourself rest and bask in it.

Which is why, instead of mentally placing my bets on how long Connor will last, I find myself smiling back—and actually meaning it. "I think so, too. He seems like a good fit for you." And it's quickly clear how much those words mean to her, because her smile breaks out even wider, and if I'm not mistaken, it looks like her eyes are shining and a bit misty.

However, I'm pulled out of those thoughts pretty quickly when my mother seems to decide that my moping around this morning is no longer a suitable activity for our afternoon.

"All right, Olive." Mom sets her fork down and claps her hands once, commanding my attention. I look up at her in surprise, and she levels me with a serious look. "You're clearly in a funk, even if you won't admit it to me, so today we're going to do something about it."

I didn't think it was possible for my heart to sink any further. "I'm fine, Mom. I just need some time to stew in it."

She shakes her head and stands up, collecting our plates

before I can shovel the last forkful of eggs into my mouth. "Stew is something you make for dinner; it's not a suitable activity. I have some errands to run today, so you're coming with me."

Could a worse decree ever be declared by a mother? Whether I'm eight or eighteen, I have *never* been a fan of running errands with Mom. It's a process that includes a lot of pit stops and takes *forever.*

"Mom—"

"Nope." Her tone is firm and she crosses her arms. "I'm pretty lenient with bossing you around, pea, but right now, this is not up for debate." She gives me a steely look as she motions toward the stairs. "So, go get ready. The groceries aren't going to buy themselves, and we have to get a move on."

"Fine," I grumble, standing up and shaking breakfast crumbs off my lap. As grumpy as I am about the prospect of being forced to go run around town with my mother all day, at least it'll be a welcome distraction from sitting and wallowing. Still, on the way out the door, I can't help but slip my phone out of my pocket and check my messages one more time, the empty notification bar taunting me. Tyler still didn't reply, so I take the risk of seeming clingy and send another.

Olive: Hey, can we talk when you get home? Things felt like they left off weird. And I could really use some time to talk to you about it.

But I'm still met with nothing. Nothing is delivering.

The rest of my day passes by the exact same way—running those dreaded errands with Mom, cleaning my room, finally unpacking my suitcase. Checking my phone constantly with not a single reply to my texts.

That's it, I finally resign to myself around 9:00 p.m. while I'm sitting on the couch with Mom, trying to distract myself with *RuPaul's Drag Race* but not quite succeeding. I've sent close to ten texts at this point, well into obsessive territory, and every single one went undelivered. Everything ranging from pleas to talk, to sending along the selfie we took on our hike, and even some stupid internet meme about coconuts that I came across during my Twitter doomscrolling. That one I was sure I'd get a response to—but still silence. *It's over. I lost my chance.* It doesn't feel unlike it felt back when Tyler and I broke up, when it was like he totally vaporized out of my life in the week that followed—no texts, no calls, not even taking the usual routes to class to avoid bumping into me.

Mom, to her credit, doesn't push me about what's wrong, even though I catch her frowning in my direction more than once, her brows furrowed. As close as my mother and I have always been, I've never felt a million miles away from her before now—not even when I was across the continent and the Pacific Ocean.

By midnight, I've finally accepted my fate and the fact that I managed to cosmically mess up the best second chance of my life. This would normally be the part of a mental crisis where I'd reach for my trusty planner and stickers and pens and washi tape and try to organize the hell out of my thoughts, figuring out what the next steps will be to solve my problem—but this time, it's a problem that seems unsolvable.

I'm so empty about it that I can't even cry, instead curling up in a ball under my comforter and listening to my breathing, feeling the sharp sting in my eyes from the tears that refuse to fall. I blew things up with Tyler, and with Delia, and she was right—I was only thinking of myself. Which is what prompts me to pick up my phone for the umpteenth time that day, but not for Tyler.

"Olive." Delia's tone is cool when she picks up. There's the soft sound of running water behind her, which means she's likely propped up in bed in her childhood room next to her exotic fish-tank that Tyler and I both admired but were never allowed to touch. One Christmas I even got her a fake little fireplace to put inside the tank—briefly, I wonder if she still keeps it there.

"Look." I take a deep breath and launch right into it. "I'm sorry. I'm really, really, really sorry. You were right about everything with Tyler, but that isn't even the point. The point is that I've been a shitty friend to you, and you deserve an apology. Of course I want to know what's going on in your life. You were one of my closest friends for so long, and I'm sorry that I wasn't there for you in all the ways I should've been. You deserve better."

"Mmm," Delia mutters. "I did. Thanks for recognizing that."

I hear a cough in the background on her end, and it brings me up short. "Is someone there with you?"

"It's my dad, down the hall," she responds dryly. "Mom moved in with my aunt across town after finding out about my girlfriend. He's working on being better and more accepting, especially since she won't be. Which is something you'd know if you hadn't ditched us all for that colossal Jackass."

The play on Jack's name isn't lost on me. "You're right. I'm sorry again, D. I wish I could take it all back."

"Well, you can't." Delia sighs. "Like I told my dad, all you can do is be better. And I hope you do, Olive. Maybe . . . maybe I'm okay with giving you another chance to try." And in her typical fashion, she ends the call before we can veer into sappy territory. But her words stick me right in the heart, and an overwhelming flood of everything I've done wrong this past year bombards me all at once. I burrow into the covers and squeeze my eyes shut, begging for some kind of emotional release, but I just feel stretched to the seams.

"I can't even cry right," I mutter in the darkness, my entire body trembling with the urge to let out the tears that won't come. "I really did screw everything up." I might have bumpily patched things over with Delia, but things with Tyler are looking as dismal as ever, text messages still going unanswered, pain still lashing at the walls of my heart. *I can't even let out the tears. Something is seriously wrong with me.*

That's my last thought as I drift off to sleep—an endless loop of *I failed, I failed, I failed.*

Chapter Thirty-One

"Pea?" Mom's gentle voice pulls me from my dreamless—and pretty terrible—sleep, and I squint in the bright light of the morning as I peek one eye out from underneath my comforter. She's standing in the doorway, already dressed in crisp linen pants and a soft-looking sweater, her face freshly washed and glowing—all indicators that I've slept in way later than I planned. I swear I dreamed hearing our doorbell as I crawled out of my murky dreamland, too, but that was probably just a UPS delivery.

"Olive?" she prompts again when I don't answer, eliciting a weak mumble from me as a response. And then what she says next stops my blood cold: "There's someone at the door for you. Delia—"

Okay, so that was *not* a UPS delivery.

"*What?*" Delia's *here,* which means maybe I've been given my chance to apologize in person, and my second thought is that the clock on my nightstand says it's almost noon and my room smells sweaty and stale, my hair is undoubtedly sticking up all over the place, and I most certainly have morning breath. Mom's face gives nothing away, though.

“Tell her I’ll be right down,” I blurt, launching out of bed and hurriedly trying to comb down my hair and tug on a pair of sweatpants. “I just . . . Give me a second.”

A bemused look crosses Mom’s face as I flail around my room, but she nods with a small smile and closes the door. As soon as she does, I finish yanking the sweatpants up over my hips, throw on my favorite worn-in hoodie, and scramble to the bathroom to brush my teeth. I’m in such a rush to get downstairs that I leave my mane of hair in a jumbled tangle on my head, hoping a few mere finger-brushes will do the trick but inherently knowing that the effort is futile.

“Where’s Delia?” I call out as I head toward the door, surprised that she isn’t standing in the foyer. Mom isn’t typically one to leave guests standing outside, and even though it’s been a while since Delia’s been around, she’s always treated this place like a second home. Probably an even more accepting one than where she resides with her parents, if we’re being honest.

“About that.” Mom’s in the kitchen, puttering around, and when she sees me reach for the door, I hear her stop the running water at the sink and take a deep breath. “Wait a second. Olive, you should know—”

But I’m not listening, already pulling the door open, revealing the face of the last person I thought I’d ever see again.

Tyler’s eyes scan my hoodie, widening in surprise. “So *that’s* where my Grateful Dead hoodie went.”

I hear Mom sigh behind us and go back to washing the dishes.

I don’t know what to do first—I want to hug Tyler, shake him, question why he went silent. I want to beg for his forgiveness and throw my arms around his neck and breathe in his scent and press my lips to his over and over and over again.

So, naturally, I do none of those things.

Instead, I zero in on the sweatshirt comment. "I can't help that it's been washed to perfection and is now the perfect amount of soft." I cross my arms over my chest self-consciously, tilting my chin up to at least hide my embarrassment and the heat rushing to my face. But I also can't ignore the happy flare of excitement sparkling in my blood, followed closely by a warmth blooming in my chest. *He is your home,* my heart and my brain both whisper to me, in sync for once in my life. *Your "home" is home.*

Tyler nods mock-seriously, clearly trying to bite back a smile. "And what did Mr. Two First Names have to say about it?"

"Nothing." *Because I kept this tucked in the back of my closet whenever he was around.* Which is probably something I should investigate later. But right now, I turn and flash my mother an accusing glare over my shoulder, where she's resting against the sink with one eyebrow raised. "What are you doing here? My mom told me that Delia was here."

"No, I didn't," she chimes in unhelpfully from the kitchen. "I was trying to tell you that Delia *texted* me and said that Tyler was dropping by, but you took off like a bullet before I had a chance to stop you." She winks at Tyler over my shoulder. "Nice to see you again, sweetheart. Been a while."

He waves sheepishly at Mom. "It's nice to see you, too, Sherri."

"Anyway." I clear my throat, stepping out onto the front steps and shutting the door behind us to cut off Mom, willing my pulse to calm back down to a normal rate. "Why . . . why are you here?" But even though I ask, we both know, those words I first texted on a whim hanging in the air between us. *If I did the math right and you're coming back tonight, can you stop over on your way home?*

Tyler takes a slow, shaky breath, and it dawns on me that I'm not the only one spiraling out from nerves right now. "I've been thinking since you left. And I have something to show you." He pulls out his phone and scrolls through his camera roll until he lands on what he's searching for, flipping the screen so I can see better. It's a close-up photo of what looks like wood, a tiny heart scratched into the surface. Instantly, I recognize it.

"You went back to take a picture of the picnic table where we got lunch?" I try not to sound confused, but I'm sure he senses it, anyway. This is Tyler we're talking about. "Why?"

"Because"—he zooms in even further, presenting me the heart—"I went back there."

I squint at the screen, searching for the J + M initials that I'd traced my finger over that day. But to my surprise, that's not what's there. Carved inside the little heart is the word *To*.

"To?" I glance up at Tyler, brows furrowed. "What's that supposed to mean? To who?"

Tyler shakes his head, exasperated, and jabs his finger at the phone. "Look closer." And there, nestled in between the two letters, is a tiny plus sign.

The heart doesn't say *To*. It says *T* + *O*.

Oh.

Oh.

"But . . . what?" The realization has my head spinning. "Why . . . how? We weren't . . . We hadn't . . ." My mind runs through every moment of that day, the hard heart-to-heart we had at the Rainbow Drive-In. There was no moment where Tyler could've done that when we were together. Which means he went back and purposefully etched those letters there. But that would've been long before he showed up on my doorstep; before I told him everything I was feeling.

Luckily, Tyler doesn't keep me guessing for long. "The day you left, I went there on my way back. I just . . . I needed a place to think, and it was nice to have some loco moco to deal with the heartache. Seems to be a theme of ours." We both laugh at this, but then his cheeks redden bashfully and he looks away from me. "I did it on a whim. I didn't mean to—I didn't even notice that I sat at the same table until I saw the other heart. But I had to put it out there into the universe. I had to . . . I had to hope. Because I've never stopped loving you, Ol, but I'm sure you know that by now." He smiles wryly. "And call me hopeful, or delusional, or whatever you want, but I think that you haven't stopped loving me, either."

"I never stopped." The honesty surprises us both, Tyler's eyes widening. "Which is why I wanted to talk to you. Seeing you those few days, Ty . . . it was a gift. More than I think I knew until I came home and realized how empty my life was without you." I swallow and watch his face, which remains unchanged, and I'm not sure if that's a good sign or a bad one. "And it took some verbal beatings over the head from a few different people to finally see it. Namely, Delia." When he barks out an amused laugh, I take another deep breath and continue. "I spent all this time running away from us without realizing that we're what I should've been running *toward*. I was wrong for implying that you weren't good enough to be with me. It was the opposite—you're a better person than I could ever imagine. It's *me* who has to do the work to be good enough for us now.

"I was stupid," I sob, ugly, snotty tears trailing down my

face. "I was stupid and selfish and scared. I tried so hard to protect myself from heartbreak that I caused it instead. And I can't even begin to express how sorry I am for that. And I can't take it back. All I can do is be better, and to start letting myself chase after the things that make me happy. And it's you." I wipe my eyes with an embarrassing sniffle. "It's you that makes me happy. It always has been."

Tyler's still standing across from me, his expression shifting to shell-shocked. Which, honestly, I can't blame him for after that massive emotional dump. My eyes skim over the picture again, staring hard at the two little letters carved into the heart. My own heart feels so sore it could burst, overwhelmed with emotion—as if he had carved those letters in my own chest.

"Ty," I whisper, heart softening. "What are we doing? Is it worth all of this?" I gesture between us, at our rapidly beating hearts and blushing faces and the nerves that are eating us both alive. "Do you really think we'll be able to find some way to meet in the middle? That you could forgive me for all the shitty mistakes I've made?"

"I mean, yeah." He shrugs. "I'd do anything for you, Ol."

Another laugh-sob rips from my chest. "I know. I heard all about the failed accounting course."

His cheeks pinken. "All right, all right, I'll admit that wasn't one of my finest moments. I was just desperate to get the girl of my dreams back."

"She's worth taking a stupid online accounting course for? I wouldn't have even *wanted* you to do that." Even as the words leave my mouth, they give me pause. Because Tyler's proven that he's willing to meet me in the middle—and I feel the rush of shame that it's taken me so long to feel ready to do the same.

Tyler scoffs, stepping forward and lacing his fingers through mine. "Olive Austin," he declares, voice no longer shaking, but steady and sure. "You're worth everything. And you must've actually knocked your head on those cliffs at China Walls if you thought for a second that I wouldn't forgive you." And before I can even open my mouth to answer, he stamps his lips on mine, and everything comes rushing back. The airport, the salt-speckled air, the sunshine and runny egg yolks and security-line kisses.

Part of me wonders what stickers I'd use on my planner's pages to document everything that's coming—more dates with Tyler. All the milestones we'll achieve together. But then I think back to that morning in Lucas and Ella's house, getting ready for our adventure day and swearing that things were going to change. *New Olive sometimes hands things to the universe to decide her fate.*

And you know what? Maybe it's fine to wing it every once in a while.

"I thought not everyone gets a fairy-tale romance?" It's hard to get the question out as I'm being peppered with kisses along my eyelids, my cheekbones, the tip of my nose.

Tyler presses his mouth against my ear in a way that evokes shivers across every part of my body. "We didn't. Not the first time." He nips my ear and I have to swallow back a squeak as he continues. "But I'd say we definitely got it right the second time around."

And in this moment, in the arms of the boy I never stopped loving, excited chills running down my spine, it clicks. *He's right.* And I've never been more grateful for second chances. I think of my lunch with Delia, with her sharp words that weren't wrong—that there's a middle ground here, somewhere, for the both of us, if we both are willing to find it. Tyler's lips feather mine for a few more seconds before he pulls back and his eyes search mine imploringly, love and excitement and a little bit of worry flitting across his face.

"Olive." His voice is strained, the panic of our second—or, I guess, third—impending implosion written all over his face. "Say something. Anything. Just please . . . please say something."

I don't even need to think about it. I open the door behind us—for Tyler, for his sweet smile, for our future. "Do you want to come in?"

Acknowledgments

It truly takes a village to bring a book to life, and I don't know where *We've Hit Turbulence* would have been without mine.

First and foremost, a massive thank-you to my agents, Marisa Cleveland and Elisa Houot, who took a chance on me and my writing, never gave up, and always encouraged me to write what made me feel excited. We're the dream team, and it's such a joy to work with both of you!

In a similar vein, thank you to Wendy Loggia and Ali Romig, who made the decision to buy this manuscript and subsequently made all my dreams come true. Being part of the Delacorte Romance family still feels like a dream, and it's because of you two that I'm able to be here. Thank you, thank you, thank you! And especially Ray Shappell, Michelle Canoni, Colleen Fellingham, Tamar Schwartz, Shameiza Ally, Noreen Herits, Josh Redlich, Cynthia Lliguichuzhca, and the entire Delacorte team who had a hand in putting this book in yours. And to the illustrious Mallory Heyer, who gave me the cover of my dreams: I'll be staring at it forever and ever and ever (and ever).

Thanks to Dave Chicarelli for the fabulous author photo! You're the only person who could get me to enjoy a photo shoot.

To Colleen Kinneary at The Neverending Story for the fabulous photo-shoot space, of course. And to my fabulous best friend and cousin rolled into one, Victoria DeBlasi Russo—your eye for design and your passion for your work is so much fun to collaborate with on this bookish dream come true. Love you, Bubba Girl!

Similarly, to my own team of fabulous coworkers, who helped me juggle my day job (as a book publicist myself!) in addition to writing my own stories—particularly Heidi Richter, Martin Wilson, Julie Paulauski, Kelly Cronin, Carlos Rosario, Lindsey Kennedy Gueron, Kasey Feather, and Darelyanel Medina. Book people are the best people, and being able to be on *both* sides of this industry is truly a dream. Nobody knows it like we do!

To my parents, Leslie and Anthony, as well as my siblings Michael and Jamie—thank you for actually listening when I told you all that I needed some uninterrupted writing time in the basement. Thank you for all the pretty notebooks throughout the years (particularly the ones you've bought me, Chick). And thank you for always making me feel like this dream wasn't a pie-in-the-sky, never-going-to-happen thing, instead treating it like something inevitable, just waiting for its moment. It's finally here! Michael, thank you for making the choice to go to UH Mānoa all those years ago, causing me to fall in love with such a beautiful place—maybe now you'll finally finish reading a book. And to all of my "second" families: the Wiens, DeBlasis, Zinsers, McIntoshes . . . and all of the Prep crew! Nobody's corner is as well stocked as mine.

To my Lola Belle and my Shelby June—the best puppies/writing assistants in the biz. Nothing soothed a long night at the desk like a cuddle from you. Lola, thank you for being my constant companion in this endeavor from the start until your very last day—and Shelby, thank you for taking the torch and already doing a fantastic job of telling me when it's time for a writing break nap sesh. I promise I'll grab you a new bone in a minute.

Jason Arthur and Kasey Carlton—what more can I say about you two? You've been champions of this book from the start, from its early concepts to its messy drafts to its cover design and every single thing in between. This book was born from both hard work and your hands helping shape it with advice, condolences, and a sympathetic ear when I needed it. How lucky I am to have two of the best writing partners in the whole world keeping me both accountable and excited about the craft. Now put your heads down and get back to your own writing! We've got work to do.

To the professors who helped shape me into the writer that I am—particularly Mary Bly, Sarah Gambito, Caroline Hagood, Paul Witcover, and Dawn Reno Langley—thank you for your words of wisdom, your encouragement, and your kind but firm editorial notes where they were needed. Even the best of writers need to rewrite, but with you all, I never felt like a failure while I was doing so, rather that I was tweaking my voice to help it shine.

I have a whole slew of bookish writing friends who are former bloggers, Bookstagrammers, and authors themselves who I can't imagine *We've Hit Turbulence* existing without. Cait Jacobs, Elle Gonzalez Rose, Thao Thai, Amber Shepherd, Emily Zinser, Mike Lasagna, Stephanie Ehmann, Chloe Maron, Ben Ace, Morrisa Shukis, the rest of the fabulous (and infamous) Brothelsprouts, the Class of 2026 debuts, and the NYC

Wayward Writers Discord—every single one of you makes my day with the writing memes, the encouragement, and the day-to-day gossip. See above about how book people are the best people. And to all my friends who kept me moving throughout the long nights and helped me celebrate the wins—including Taylor McIntosh Schneider, Alex Koopman Mezzacappa, Emily Zinser, and Danielle Raynor, just to name a few of the (many) of you out there!

I'll be honest: A solid 90 percent of this book wasn't written at the comfort of my desk. Rather, it was written at my favorite rickety table at The Bean, next to the wall of cold brew drips, a sweating cup of frozen hot chocolate (don't forget the toasted marshmallow syrup) by my side. Sundays at The Bean are still my favorite thing, so I'd like to extend a heartfelt thank-you to the staff for being the best around, and the venue itself for being the best place to write on Long Island, hands down.

K. L. Walther and Sarah Dessen—to put it simply, this book would not exist without your writing inspiring me from my teen years and beyond. A big part of the reason I am the writer I am today is because of the awe I felt when picking up your stories. Thank you for helping me find my voice and the courage to actually dream of spinning it into a story for others to read. I hope one day readers feel the same warm fuzzies when reading *my* books that I always felt when reading yours.

To the locals and native people of Hawai'i—your islands are some of the most beautiful places I've ever known. Thank you for the time, care, and attention you give to every aspect of your home, and perhaps most importantly for sharing your culture with the world. It's my hope that anyone who finds themselves passing through will stop and take a moment to appreciate the sheer artistry and ancestry encapsulated in every inch of space. It's truly a jewel like no other.

James P. Egbert is someone I wish I could hand this book to, and maybe in another life, I'd have the chance. Mr. E, I miss you every single day, and I wish you were here to hold this book in your hands, flip through its pages, and realize that all those years of entertaining my rambling story ideas between class periods weren't for nothing. I'll always wish I stayed an extra five minutes. Wherever you are, I hope you can see this—and that there are plenty of good books to read.

Last but certainly never least, to Matthew—without you, I wouldn't know what love truly feels like, let alone how to write about it. I love you forever and for always, more than you'll ever know. I loved you then, love you now, and will love you later. Want to go on a Taco Bell run?

About the Author

Jessica L. Cozzi crafts swoonworthy romances for teens to show that there is always love in the world if you're willing to find it. She is a publicist at William Morrow, an imprint of HarperCollins, and is also a former YA book blogger. She has a BA in creative writing from Fordham University and an MFA in young adult fiction writing and professional writing from Southern New Hampshire University. Her literary passion lies in young adult stories, including any and all contemporary romantic comedies. *We've Hit Turbulence* is her first novel.

jesscozziwrites.com
@jesscozziwrites

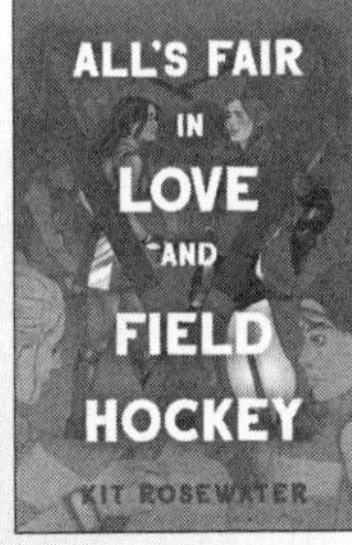

IT'S A LOVE STORY.